RAVES FOR FROM DARKNESS

"*From Darkness* is deeply romantic, in both senses of the word. It's moody and atmospheric yet passionate and endearing. This story broke my heart with its fraught relationships and stitched me back together again with its gorgeous words."

—ALEX BROWN, Tor.com

"A story that takes the reader on an edge-of-your-seat ride through love, loss and redemption."

—MARK SMITH, bestselling author of *The Road To Winter*

"Set in two richly imagined, juxtaposed worlds and cleverly infused with Greek mythology, *From Darkness* is an atmospheric tale of grief, courage and first love."

—JULIA EMBER, author of *The Seafarer's Kiss* and *Ruinsong*

"This delicate story combines suspenseful twists with emboldening love, threading miracles out of the bleakest moments."

—*Foreword Reviews*

"An atmospheric read... The book's greatest strength is its sense of place; the pine plantation and terrifying sinkholes come vividly to life."

—*Kirkus Reviews*

FROM DARKNESS

A NOVEL

KATE HAZEL HALL

interlude press • new york

ISBN 13: 978-1-945053-98-6 (trade)
ISBN 13: 978-1-945053-73-3 (ebook)
Library of Congress Control Number: 2020939800
Published by Duet, an imprint of Interlude Press
www.duetbooks.com

Cover and Book Design by CB Messer
10 9 8 7 6 5 4 3 2 1

interlude press • new york

For Maya and Kendra

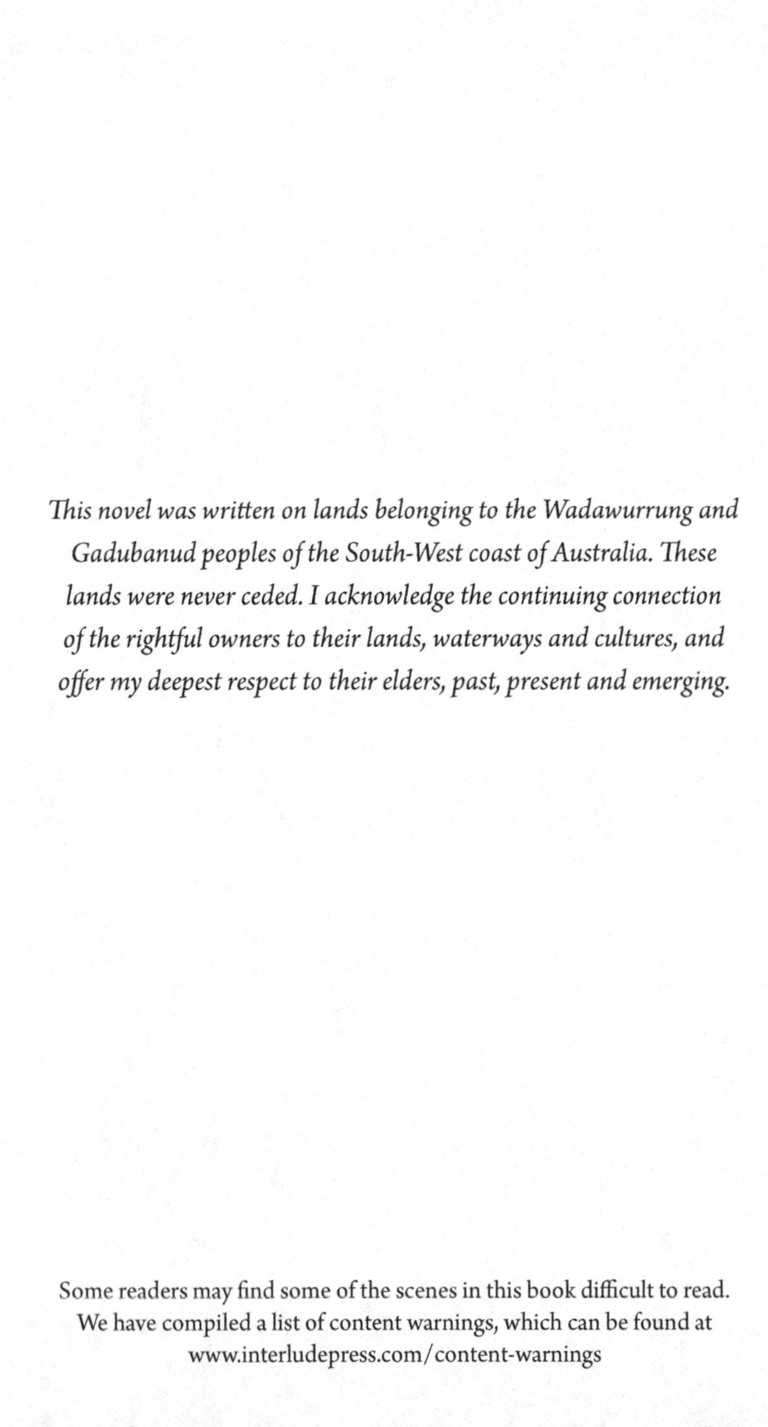

This novel was written on lands belonging to the Wadawurrung and Gadubanud peoples of the South-West coast of Australia. These lands were never ceded. I acknowledge the continuing connection of the rightful owners to their lands, waterways and cultures, and offer my deepest respect to their elders, past, present and emerging.

Some readers may find some of the scenes in this book difficult to read. We have compiled a list of content warnings, which can be found at www.interludepress.com/content-warnings

1.
Anniversary

Ari watched a wave slip through the deep blue channel between the reef and the rock. She dug her thumbnails into the soft pads at the tips of her fingers, one by one. Pointer, Tallman, Ringman, Pinkie. Pointer, Tallman, Ringman, Pinkie. Pointer, Tallman, Ringman. To stop herself, she crossed her arms and tucked her hands away. What if she didn't have the guts to do it? "Of course I'm going to do it," Ari told herself. Her voice sounded squeaky against the deep hum of the sea.

As she stepped cautiously over the sharp bits of the reef, Ari glanced over her shoulder at the empty beach, then checked the two headlands and finally the horizon. The beach was called Seal Cove and it was deserted. It was too early in the morning for tourists, and fishing boats never came close to shore in the rising swell: perfect conditions for an anniversary swim. Ari's feet sank into the slick sponginess of sea lettuce and slid on the tight green beads of Neptune's necklace. Despite the summer heat, the seawater was freezing, and Ari tried not to think about how icy it would be when she plunged in.

"It's too cold!"

"Baby."

"All right then, I'll show you."

Laughing, Ari watched Alex pull her dress over her head and throw it down, furiously, on the reef. When Alex got cross, she sometimes did silly things, but Ari knew her friend would swim the channel now. Dare or no dare, she would do it just to prove that she wasn't a baby.

"Well, come on then, Ari. This was your idea."

Alex was poised on the edge of the reef: a tall, skinny, black-haired girl in a faded olive-green swimsuit. The ocean glittered under the midday sun. Waves ambushed the rocks and turned Alex's ankles white with spray. Ari slipped off her singlet and jeans and stuffed them into her backpack, where she also had a towel, a plastic drink bottle full of lemon soda, and some sandwiches for after their swim.

"Hurry up, Ari, the tide's coming in!"

Looking past Alex at the waves crashing on the edges of the reef, Ari saw that she was right. A nagging little voice inside her whispered: it's already way too high, *but she ignored it and picked her way carefully over the rocks to join Alex, who was making funny faces at Ari and windmills with her arms.*

"Are you ready, Your Highness?" Alex gestured dramatically at the grim, gray rock surrounded by swirling water about twenty yards off the reef. "Danger Island and the Cave of Sorcery await us."

Ari gave her warrior salute, and they dived together, into the cold, inky channel.

Alone on the edge of the reef, Ari closed her eyes, remembering. At nine and eleven, she and Alex had been too old, really, to still be playing princesses and warriors. Alex's parents were worried that their almost-teenage girl was still hunting imaginary dragons in the pine plantation. Cass, Ari's mother, didn't mind the make-believe, but she agreed that Alex and Ari should be encouraged to do other, more normal, things. Beth and Nate decided that Alex should join the netball club with the local girls, and Ari was offered a pony and a future of Saturdays filled with pony club meetings and gymkhanas. But Alex hated netball, and Ari only wanted to ride her mother's rescue Clydesdales. She loved their gentleness and their shaggy feet and she thought that their great, patient strength made them closer to the heroic steeds of legend than any well-bred, pampered pony. Ari and Alex were happiest when they were together, playing warrior queens, dressing up, dressing the horses up, fighting dragons, and shutting out everything but the world that belonged only to them. Eventually, their parents gave up and left them alone, and so the mermaids and sea monsters of Seal Cove flourished where they might have become extinct.

Ari had vague memories, assisted by photos and her mother's recollections, of Alex towing her around in a homemade wagon when she was tiny, of trips to the wildlife park and the movies in Port August, and of a playground with a rusty metal roundabout that always made her feel sick. She remembered climbing trees and falling out of them, and Alex holding her hand while one of their mothers tortured her with Dettol. But she had much clearer memories from when they were older: ordinary, school holiday memories, like swinging on the old tire under the ghost gum near the beach, riding their bikes along the hot, dusty orange road to the camping area to buy ice creams from the kiosk, or running squealing with a bunch of other kids through the sprinklers on the Stonehaven football field. She remembered playing cards with Alex in the cargo bed of Beth's rusty old pickup while their mothers did the kind of grocery shopping that meant they wouldn't have to drive back into town for weeks. If the girls behaved themselves in town, they got to travel all the way home in the back of the pickup. And there were the long summer days spent swimming, and exploring rock pools, and trying to build rafts out of driftwood. Ari had a hoard of perfect moments with Alex and she kept them carefully in her memory so that they would always be there.

But it was their private world, the place only they shared, that she remembered most of all. On the long, winding bus trips to school on foggy winter mornings, Alex and Ari would sit together, heads bent over Alex's sketchbook as she drew mountain ranges and rivers, immense deserts and dark, dangerous forests, while Ari made up the people, animals, and magical beings that populated these wondrous landscapes. The other girls stopped trying to include them in their groups after a while, and Ari and Alex didn't care. They were inseparable, and the rest of the world was irrelevant.

The water was cold, and the current much stronger than Ari had thought it would be. Alex surfaced beside her, and they began to swim, cresting small waves like seals and paddling strongly down them. The undertow tugged at their legs, but they were both good swimmers. Alex wasn't quite as good as Ari, and Ari knew that this bothered her friend more than she would have admitted. Being two years older meant that Alex was superior in many respects. She could run faster and lift heavier things. But swimming was something Ari did better than most people. Every year, she won all the races at the school swimming carnival and infuriated the sports teacher by refusing to compete in inter-school swimming competitions.

For Ari, the public pool, that over-chlorinated aqua lozenge next to the Stonehaven tennis court, was something she swam in because she had to. But the ocean, that was home. She had trained herself to hold her breath for well over two minutes, just so that she could stay underwater longer in the cool, buoyant stillness of the sea. Down there, in the silence, Ari would swim like a dolphin or a mermaid: arms folded back against her sides, moving her legs together so that her body rippled through the water. Her favorite time to be underwater was on sunny days when the sea was still and quiet. On those days, the water was so clear that swimming was a kind of flying, and the sun-dappled sand of the ocean floor became a continent, with its own mountain ranges, deep valleys, and tall dark forests of kelp. Ari would gaze down at this strange and beautiful land from a great height, then plummet gannet-like to the bottom, just for the thrill and the unbounded joy of swimming in deep water.

Ari knew that Alex was secretly afraid of swimming out of her depth. But because she was two years older, because she hated to be beaten at anything, and, mostly, because she couldn't deny Ari anything, on the day of their Danger Island swim Alex paddled strongly through the waves beside her, and Ari could see her friend making an effort to keep her gaze fixed on the surface of the water. The channel was much wider and the rock much farther away than it had seemed from the reef. Ari claimed it was less than twenty yards, "not even as long as the swimming pool," but it was clear that Alex had her doubts about this estimate. In any case, the waves and the sweeping current made swimming much harder and much more tiring. Finally, though, Danger Island rose, tall and imposing, and they paddled the last few yards and clambered triumphantly onto the slippery rocks at its base.

"We made it!"

"Let's find the cave, quickly." Ari stood up and gripped the sheer sides of the rock with her fingertips. She suddenly felt anxious about her mother and Beth, who had, of course, told the girls never to dive off the reef, but who had not imagined that their children would ever attempt to swim the treacherous channel between the reef and the rock. And the tide was coming in much quicker than Ari had bargained for. Looking back across the channel, she could already see little waves washing over the long, jagged reef that was their only way back to the shore.

"I think it's this way. Come on, Ari, what are you waiting for?" Now that the swim was over, Alex was wildly excited, itching to explore the rock. She scrambled nimbly over the shale stones that lay piled up, like a

little gravelly beach, along one side of the rock. Huge Pacific gulls circled silently or perched on top of the rock, and the girls saw bits of bleached driftwood like skeleton fingers poking over the edge. The stones crunched underfoot with twiggy nest scatterings—brittle shells and tiny bones—and the waves slapped against the boulders, clawing the gray shoal with white fingers of foam. Like magic, the cave appeared, a dark hole in the wave-worn face of the rock. Ari and Alex had seen the cave only once, and that was from the deck of Dawso's fishing boat. Now they were actually standing at its entrance and they high-fived each other, laughing triumphantly, while all around them the sea heaved and fell in surges, like a restless giant breathing.

Ari put her towel on a dry rock and pulled absently at the straps on her swimsuit. She still wore the faded black one-piece that her mother had bought her for school swimming sports two years earlier, but the swimsuit was getting very threadbare and the straps were uncomfortably tight. The last time she'd dived into this channel, Ari had worn a little girl's suit, with pale blue and white stripes and a ruffle like a ballet skirt. Seven years ago.

Seven years ago, she had curled her toes over the edge of this same reef, ready to swim to the island with Alex.

Seven years ago, two children dived into the ocean from a reef and swam across a notorious undertow to a large rocky island.

Seven years ago, two children watched from that rock as high tide swept in and buried the reef under six feet of water.

Seven years ago, two children tried to swim nearly a mile through rough seas to reach the shore.

Only one child made it.

2.
The Lost Girl

Ari put both hands flat on the reef's edge and hauled herself out of the water. The sun warmed her back and shoulders as she sat to catch her breath. The island looked small and insignificant now that she had been there and back once more. Plunging into the sea had been the worst part. Ari had been dreading the dive from the reef into the channel; she'd been afraid that the cold depths would suck her down as they did in her dreams. Some of the drowning dreams, as she secretly called them, were not terrifying at all, but gentle. Lulled by the ocean's quiet rocking, Ari would find herself able to breathe underwater. In these dreams, Ari wandered calmly along the seabed until a familiar figure appeared, wavy and indistinct, but with its arms stretched out wide to welcome her. Ari would wake up from this kind of dream feeling comforted, or at least untroubled. But then there were the other drowning dreams, and these were horrible ordeals, full of panic and fear and pain.

The worst nightmare was the one where Alex floated, pale and still, just under the surface of the water. "I'll get her! I'll save her," Ari promised Beth, who ran back and forth along the beach calling for her child. But no matter how far Ari swam or how desperately she reached for her, Alex floated just out of reach. Each time, just as Ari touched the tips of her lifeless fingers, the current snatched her away. In the dream, Ari found herself alone, treading water in an empty ocean, until Beth's sobs and her own grief became one and she woke, usually to a soaking wet pillow and her mother's voice calling her name. After Alex's funeral, the dreams had been particularly bad but, as the years passed, they had become less frequent, until they seemed almost like the memories of nightmares that belonged to somebody else. Living with the guilt was harder. "It wasn't your fault," they all said, even Beth and Nate, who had every right to hate her for causing the death of their only child.

Then, one day, about three years after Alex went missing, Cass came into Ari's room and held her tightly and told her that Nate had left Beth and gone back to Crete. She had to hold Ari very tightly for a long while after that. Those weeks and months following Nate's departure were, in a sense, even worse than after Alex's death, because then Beth began to fade away. She took all the pills the doctor prescribed and she let Cass and Ari look after her; she opened her mouth when they wanted to feed her and lay down obediently when they asked her to sleep. But loss had eaten her from the inside. Beth was taken to the psychiatric ward of a large public nursing home in Port August.

Ari sometimes thought that it might have been a little easier on Beth and on everyone if they had found Alex's body. It was the not knowing: that tiny, desperate uncertainty that lingered in the heart, that was hardest to bear. They hid the newspapers from her, but Ari read the headlines on the newsstands outside the general store. Alex wasn't Alex anymore. She was "Eleven-Year-Old Girl Drowned," or Stonehaven's "Local Tragedy." She was "Alex Cohen Still Missing, Hope Fades." Helicopters and boats had searched the ocean around Seal Cove for weeks, and Beth and Nate had hired fishermen and charter boats to keep searching for months after that. But they never found any trace of their daughter.

For years Ari sometimes let herself imagine that Alex had been swept out to sea and picked up by a foreign fishing boat or that she'd been washed ashore on a desert island, just like a story in a book.

She learned, as time wore on, to forget these childish fantasies. In the end, loss was loss, with or without a body to prove it.

Cass tried desperately to convince Ari that Nate's desertion and Beth's breakdown were not her fault, just as Alex's death wasn't her fault. For Ari, though, guilt multiplied inside her like some ugly and unstoppable weed. She learned, as she grew up, to conceal it so that others, especially the psychologists and grief counselors whose business it was to ferret out such guilt, would think that she had forgiven her nine-year-old self for drowning her best friend and destroying her best friend's parents. But Ari had come to terms with the truth. The guilt would never go away. Like grief, it might continue to wilt and bury itself deeper inside her, but no amount of self-loathing would erase it. So she lived with it, getting on with the business of being a teenager, which often took so much concentration that it blocked out, sometimes for long stretches of time, the horror and the misery of Alex's death.

Ari wrung the seawater out of her hair and watched a cormorant dive for fish just past the channel. She didn't know, exactly, why it had seemed so important to swim to the rock on this particular day. But she did know that nobody could know about it. Her mother would be horrified, even though Ari was nearly seventeen and a very strong swimmer. Ari's mother, who was very perceptive and understanding about a lot of other things, would not understand the way the ocean pulled at Ari, lured her, as if it wanted to swallow her too. Plunging into the freezing water this morning had been a private memorial service, an homage to Alex, but there were other darker and ill-defined impulses that had to do with sacrifice and surrender, and these feelings were so secret she barely admitted them to herself.

Now that she had made it out to the rock and back, Ari was astonished that she and Alex could have dived so cheerfully into this same patch of ocean seven years before. What were they thinking? Looking at the channel, she saw for the first time just how dangerous it was. There was a telltale patch of dark water, about halfway across. If you knew what to look for, this was the sign of a vicious undertow. Ari had tried not to think about it while swimming across the channel. Maybe the swim was easier today because she was older, and taller, and the channel didn't seem so wide. Maybe she was just lucky. But, as she measured the distance between the rock and the beach, she saw, clearly and unequivocally, that no child could be expected to swim that far and survive, especially against the undertow. The fact that one of them had made it at all was, as everyone said afterwards, a miracle.

As the sun rose higher, Ari began to think about the long, hot walk home. Even during school holidays there were animals to feed, her bedroom to tidy (if she got around to it), and last night's dinner dishes that she'd promised to do in the morning, which was now slipping away.

Wrapping her faded old towel around her waist, Ari began the slippery walk back across the rocks. As she passed a particularly deep rock pool, Ari stopped to tuck in her towel, and was mesmerized by this small patch of stillness so close to the crashing waves. She squatted to peer in and was startled by her own reflection caught in the mirrored surface of the pool. Long wet hair dangled on either side of a small, freckled, and slightly sunburned face. Her nose and lips were small, too, like her mother's, but her eyes were large, blue-green, and fringed with dark lashes. "You have your father's eyes," they told her, and although she didn't see her father very often, she had photos which showed her this was probably true.

O

AS SHE RINSED HER SANDY feet with the garden hose, Ari noticed that the house seemed very quiet for this time of the morning. Neither her mother nor Nick were big on sleeping in, and both of them were usually busy in the kitchen by this time or, as it was Sunday, absorbed in their weekend ritual of tea and newspapers on the veranda.

As she entered the house, Ari called out, wondering, for an embarrassed moment, whether her mother and Nick might be in bed but *not* sleeping. Clearly, they'd been doing a bit of that sort of thing because Ari was going to have a little half-brother or -sister. The baby was a surprise for all of them. Cass had not thought she would be able to get pregnant again and she had once confided to Ari that she sometimes worried whether Nick wished, maybe just a little, that she had been younger when they met.

"I was only forty then, and so we tried for a while, but it just didn't happen," Cass had recalled, twisting her fingers together. "We talked about it a lot. Nick wanted children of his own, but he didn't meet anyone special until . . ."

Ari smiled. "Until he met you."

Her mother patted her cheek. "You know, Ari, Nick really feels like you belong to him now. He feels like a dad and he really does love you like a father."

Ari wasn't sure how to respond to this. Her own father was essentially a stranger living in her photo albums, but he still belonged to her. He visited every now and then, he sent presents at birthdays and Christmas, and he often talked about flying Ari to Scotland so that she could stay with him and meet her stepbrothers and stepsister. So far, the trip to Scotland hadn't happened, but Ari liked to imagine it. If people had the same eyes, then they might be similar in other ways, too, and Ari thought maybe her father, if she got to know him, could tell her things about herself that she hadn't quite figured out. Mostly, Ari thought it would be good to have someone of her very own to belong to, the way Cass and Nick belonged to each other.

She had often wished that she wasn't an only child but, until a few months ago, Ari had supposed that this was the way things would always be. Nick and Cass had talked for a while about adopting a child, and Ari had heartily endorsed this idea. A little brother or sister would have made them two and two, and not just two and one, which was sometimes lonely. But the adoption process turned out to be so complicated and expensive that they reluctantly put the idea on hold, and all of them, Nick, Cassandra, and Ari, had accepted that they would probably always be a little family of three.

So it was difficult to know who was most stunned when Cass, looking flushed and bright-eyed, stumbled out of the bathroom one morning, held up a little plastic stick, and said, "Um, I think we're going to have a baby!"

Ari was thrilled at the prospect of a little half-brother or -sister, but she was also worried. *Was* her mother too old to have a baby?

"Honey," her mother reassured her, "women have perfectly healthy babies at fifty and even sixty. I'm only forty-eight. Relax."

But Ari couldn't relax, not completely, because her mother—who never got sick, who could chop mountains of firewood and rescue cows when they got stuck in the mud and still have energy left over to help Ari with her algebra—her strong, sunny, dependable mother, started throwing up, and not just in the mornings but all day long. She was pale and tired, but she seemed ridiculously happy.

"It's all completely normal," Cass would tell Nick and Ari. "Just ordinary morning sickness. It will go away in a few more weeks." And she would give them a thumbs-up before bolting through the back door to vomit on the azaleas.

Cass was right, of course. The morning sickness did go away, and now, a few months later, she was her usual robust self, complete with a little round belly that fascinated Ari. She and Nick had a five-dollar bet on who would be the first to feel the baby move.

Ari took a deep, happy breath as she entered the coolness of the kitchen. It was Sunday and school holidays, and she had weeks and weeks of sunshiny days to look forward to. And it was amazing to think that in a few short months there would be a tiny baby in the house, a baby that would be extra special because it would make them, Nick, Ari, and Cass, seem more of a family. She opened the fridge and grabbed the orange juice.

As she turned to the kitchen bench, she saw a folded piece of notepaper with her name scrawled on it resting against the fruit bowl:

Dearest Ari,

Please don't worry. Your Mum's had a bit of a scare, and we've gone to the hospital. Couldn't wait for you. Don't know how long we'll be. There's money in the envelope on the bench, and Cass says there's food in the freezer. Please go over to Claire's house. She's expecting you.

Call me on my mobile when you get this. I should be in range by then.

Don't worry. Everything will be fine. Love you,

Nick

Ari collapsed onto a kitchen chair. She felt dizzy, as if she might be sick. Not more loss. Not the baby. Please no. The phone was on the table. Her legs were wobbly, and her heart thumped painfully inside her chest as she dialed Nick's mobile number. A few minutes later she tried again. Ten minutes and several calls later Nick answered. His voice sounded strange, as though he was speaking with his hand over the phone. He told Ari that they had just seen the doctor at the little hospital in Port August.

"What's wrong with Mum?"

Nick's voice was very gentle as he answered. "They think she might be in premature labor, honey. They're going to fly her to the special women's hospital in the city. She'll get the best care there, and so will the baby. I'm going with her. And, Ari, I'm sorry, but we might be there a while."

Ari didn't say anything.

"Your mum's worried about you, Ari. I told her I'd tell you to stay at Claire's, at least at nighttime, and that I would call you every day."

"Can I speak to Mum?"

"The nurses and doctors are getting her on the stretcher to go in the helicopter now. Can you believe it? A free helicopter ride and we can't even enjoy it. Sorry, that was a terrible attempt at humor."

Ari could hear the strain in his voice. "Please put Mum on," she begged. "I want to tell her I love her." There was a long pause.

"Ari, sweetie, she's a bit upset at the moment. I promise to tell her you love her as soon as I can. And, Ari? Try not to worry. The doctor said it's amazing what they can do to stop labor these days. Your mum is fine, and the baby is doing okay at the moment. I have to go. Promise me you'll go to Claire's now? She's expecting you."

"I promise. Nick?"

"Yes, honey?"

"Will you call me at Claire's as soon as you know *anything*? Anything at all? Promise?"

"I promise," he said.

Ari stood up and hung the phone back on the wall. She was oddly calm as she began, mechanically, to gather some bits and pieces to take to Claire's. In her bedroom, she pulled a pair of faded denim shorts over her swimsuit and grabbed her backpack from her wardrobe. The house was horribly quiet; it screamed at her in its emptiness. The morning light streaked through the windows and across the floor, but Ari's arms and legs were goosebumped, and she shivered.

As she came out of her room, the phone rang. She sprinted down the hall and grabbed it. "Nick?"

"Ari, honey, it's Claire. How are you doing?"

"Oh, hi. Yes, sorry, yes, I'm okay." Ari swung her backpack onto the kitchen table and put the juice back in the fridge. She half-listened to Claire apologize for not picking her up and to her explanation about the Volvo, which was having one of its regular long stays with the mechanic.

"I would walk across to meet you, but Sam's not home yet, and I can't carry the twins all that way."

Ari reassured Claire that she was fine; concerned about her mother, but otherwise fine and perfectly capable of walking the few miles to Claire and Sam's place. Since Sally, the elderly border collie, was not up to walking all the way to Claire's, Sam would pick her up later. Ari or Sam could return tomorrow to feed the horses and the four ex-dairy cows Cass had managed to save from the saleyards. As they made arrangements, Ari was deeply grateful that Claire knew her so well. Ari didn't have to explain how much she needed that walk across the fields and through the bush.

She hung up and, from force of habit (Cass's, not hers), picked up her wet towel and carried it into the laundry. The trough was full of towels soaking. Ari saw Nick's beach towel, the palm trees and faded stripes just visible under the dark red water. The trough was full of towels, and the towels were soaked with blood. With a gasp, Ari hurtled through the back door and started running.

Though she was running furiously, heedlessly, the scorched fields and the old farm sheds seemed to hover around her in a steady blur instead of whizzing past and disappearing. Ari put on speed. She looked only at her feet, bare and brown and calloused, as they flashed beneath her. But speed alone wasn't enough to stop the tears, and soon her nose was so blocked from crying and her eyes so blurry that she was breathless and blinded and had to slow down.

As she approached the line of trees that marked Wyndham's boundary, Ari tried to choose the least prickly patches of stubble and she wished desperately for the shade of the bush. Her feet and eyes and chest were burning. Her feet were the worst. Ari lifted first one foot and then the other and cringed as she examined their raw, red soles.

Her mother was very stern about proper footwear, especially in summer. "Boots!" was the habitual call as Ari dashed out the farmhouse door. "I'm going *swimming*," she would complain, but mildly, because she knew her mother was right. Only last summer, a black snake bit Amy Drouin as she walked from the caravan park kiosk to the beach. She spent weeks in the hospital, and, when school started in the autumn, people whispered and stared, even though they'd been told not to. The venom had caused a lack of oxygen to her brain, and poor Amy had suffered a minor stroke. The left side of her face had slipped, her left eye-socket hung down, and parents from Port August to Stonehaven referred to this cruel landslide every time a child was caught with bare feet in summer.

Looking at her feet, Ari thought about Amy Drouin and wished she had stopped to slip on her boots. As well as being barefoot,

Ari had bolted out of her house wearing only her threadbare black swimsuit and a pair of shorts. She'd left her backpack full of clothes on the kitchen table. Claire or Sam would lend her some clothes. But what about her feet?

As she stood, irresolute, an image of the bloodied laundry trough nudged at the edge of her consciousness. She pushed it away and tried to figure out what to do. She was over halfway to Claire's, and Claire was waiting for her. Going back for her clothes and boots would take ages, and that would worry Claire. But there was the bush to negotiate before the fields began again, and Ari understood, as did every farm kid, that to go into the bush in bare feet in the middle of summer was just about the stupidest thing you could do. She sighed and turned around. The long swim, almost forgotten since she'd been home, and the shock of the bloodied towels and the mad dash across the fields had made her whole body abruptly, achingly, tired. She began the long walk uphill. She trod gingerly, sticking to the sandy dirt of the rutted cow-tracks to ease her swollen feet. She would have to call Claire and tell her not to worry, and she would have to think up a plausible explanation for her delay.

Ari didn't want to tell Claire or Sam, or anyone, about the blood-soaked towels or the fear that was suffocating her. She was wrapped up in that fear. It was an intensely private suffering, and the only other people who could share it were far away, over six hours' drive away by now, in an unknown hospital among strangers. She would just have to call Claire and make something up.

The midmorning sun was fierce on Ari's head and bare shoulders, and she had to shield her aching eyes when she looked up to gauge her distance from the farmhouse. As she peered into the shimmering heat haze, Ari stopped. A dark figure stood on the track just a few yards uphill. It did not move, but it seemed to shimmer and flicker in the heat. Here was an intruder, where nobody ever came, and Ari knew by the sudden chill in her bones that it was waiting for her.

Like a hare frozen under the hawk's shadow, Ari held her breath, fists tight by her sides. Then the shadowy figure seemed to flow downhill toward her, coming closer, transforming from a backlit silhouette into a young woman not much older than Ari. She was tall, with long black hair and grayish-green eyes that seemed as though they might swallow the world and Ari too. They were beautiful eyes, but they had purple smudges, like fading bruises, under them. What did those eyes remind her of? Though her skin was much darker than Ari's, she was pale, and her face reminded Ari of the faces of the city people who came in buses to Stonehaven Bay each summer, people who lived in the shadows of tall buildings and rarely saw sunlight. She wore a long black cloak, and its hem rippled eerily in a breeze that wasn't there. Ari was afraid, but this wasn't like the vague unease that came when random backpackers or hikers asked to use the phone or the terror that savaged her when she had nightmares. It was like the prickly chill, the skin-crawl she felt that time she thought she saw a ghost in the hallway.

"Are you lost? The road's back there." Ari pointed over her shoulder. The tall girl said nothing. Ari shivered. Gooseflesh prickled her arms. "I think maybe you should leave now. You're trespassing. If you need money or whatever, I'll have to ask my parents." As she spoke, Ari heard the hollowness in her own words. This wasn't that kind of stranger. Was she even real? Ari's neck and cheeks were fiery with fear.

The tall girl sighed and moved closer to her. When she was close enough to breathe on her, she whispered softly, "Don't be afraid, Ari," and then fear speared Ari in the chest. She rubbed the goosebumps on her arms and tried to breathe normally.

The stranger put her hand on Ari's shoulder. Ari yelped as something pierced the side of her foot. She looked down, more surprised than shocked, and saw a long, striped snake on the dusty track. Its head was raised to strike, and it did, biting her twice more before she could move.

Ari screamed, a high thin sound in the windless field. The stranger clapped her hands, and the snake slid unhurriedly away. Ari clutched her foot, gaping soundlessly with the pain. Her foot was on fire, and the fire was spreading up her ankle. She staggered, and the stranger caught her and let her sink to the ground. Then she knelt and cradled Ari's head and shoulders on her lap. Ari bucked and writhed against the throbbing in her foot, but there was no escaping the pain. Every movement made it worse. The stranger held her shoulders. Was she trying to calm her or restrain her?

"Help me," Ari gasped. "Do you know what to do for snakebite?"

The stranger looked at her and gave her a sad little smile. "Even if I did, I'm not allowed to stop this, Ari. This is your time. You die here, today, from this snakebite, and I'm not allowed to interfere. I can ease your pain a little, perhaps." She placed her hand on Ari's foot, and coolness began to flow into her skin. The pain ebbed slightly. "Is that better?"

Ari unclenched her jaw and tried to breathe normally. "What did you do? And how do you know my name?"

"I am the Summoner. I'm here to collect you and to guide your soul across the river to its final resting place."

Ari turned her head to look at the bleached fields under the noonday sun, at the bright blue line of the sea beyond the hills. She watched the white clouds of cockatoos circle the oasis of the farmhouse and orchard, their familiar screeching turned to razors in her ears. Then, finally, making herself do it, she looked up at the face of the stranger, who averted her eyes. A ghostly aura marked her off from the everyday world, like a neon sign advertising her strangeness. Ari felt the venom travel in a river of pain up her leg; she knew enough about tiger snakes to know that multiple bites were often fatal. This Summoner, whoever she was, could be telling the truth. Maybe she *was* a messenger of death come to collect her. But Ari was stubborn and she wasn't going to cower and be afraid. At least, not on the outside.

"I'm not going anywhere with you," she stated flatly.

The Summoner looked away. Ari admired the firm line of the other girl's jaw, and the way her hair fell in dark waves past her shoulders. She opened her mouth to speak but cried out instead as the pain raged up her leg.

The Summoner rested her cold hand on Ari's shoulder. "I'm sorry. You don't have a choice. The poison is spreading. First your muscles will atrophy, and you will not be able to move. You may feel sick and disoriented. It often happens that way with snakebite. Then the poison will reach your heart, and your heart will stop. When that happens, your soul will leave your body, and you must follow me to the underworld." She pointed back toward the scrub. "There is a portal there, just under the rock ledge where the trees begin. When your heart stops, you must come quickly. The great river is rising, and the ferryman will not cross it at high water."

Ari shook her head. "Even if I die," she growled, "I'm not going with you."

"It's your time, Ari," the Summoner said dispassionately. "I'm here to guide your soul to the Fields of the Blessed, and you would be wise to follow me. If you choose to linger here, your soul will be but a whisper on the breeze. Without a body to house it, a soul does not belong to this world. If you do not follow me, you will become what is known in the land of the living as a haunt, a ghost. Your soul will linger in this place, lost and alone, forever."

Ari tried to ignore the panic singing in her veins. She closed her eyes so the Summoner wouldn't see her naked fear. An image of the bloodied laundry trough swam before her eyes, and she struggled to sit up.

"Come on, Ari," she told herself. "Fight. Fight for Cass. Fight for your baby brother or sister. Get up." But she couldn't move her leg, and thrashing around just made the pain even more excruciating. She closed her eyes and tried to stop the tears that would make it impossible for her to speak. "Please," she whispered desperately. "Please. My mother might lose her baby. I can't leave her now. Please help me. You're supposed to bandage the wound and immobilize the whole limb. If you help me to the house, I'll tell you where the first aid kit is, and we can call an ambulance. Wait! I know they keep antivenin at the general store in Stonehaven. If I could just get to a phone, I could ask somebody to bring some here. Please. Please?"

Even as she begged, Ari knew it was too late. An ambulance from Port August, or even a delivery of antivenin from the general store, would take much more time than she had left.

Ari thought she saw pity in the Summoner's eyes as she answered: "Ari, I'm only a messenger, a guide. I do not decide who may live and who must die, any more than you do."

Ari squeezed her eyes shut, and tears forced their way under her eyelids. She pictured her mother, lying helpless in some strange hospital bed, and she did something she hadn't done for years. She called for her mother, like a terrified child who knows only one source of comfort and aches for it with all her being.

The Summoner shifted uneasily under her. She lifted Ari's head and shoulders gently and lowered her to the ground. Ari curled up in a ball, whimpering. The Summoner stood up and moved away from her.

Ari hugged her knees tightly. Her stomach tensed and cramped, and the world began to tip sideways. It felt as if she was spinning around and around on the hillside, or was the hillside itself spinning? She wanted to be sick. Everything was blurry. Ari uncurled, put her hands flat on the grass, and pushed. Her arms still seemed to be working, at least, and she pushed herself up until she was sitting upright, legs stretched out in front of her. The leg with the bite had become a lump of dead wood, and she had to lift and position it, the way she'd seen people in wheelchairs do with their lifeless limbs. She ignored the Summoner, who stood quietly nearby, watching her.

Ari tried to focus on the farmhouse and gauge the distance she needed to crawl. The effort of squinting, of trying to bring her house into focus, made tiny nauseating lights whirl in front of her eyes. Ari was truly frightened, and she couldn't tell if it was terror, or the poison, that was making it so hard to think clearly. She kept telling herself to crawl, to get up on her hands and knees and crawl to the house. Maybe there was still enough time. Surely, if she could just get inside, she could phone for help, put a pressure bandage on her leg, and wait. The ambulance people would tell her what to do.

"Crawl, Ari," she told herself. "Do it." But her leg wouldn't move. She turned her head, making the world tilt again, and glared at the Summoner. "How can you just stand there and watch me die? Don't you have any compassion?"

"I'm not allowed to feel emotions," she said simply. "It's part of the job. It's so that I don't become involved."

Ari considered this. The Summoner looked real, looked human enough, except for the unearthly glow. But she had seen sympathy in her eyes, she was sure of it. Maybe she would still help her.

"Were you a person once? I mean, a living person?"

"Yes."

"And now you're, what? A ghost?"

"Not quite," the Summoner replied mildly. "The correct term is shade. Ghosts are unquiet spirits. Shades are . . . different. You'll see."

"What happened to you? I mean, if you don't mind me asking, how did you, um, get like this?"

The Summoner gave a short, mirthless laugh. "I don't know. I woke up in the dark. There were people bending over me, but I couldn't see their faces. They gave me a drink. I was so thirsty that I would have drunk dust or poison. But it was just fresh water. I drank it, and that is the first thing I remember about being in the unlit realm."

"Was it long ago?"

"What is 'long ago'?" She shrugged. "I don't know what that means anymore."

"Can't you feel anything? That must be awful."

The Summoner shook her head. "I don't really know. Most of the time I just do what is required of me. Sometimes, when there are no new souls to guide, when I am alone, then I try to think about my life before. But it is not a profitable pastime. Besides, it is forbidden."

"By who? Who's in charge? I'm guessing it's not an old man with a beard and white robes. But you said something about a ferryman and some river. This underworld of yours, it's like the Greek version, right? Hades and the river Styx and all that?" Ari pushed her tangled hair behind her ears and raised an eyebrow at the Summoner. I can't believe I'm buying any of this, she thought, but she might as well know that I read books. Ari was surprised that, in the middle of her dying, it would matter to her what this ghostly older girl thought.

The Summoner seemed to weigh something in her mind. She glanced over her shoulder before replying in an undertone: "Since you have guessed so much, I suppose I can tell you something about it." She licked her lips. "There *is* a great lord. Probably the most powerful and feared ever to walk the unlit halls. And we, the inhabitants of the underworld, cannot understand why he has been allowed to grow in power so that all the other gods and goddesses are daunted. But you do not need to fear him. Your path will be free from all fear, and that is a promise. I will make sure that you do not falter on the road." The Summoner stopped and looked at Ari with what seemed very much like astonishment. "I don't know why I told you all that."

Returning her gaze with as much composure as she could, Ari thought perhaps this Summoner was much younger than she looked. Her expression, wide-eyed and earnest, was oddly childlike. It was also disturbingly familiar.

There was a lump in Ari's throat as she swallowed. What if this was real? What if she died, and the face of this ghostly Summoner was the last face she ever saw?

The fields and summer skies faded away. It seemed as though Ari was sitting in a train that was moving away from a crowded platform. Everyone she loved, all her acquaintances—school friends, teachers, shop owners, every person she had ever met, as well as Sally and the horses—she had to say farewell to them forever. The train would not go backward, nor could she jump from the carriage and rejoin the people on the platform. She was hurtling into the dark unknown, an underworld ruled by some terrifying god of the dead. Ari did not consider herself religious and she had deliberately and steadfastly refused to consider what happened after death. Now that she was about to find out, she thought tearfully of the pearl-colored gates and benevolent angels of her primary school religious education classes and wished that she could step off the train hurtling into darkness and onto a prim golden stairway leading to a place of safety in the clouds.

Ari tried again to move her leg. The Summoner's touch had eased the agony, but the limb was swollen and hot. The skin around the puncture marks on her foot was black and puffy. Ari moaned as another bout of nausea and dizziness claimed her. The world no longer made sense. Her vision was failing, and Ari's throat tightened as she struggled to breathe. She gave up trying to sit upright and let herself fall sideways onto the grass. There was a dreadful ringing in her ears, and Ari wrapped her arms around her head.

Without looking up at her, Ari asked the Summoner how much longer she thought it would take. She didn't reply. Ari watched helplessly as the trees began to drip and twist and run into one another, like oil floating on a puddle. The seagulls were monstrous, and they circled like white pterodactyls above the melting trees.

She closed her eyes and whimpered. "It's not real," she told herself. "It's just the venom, and it'll be over soon. Make it stop. Please make it stop."

Something brushed the soft skin under Ari's left arm and she opened her eyes. The Summoner was on her knees beside her. She drew her hand away, and Ari saw that her hand was shaking. The Summoner was staring at Ari's armpit, where a row of thin white scars began, and her gaze followed the pale lines down along the side of Ari's breast until they stopped just above the seam of her old black swimsuit.

"Ari, how did you get those scars?"

"I fell off some rocks when I was a kid. So what?" Ari clasped her arms over her chest. The Summoner's face looked paler than before, and she was breathing shallowly. Her dark eyes were wide with an expression Ari couldn't identify. "What is it?"

The Summoner's voice shook as she pointed at Ari's left arm. "You fell from a cliff above the crashing waves. It was a long way down. You screamed, and it sounded like seagulls."

"I was eight years old."

The Summoner closed her eyes. "I saw it. I saw you fall. I thought you would die."

"I grabbed at some grass growing from a ledge on the rock."

"You broke your fall, but your left side was all grazed, and there were some deep gouges that needed stitching afterward."

Pulse thumping, Ari stared at the Summoner. "How do you know about that?"

"I see it, in my mind. It's very clear, like a picture. I was there. I watched you fall." She leaned over and took Ari's face in her hands, fingertips like cold feathers cradling her cheeks.

"I know you, Ari." The Summoner's dark eyes were bright with tears. "I *know you,* but I have forgotten *my* name. Say my name. Please?"

"No way," breathed Ari.

"I was there. I pulled you back up the cliff."

"No."

"I held your hand while the doctor stitched your wounds. Cass, that's right, isn't it? Oh gods, *Cass* said you were only being brave because I was there."

Buried grief beat its wings in Ari's chest. Anger and a new fear fought inside her. She pushed the Summoner's hands away. "You can't be her. You're the wrong age, for one thing."

"Ari, please?"

"What is this? A sick joke? Leave my memories alone. After all, they're all I have left."

The Summoner just stared at her, her eyes shining. She smiled. "I *remember.* That's the word, isn't it? I remember that our mothers wouldn't let us go to the beach alone for ages after your fall. That was when we discovered the pine plantation. Do you remember the castle we made in there? Nobody ever found it, did they? I wonder if it's still there." She slid her arms under Ari and lifted her as though she weighed nothing at all. The sudden movement made the world spin and the pain flare in her leg, and Ari screamed and thrashed in the Summoner's arms. She held her close. "I'm sorry, Ari," she said urgently. "I didn't know it was you. But I'm going to save you. I don't care what they do to me."

Ari stared up at her. Above their rings of shadow, the Summoner's eyes were clear and very human. She knew those eyes. The lines of her face might be different, and her height, and the strength of her arms, but only one person in the whole world had eyes like that.

She whispered her name, and the Summoner nodded grimly. "Hold on," she told her.

3. Old Friends

Ari woke, briefly, to movement, and to a searing pain that flamed up and down her left leg. Her head was pressed against something warm and soft and was bumping slightly against it. There was a rushing sensation and a blur of lights and colors. Strong, slender arms held her, and she remembered Alex. Alex was back. She was grown up now. She had been telling Ari she was going to take her somewhere, but she couldn't remember where. Then, much later it seemed, she felt herself being lifted by many hands. After a confusion of noise and movement and a sudden sharp pain in the back of her hand, everything went dark again. In that darkness, she was aware of somebody calling her and she struggled to break the surface of whatever was keeping her from life.

When she opened her eyes, she saw Claire talking to a doctor and a nurse reaching up to attach a bag of clear liquid to a tall silver pole. That's a drip, she thought. I'm in a hospital. Oh God, that hurts.

"She's awake!" cried Claire. "Ari, honey, don't move. It's going to be fine. You'll be fine."

Claire was crying, and Ari wanted to comfort her, but another wave of pain rushed up from her ankle and her stomach twisted. She retched violently, and the nurse held a plastic bowl under her chin as she vomited again and again.

Ari heard the doctor reassure Claire. "It's just the antivenin. We had to give her another large dose, I'm afraid. I still don't understand how she made it all the way to the Stonehaven store from Wyndham.

She can't possibly have walked all the way after being bitten like that."

"She's confused, probably," murmured Claire.

Ari screamed as the pain took over her body again. The doctor said something to the nurse, who rushed from the room. "I'll give her something a little stronger for the pain. It might make her sleep, also. Have the parents been contacted?"

The nurse came back with another bag and hooked it onto the pole. A thin tube snaked down from it and Ari watched the liquid trickle along its length as they attached it to one of the plastic needles taped to the back of her hand. A sickly warmth began to steal into Ari's veins. The pain dwindled, gave a last throb, and then ebbed away.

Smiling, Ari reached out to Claire and whispered, "I'm sorry you had to come all this way. Have you seen Alex?" She gripped Claire's hand tightly. "She's come back, Claire. She's grown up now, but it's her, it's really her! I think she saved my life!"

Claire, stroking Ari's hair, put her hand over her mouth. "Oh my God …"

O

IT WAS NIGHT, AND THE lights in the ward were turned down so that the patients could sleep. But there were so many machines, and all of them had glowing or flashing lights. Some of them beeped loudly at intervals. Nurses drifted like pale green ghosts. Ari rubbed her eyes and felt a sickening little sting as she knocked the drip needle in her hand. She was horribly thirsty. There was a plastic jug of water on the bedside table and an upturned glass on a folded paper towel. Ari struggled to sit up. She was groggy and weak, but she managed to pour water from the jug into the glass and drink it, then another glass, and another. She fell asleep to the incessant beeping of a machine next to her bed.

In the morning, a nurse came and took her temperature. She also offered Ari a bedpan, which she indignantly refused.

The nurse laughed. "I'm glad you're feeling better. I'll help you to the toilet. You could have a shower, too, if you like. Then, if you're up to it, some food. Are you hungry?"

Ari smiled. "Yes."

"You're a very lucky girl," the nurse told her as she turned on the shower. "The doctors are all trying to figure out how you survived."

Ari didn't say anything. She just sat on the plastic shower chair, closed her eyes, and let the warm water stream over her head and shoulders and down her back. I'm alive, she thought fiercely. I'm alive.

After a surprisingly tasty hospital breakfast, Ari lay back on her pillows and tried to stop thinking about Alex. She was filled with so much joy and gratitude she thought it might cascade out of her at any moment, and she wanted her to be there, to be part of it, to receive her share of it. In the early morning, Nick had called. Her mother was doing well. The doctors had been able to stop her labor, and the baby was holding steady. Cass would have to remain in the women's hospital in the city for some time, possibly months, but Nick was coming back to Port August later in the week to see Ari in the hospital, and then on to Stonehaven to collect some of Cass's things.

"I want to stay with her, Ari. Do you mind very much if Claire looks after you a bit longer? I was frantic with worry when she called me. I couldn't believe it. First Cass and the baby, and then you being bitten by a snake. But you're okay, thank goodness. I want to be there, to look after you, but Cass needs me, really needs me right now. I hope you understand."

Ari had assured him that she understood. "But can't I come back to the city with you? I want to see Mum!"

"Of course you can. But let's get you completely well first. I still don't know if keeping this from her is such a great idea. She's bound to find out eventually."

"She has to be protected from any shock or stress. You said so yourself."

"Right." Nick sighed. "You're right, of course. Well, we'll keep telling her that you are safe and well at Claire's, but—Ari?"

"What?"

"Please take care."

"Of course."

A nurse poked her head around the curtain of Ari's cubicle. "You have a visitor."

And there was Alex, dressed in jeans and a faded T-shirt, holding a bunch of flowers and smiling down at her.

Tongue-tied and shy, Ari smiled back. Alex laid the bunch of flowers on Ari's bed and sat stiffly in the chair beside her. "How are you feeling?" she asked, her voice cheerful. Ari saw that she had lost her eerie, unearthly aura, that her skin was not as pale, and that she seemed more solid, more ordinary. The dark circles under her eyes had faded.

But Ari wasn't in the mood to tackle mysteries this morning. Happiness flooded her, so much that she thought it must be overflowing into the world. "I feel, I don't know. Like bursting!"

Ari told Alex about her mother and the baby. "Nick said the doctors discovered straight away what was wrong with Mum. They said it's quite common and they can manage it, but she'll have to stay in bed for the rest of her pregnancy. That's another four months! Can you imagine? Cass will go completely insane. She hates being in bed even when she's sick, so being forced to lie still with her feet up for months will drive her nuts. She'll do it, though, of course, if it's the best thing for the baby."

As Ari talked, she relaxed and Alex seemed to relax also, drawing her legs up to sit cross-legged on her chair, like a child. When she and Alex had recognized each other on the track yesterday, Ari had only noticed how much older Alex was. Now, in the soft morning light, she could not help but be aware that this grown-up Alex was incredibly, almost impossibly, beautiful, with her flawless skin, that long, dark hair, and eyes of such a deep greenish gray they seemed black. She remembered the warmth and softness of her chest and the strength of the arms that had, somehow, carried her all the way from Wyndham to the general store in Stonehaven. And yet, Alex herself seemed completely unaware of her own allure.

A young nurse came to take Ari's temperature and she didn't just glance at Alex; she stared, her lips slightly parted, as Alex laughed at something Ari said.

"I see you ate all your breakfast. That's a good sign," chirped the nurse as she picked up Ari's tray. She batted her eyelashes at Alex. "Would you like me to get you something? It's very early. Maybe a coffee?"

Alex just smiled politely and shook her head. The nurse seemed reluctant to leave. She fiddled with Ari's drip, took her blood pressure, checked the wound on her ankle, smoothed her sheets and blankets, and picked up the flowers. They were tied with string. "I'll put these in water for you." As she left, she tucked her wavy blond hair behind her ear and stared again at Alex.

Ari could have sworn the nurse was blushing as she disappeared behind the curtains of the cubicle. "That nurse likes you," laughed Ari. She watched Alex closely to see how she would react.

Alex looked confused. "Why would she like me? She doesn't even know me."

Ari changed the subject, but when the nurse returned a few minutes later with her flowers, beautifully arranged in a glass vase, Ari pretended to fiddle with the TV remote while the nurse placed the heavy vase on her bedside table next to Alex. She had to lean over Alex slightly as she did this, and Ari saw that her uniform was a little too tight, and the top few buttons were undone. But Alex was staring up at the TV with rapt attention, and, in fact, craning her neck a little to see past the nurse. The nurse must have taken the hint, because she left without saying anything.

Ari and Alex sat silently, watching the morning news program. Ari reached out to touch her flowers. "Where'd you get these? They're beautiful, by the way, thank you."

"I picked them. There are so many lovely gardens here. I looked for belladonna lilies and pale pink roses. I remember they were your favorites. I waited until it was dark, of course."

"Of course."

There was an awkward pause.

"And the clothes?"

"Somebody's clothesline in Stonehaven."

"Oh."

"Are they, you know, suitable? I didn't know what to take. Everything is so different. Nothing looks familiar." Alex's voice trembled a little and Ari reached across to touch her hand.

"They're fine. Very, um, normal. When I get out of here, I can lend you some of my clothes. Or we could go shopping. I've got some money saved up, and we could get the bus to the city, see Mum, and then go get you some awesome clothes. After all, it's a special occasion, you returning and everything. Cass will be so thrilled. Oh, but we need to wait until she's had the baby, because she mustn't have any shocks. But that's all right, we'll keep you a secret and then we can surprise her." Ari paused. She heard herself babbling, but she couldn't find the words to tell Alex what it meant to see her again. She carefully avoided her old friend's gaze as she said, softly, "So many people have missed you, Alex."

There was a long pause. Alex stroked the velvety petals of one of the pink roses she had stolen for Ari. The television twittered in the background.

Ari suddenly went cold all over. "You *are* staying now, aren't you?" She heard the fear in her own voice. "Because if I lost you again, I think it really would be the end of me."

"I'm not going anywhere." Alex patted her leg awkwardly. "I can't go anyhow. The portal, the one we were supposed to take, is closed. We missed it. So, I guess you're stuck with me." She smiled with one side of her mouth, a quirk Ari remembered well.

"For how long?"

"Don't ask me questions like that, Ari." Alex was suddenly, visibly, distressed; her forehead was beaded with sweat, and her breathing, if it was breathing, was fast and shallow. She leaned back on her chair and stole a glance through the curtains as though somebody might be listening. "I'm not really supposed to be here, and neither are you. I don't exactly know why we have been allowed to stay or why I haven't been called back."

"What do you mean, 'called back'? You have to tell me something about all this, Alex. I nearly ended up dead and on my way to some kind of weird afterlife that sounded a lot like Hades." Ari struggled to recall their uncanny, incoherent conversation in the field. "And you said… I remember now. You said you were going to save me and that you didn't care what they did to you. Who's 'they'? Why are you in trouble?"

Alex stood up suddenly. There wasn't much room to pace up and down in the cramped space of Ari's cubicle, but Alex moved along the length of the bed restlessly, stopping to stare out of the tiny window each time she reached it as though slightly hypnotized by the sun.

At last, she perched on the edge of Ari's bed and looked directly at her. "Because I broke the rules, Ari. I'm not supposed to mess with fate, with the order of things. The more we talk about it, the more we draw attention to ourselves. Somebody," she lowered her voice to a whisper, "somebody is *always* watching, watching and listening."

Ari reached up to touch Alex's face. It was warm. "You feel real," she whispered.

Then, before Alex could move or protest, she sat up and slipped her hand under her T-shirt, placing it gently just below Alex's left breast. Ari closed her eyes and concentrated, trying to listen through the palm of her hand. But she felt nothing. Alex's skin was warm and silky, but too still.

"No heartbeat."

"No. I'm sorry, Ari. I can't explain." She shrugged helplessly. You will have to accept that I am here, but not *really* here. Can you do that? Can you take it on trust?"

Ari bit her lip. "Am *I* really here?"

Alex laughed. "See for yourself." She pointed to the heart monitors stuck to Ari's chest and then to the machine that measured her heartbeat. A little red neon heart thumped on the screen with a reassuring rhythm. But Ari could feel her heart anyway. It beat strongly and it had quickened perceptibly when she'd pressed her palm against Alex's body. She wanted to touch her again, not to find out whether she was real, but to feel that fiery tingle along all her veins, that sudden tension that made her hold her breath. She wanted to know if Alex had felt it too.

They were silent. Alex seemed preoccupied, and Ari was tired, too worn out to keep questioning her about possible threats from the underworld. Her foot ached. She lay back against the stiff hospital pillows and closed her eyes.

The curtains rustled, and Ari's doctor came in to examine her. She greeted Alex cheerfully and admired Ari's flowers. Alex disappeared tactfully behind the curtain. As Doctor Roberts inspected her bite wound, Ari gazed at the vase with growing wonder. How did Alex remember? Belladonna lilies and pale pink roses were, indeed, her childhood favorites. She had forgotten, but Alex still remembered.

Belladonna lilies, deadly to horses and cows, had always filled her bedroom in summertime. It had been Ari and Alex's job to take a wheelbarrow out into the horse paddock and dig them up, along with the Scotch thistles and capeweed that tried to invade the pasture. But Ari couldn't throw the pretty pink flowers on the bonfire heap with the other weeds, so she filled jars and jugs and bowls, and the house smelled, as Cass complained, perpetually like paddock-lilies. Pink roses, too, how did Alex remember that she had loved them? It was a fragment of a memory, half-forgotten until Alex reminded her.

Laughing, they ran across the last open stretch of meadow and paused, reverently, as they always did, at the entrance to the pine plantation. They loved the bush near the beach for what it was—homely, familiar, with its spiky, sea-twisted Moonah trees, bright blue fairy wrens, sandy soil and speckled sunlight. But the old pine forest was the forest of adventure and mystery, the forest of fairy tales. A solitary little girl in a scarlet cape skipped through here, like a red rag to the wolf. The abandoned children scattered their breadcrumbs in here; the princess was imprisoned in a tower in here; and, somewhere in the green center, a beautiful girl lay entombed in a glass coffin. And there were darker, more fearful fairy-tale creatures who lurked here too. That was why they never came after dusk. But it was a bright spring morning, and Ari and Alex were not afraid.

Together, they ran through the avenues of trees until the ground began to slope sharply downward. Then they picked their way down the loamy slope toward a small clearing at the bottom. This was their great discovery, their special place. A tiny creek trickled through the basin, and the mossy green grass in the clearing was sprinkled with miniature white daisies.

Once, long ago, a house had stood here, made solidly from sandstone blocks, now crumbled and scattered. The stones just lay on the ground, some of them quite deeply embedded in the rich earth. The children looked at each other in delight. Tree houses they had in plenty. Cubbies had come and gone. But here, in this secret little valley, hidden away from the rest of the world, here they could make something more permanent—a castle, in fact. And this castle, which soon filled all their time, began to take shape in an amazingly satisfying way. They dug up the blocks of stone and laid them carefully and they fashioned beds and chairs and even a table from the fallen branches that lay everywhere on the forest floor. Ari coaxed some pretty crockery and old bed linen from Cass, and Alex dragged a roll of carpet from under her house all the way to the pine forest.

When the castle was finished, they sat on the outside bench they had constructed and critically surveyed their masterpiece.

"It needs a moat and drawbridge," declared Alex, "just to finish it off."

Ari looked at the bare earth where they had pulled up the stones.

"It needs a garden," she said softly. "I bet the people who lived here long ago had a garden." She jumped up and inspected the tangle of foliage next to a half-buried line of stones they hadn't bothered to pull up. Among the weeds and grasses and blackberry brambles Ari thought she had seen a glimmer of color. She parted the weeds, pricking her fingers

on the brambles, until she revealed a young rosebush, green and pliant and graceful, and already bearing diminutive, close-furled buds. The tip of each bud was pale pink.

"I'll water you, little pink rose," she promised it. And, in the days and weeks to come, the roses bloomed in the enchanted clearing in the pine forest. The roses still bloomed as spring turned into summer, and then to autumn, and the children never returned.

The phone on her bedside table rang just as Doctor Roberts was scribbling on Ari's chart. It was Nick.

"Hi, sweetie." He sounded tired and anxious. "I'm just outside your mum's room. She wants to talk to you, and I've told her you're at Claire's, got it?"

"But what if she rings Claire?"

"Claire agrees with you, of course. She said it would be better if we didn't tell her where you are or what happened until after the baby is born. No stress." He sighed.

"Claire's right," said Ari. "Can I speak to mum?"

"Just putting her on now."

Tears slipped down Ari's cheeks when she heard her mother's voice.

"Ari? Oh, my darling, I miss you!"

"Mum? Mum, I miss you too!"

They both started crying then, but Cass kept sobbing and trying to talk at the same time, so they ended up laughing. Dr. Roberts waved a silent, cheerful goodbye and left them to it.

After blowing her nose, Ari started to wonder. Had Cass guessed that something had happened to her? She had an uncanny mother's knack for uncovering concealment of any kind. But Cass just seemed happy to talk. Ari listened as her mother told her about the big city hospital where she was staying and the amazing view from the window.

"Oh, Nick says to tell you he's glad his mobile is working here. We're using his phone because the hospital charges way too much to make outside phone calls. Ari, tell me, how are you doing? Are you very lonely at Claire's?"

"Lonely? At Claire's? Are you kidding?" Ari forced a laugh. She hated lying to her mother. But the doctors were happy with her progress, and it seemed likely they would let her out soon, and then she *would* be at Claire and Sam's chaotic little beach shack and it wouldn't be a lie. "Those twins make more noise than all the children in the world combined," she said cheerfully. "But I want to know about you. And about the baby. Please, Mum, you know what Nick's like. He won't tell me anything at all. Are you all right, really?"

"Yes, we really are all right. Both of us. But, Ari, they want me to stay here until the baby is born. And it's likely she'll have to be delivered early, so hospital's a good place to be, all things considered."

Ari caught her breath. "She?"

Cass swore mildly. "Oops. That slipped out, didn't it? They did so many ultrasounds, honey, that in the end I cracked up and made them tell me what we were having. You're going to have a little sister."

Ari was speechless. She had loved the idea of the baby, but now it wasn't "the baby" anymore. It was a little girl. A sister. Someone to dress up and play dolls' houses with. Somebody to cuddle and read stories to, and, later on, someone to share secrets with. A sister. Ari talked happily to her mother for another half hour, making plans to come to the city to visit and to help her mother and Nick think up the most beautiful girl's names for the baby.

"I'm stuck, because I always thought Arielle was the prettiest name I had ever heard," said Cass and she gave a loud sniff. "God,

I'm turning into a leaky tap in here. I seem to cry at the drop of a hat. But I'm just so relieved, and so grateful, and a bit frightened too, I'll admit it. The doctors keep telling me how lucky I was not to lose her and how careful I must be from now on."

"You see?" Ari cried, "That's what Nick's been keeping from me! He just keeps telling me you're fine."

"I *am* fine. And you're not to worry, little worrier. Promise?"

Ari promised, told her mother she loved her, and hung up. Outside her window, the sky was a hot and brilliant blue.

O

"WE HAVE TO FIGURE OUT what to tell people about you." Shielding her eyes from the sun, Ari peeked under her hand at Alex. She looked impossibly normal sitting on one of the cast iron park benches in the hospital grounds. Sunlight flooded the bright lawns and flowerbeds, and, as she and Alex drank smoothies and talked, Ari thought they probably looked like two ordinary teenage girls enjoying the morning. But Alex's identity was a problem neither of them could figure out

Alex had started introducing herself as Anna, and Ari tried to remember to call her that when other people were in the room. The hospital staff, in any case, just assumed that Alex/Anna was either Ari's best friend or girlfriend, and it was simple enough to play along with that.

But Claire was clearly troubled by the sudden appearance of this stranger in Ari's life, and Ari sensed the weight of her anxious, unspoken questions. Who was this older girl? Somebody from school? Maybe a girlfriend? Why hadn't Ari told anyone she had a girlfriend? Did Cass and Nick know about her? She didn't ask any of these questions, and Ari was grateful for that. But Ari could tell that Claire was very curious to know what Alex had been doing at Wyndham when she found Ari half-dead from snakebite in the southwest field. Had it been arranged that she would visit that day? And why would Anna, or any visitor, finding nobody at the house, set off through the fields to hunt out its inhabitants? It was a very strange coincidence that this Anna girl had happened to find Ari just in time to save her. Claire would not have forgotten, either, what Ari had told her when she first woke up in the hospital. She was clearly worried, and Ari thought about telling her the truth. Surely, if anybody could believe the impossible, like Alex returning from the dead, it would be Claire.

Alex wasn't at all sure. "Let's assume that Claire believes you." She put their empty smoothie containers into a nearby bin and sat on the lawn next to Ari's wheelchair. She stared at the grass. "What will she do next? Who else might she tell?"

Although she was looking down on the top of Alex's head, Ari heard the tremble in her voice. She tried to choose her words carefully. Grief had opened a chasm in each of them and between them, but Ari was unsure if Alex could feel this the way she, Ari, did. So she asked Alex, as gently as she could, if she wanted to see her mum. "Maybe not straight away, maybe when you've had a chance to get used to being back?" Alex didn't reply, just hugged her knees and stared at the ground. Ari took a breath and tried again to find the right words. "I visit her once a month, with Cass. She seems to like seeing us."

Alex remained silent, but her head fell forward onto her arms and stayed there. Ari wanted to hug her, to comfort her in some way, but even though Alex was within arm's reach, she might as well have been on a distant star. Ari saw, suddenly and clearly, that it might be possible to measure seven years in space as well as time. Those years had kidnapped their childhood closeness, whisked it away, and substituted this new strangeness of their grown-up selves. She patted Alex's shoulder awkwardly. "Alex? I'm sorry. This must be so hard for you."

Alex looked up at Ari then, but her eyes weren't filled with sorrow, or pain. She looked remote, even detached, and Ari wondered if the Alex she once knew so well was still there, behind that opaque expression. "What's hard is that I can't *feel* like I should," she said bleakly. "I've returned from the afterlife to discover that my father took off back to Greece and my mother has been in some psych unit in a nursing home for years. And suddenly, I can go and see her! I can just walk up to her and say, 'Mum. It's me. I'm back.' But she wouldn't know me. I'm not the little girl she lost. Or, if she does manage to believe that I'm her daughter, wouldn't that just make things worse? What would that do to her? How could I explain why I'm older, where I've been?"

"Maybe you wouldn't have to," said Ari softly. "Beth might be able to—what was it you asked me to do earlier? Take it on trust. Like me."

Alex looked sidelong at Ari, her wry, one-sided smile accentuating her perfect lips. "Except that you are not going to be able to do that for long, Ari. You're bursting with questions."

"I won't ask them if you don't want me to. I know how to keep quiet," said Ari, a little indignantly.

Alex leaned back on her elbows and squinted at the sun. "I know I should feel sadness, and grief for my parents, and also fear for myself. I also know that I should feel fearful for you, and no, you can't ask me why. I'm happy; I think that's the right word, happy to be here. And I want to stay. I should be able to feel hopeful that we've been allowed this much time or even more hopeful that we have, just maybe, escaped notice for a while." She shook her head. "That's an awful lot of emotions to process. But I don't think I'm feeling any of them properly. I just feel numb. It's like I'm only half awake, or like parts of me have been frozen."

"But," said Ari, treading carefully, "maybe if you did see Beth, maybe something as intense as that would, I don't know, release something inside you, make you feel things properly again."

Alex looked up at her. Their eyes met.

"I felt something when I first recognized you."

Ari's cheeks flushed. Did Alex have to be so attractive? It was very distracting. The Alex she remembered had been a good-looking girl, but not... she hunted for the right word and blushed even more fiercely as one word suggested itself. She dipped her head so that her hair swung in a curtain across her face. But Alex had also looked away. She was staring at a tiny black and white willy-wagtail splashing in a nearby birdbath. Little diamond drops of water fountained out of the shallow bath, and the sun pierced each one as it rained down. Magpies warbled overhead.

Alex tilted her head to look at Ari again, but Ari found that she couldn't meet her gaze for long. Alex spoke haltingly, as though trying to remember certain words. "It's incredible, you know? Being back. Everything is so beautiful, so vivid. I didn't realize just how much I'd missed the sun and the light. Life is, I don't know, wonderful? Special? I don't know the words." She shook her head and laughed. "I'm glad I'm back. I seem to be able to feel gladness. Or something like it, anyway."

Ari wanted so much to ask the questions that she sensed Alex was avoiding, but she held her tongue. Let her be, for now, she told herself. Alex closed her eyes and tipped her head back to the sun. Ari dug her thumbnail into her fingertips. How long had it been since sunlight had warmed Alex's skin? Had it really been seven years? She wanted to take Alex by the hand and run away with her again the way they used to when they were children.

Memories came bubbling to the surface. When she was allowed to go home, she would take Alex back to their special places: to the pine plantation, to see if anything remained of the little castle of stones they had built there; to the creek where they used to catch tadpoles; and to the beach, their beach. I'll help her remember, Ari promised herself. It will be how it used to be, just Alex and me, together. Except, whispered a voice from deep inside of Ari, that it isn't the same. When you were nine, Alex was your best friend. But now, she's older and breathtakingly beautiful, and her T-shirt is clinging to her in ways that make you forget everything else. Whatever happens next, things will never be the same between the two of you.

O

LATE AFTERNOON SUNLIGHT RAKES THROUGH *the trees and the children pause, struck momentarily by the architectural symmetry of dark, pillar-like trunks and slanting beams of light. Outside of the pine plantation, summer heat smothers everything, but here, in the cathedral of trees, there is endless space and the cool sponginess of pine needles underfoot. Princess Arielle begins to walk, slowly, her long white robes trailing along the loamy ground. She holds a small posy of daisies, and her hair is crowned with them. Her sword drawn, the warrior queen waits behind a tree. The princess is weeping. Her father is away fighting in an enemy kingdom. The queen has been imprisoned in the castle tower. Her cruel uncle, motivated by greed for the kingdom's gold, has decreed that the princess must marry his son: an ugly, dim-witted lout whose chief pleasure is hunting and killing innocent creatures for sport.*

But as the princess walks the long aisle toward her doom, the brave warrior queen springs out from behind a tapestry. Her sword flashes as she fights off the uncle's henchmen, takes the princess by the hand, and runs with her back down the aisle of the great cathedral and out into the sunshiny meadow where her trusty steed is grazing. Queen Alex is a little too short to jump astride her horse, but fortune favors the brave adventurers by providing a handy gate they can both climb to reach the patient horse's broad back. They canter off, the princess clinging tightly to her rescuer, her daisies scattered on the grass.

"Wait!" Queen Alex reins in her mount. "We cannot abandon your royal mother to such an evil fate. We must rescue her!"

"Of course," agrees the princess.

But just as they decide to turn the horse around, Princess Arielle notices one of the peasants from a nearby farm waving furiously at them.

"Could be trouble," says Queen Alex doubtfully. The peasant woman continues to wave, then cups her hands around her mouth and shouts. They can't hear her, but her meaning is quite clear.

"Let's go home," says Ari. "I bet my Mum's already asked your Mum to stay for tea."

"C'mon, Rusty." Alex gives the big, gentle Clydesdale a squeeze with her legs, and the children are carried safely homeward.

While the nurse checked her temperature and scolded them for sitting in the sun without hats on, Ari thought of all the memories she and Alex shared. She would help Alex remember. And she'd try hard not to think about Alex in *that* way. Besides, Alex might like boys or just not be interested in her, like that. She would have to get to know this new, grown-up Alex. Ari didn't ask herself what she would say when Alex remembered how she died. She pushed that memory into a corner of her mind where her darkest fears lived and shut the door on it.

O

AS HER RELEASE FROM HOSPITAL drew closer, Ari listened anxiously while Claire made arrangements over the phone with Nick. Nick wanted Ari to stay at Claire and Sam's under some form of benevolent house arrest. Ari protested loudly and pushed to be allowed to spend her days at home. Claire argued that Ari needed some solitude during the daytime and that, at sixteen, nearly seventeen, she could surely be relied upon to turn up just before dark each day. She could eat with them and read bedtime stories to Jack and Oscar. Claire agreed, and this was one of the things Ari loved about Claire, that it was perfectly reasonable for Ari to walk over at dusk, or even after sunset, that she knew her way through field and forest the way she knew how to walk half asleep into the bathroom in the middle of the night. Even after the snakebite, Claire trusted Ari enough to know that she would be much more careful in future. Ari was allowed to spend as much of her time at home as she wanted, but she would always spend the nights at Claire and Sam's. Sally-dog would stay there all the time, using the basket that had been lovingly prepared for her by the twins. Ari would continue to work part-time at the Stonehaven pub when she was completely well.

These arrangements hadn't come without their fair share of lectures, though, from the doctor who discharged her from the hospital, to Nick, anxiously pulling his beard and peering through his glasses at her when he came to visit, to Claire's gentle but firm remonstrance about the importance of not taking risks, especially while Cass's health (and the baby's) was still precarious.

On the day she was discharged from Port August Hospital, Sam and Claire gave her a coming-home gift: a pair of steel-capped Blundstone boots. Ari laughed when she opened the box, but Dr. Roberts looked very solemn as she told Ari, once again, how close she had come to death from snakebite.

Later, after Ari had thanked the nurses and was signing forms at the discharge counter, she overheard Dr. Roberts talking to Claire and Sam.

"She doesn't know, and I don't think she needs to know, but we're considering her recovery a medical oddity, a bit of a miracle, really. She had to have been lying in that field for at least an hour before her friend found her, and then she had to walk the three or four miles up the road to the general store. Even if her friend carried her some of the way, that's incredible." The doctor lowered her voice. "And, I don't think there has been a recorded case of anybody resisting tiger snake venom for the length of time that she did. We had to administer shockingly large doses of antivenin when she came in and we had very little hope, because…" The doctor lowered her voice still further. "…because her heart had completely stopped. We had to resuscitate her twice. She should be dead, or at the very least severely brain-damaged, but she's in perfect health. I just don't understand it, and neither do the colleagues with whom I've discussed Ari's case."

"Maybe it is a bona fide miracle," said Sam. "But our Ari, she's a fighter."

"She's very strong," added Claire.

Ari thought she detected a warning note in Claire's voice, but Sam went on in an undertone: "She made this incredible swim at Seal Cove when she was nine or ten, but her friend, a girl two years older than her, drowned trying to swim the same distance. You might remember if you've lived here for a bit. Little Alex Cohen—her parents were the managers at Smythson's about ten years back."

"I remember," said Dr. Roberts. "Poor Beth. Beth, and... Oh, I can't remember the father's name."

"Nathaniel. Nate," said Claire reluctantly.

Ari closed her ears. She knew the next part of this story, and it made razors twist in her belly.

"Beth is still in care, I understand? At Sunnymead?"

"Yes," said Sam. "She never got over it. Alex was her only child."

"And the father?"

"Nate."

"Yes. Nate. He left her just a couple of years afterward. Is that right?"

"It was terrible. A tragedy." Claire sounded anxious. "Honey, I think we should get Ari home. She must be itching to get out of here." She stopped, and then seemed embarrassed as she added, "I mean, out of hospital. You've all been so fantastic, and we owe you so much."

"Yeah," added Sam. "Thank you, Doctor. We'll keep a close eye on her."

Ari picked up her bag and waved as cheerfully as she could at Sam and Claire when they came around the corner.

4.
Strange Tales

Ari washed the last dish, placed it triumphantly in the rack, and untied her apron, all in one swift motion. The bistro was finally empty, thank goodness, but the bar was filling up as the usual Friday afternoon crowd filtered in.

Nick had firm rules about Ari working in the hotel. "No bar work until you turn eighteen. Stay out of the bar, and don't hang around outside in the beer garden, especially where people are smoking. If I'm not there, Jodie's in charge, but you can help her with locking up, doing the rosters, the safe, putting the wages in, that kind of stuff."

Once she was considered well enough to work again, Ari found herself doing all of this and more, but she was under strict instructions not to tire herself, and so Jodie made sure that her shifts were kept short. Nick was concerned about leaving the pub without a manager during the holiday season, but Ari reassured him that they had plenty of staff and that Jodie was holding the fort with her usual capable confidence. Ari had been out of the hospital for two weeks, and life had settled into a new routine. Claire would run her up to the pub around midmorning, and Ari would do paperwork, help in the kitchen, serve meals, and wash up. Then, in the afternoon, Jodie would drop her off at Wyndham, where she would call her mother, feed the cows and the horses, collect the mail, water the veggie patch, and spend some time with Alex, who was sleeping in her bedroom.

Alex had initially been very worried about this arrangement.

"It's totally fine," Ari told her as she placed some towels and a pair of clean summer pajamas on her bed. "Nobody will suspect anything.

We won't get many visitors, especially now that people know that Mum and Nick are staying in the city. All my school friends have gone away for the holidays. Nobody will bother you. And don't worry about Claire. She's terrific but, I agree, she wouldn't really understand. We'll just have to keep you a secret. I told her that Anna had to go on holiday to Queensland with her parents and that I would catch up with her when school started. I said we were pretty close, and we just left it at that. Claire's great, she doesn't ask heaps of questions like most adults."

Ari busied herself with folding and hanging up some new jeans and shirts she'd bought for Alex. Ari had asked Claire to take her shopping on the way home from hospital, pretending she needed the retail therapy. Alex seemed grateful for the new clothes but not at all curious about how Ari had obtained them. She probably hasn't had to think about clothes for years and years, Ari thought.

Alex was wandering around Ari's room. She stopped to examine a small, silver-framed photo on her bedside table. It showed the two of them, aged six and eight, sitting high up on Rusty's back. Staring intently at the photo, Alex sank slowly onto the bed. The picture was slightly grainy and overexposed, taken on a bright summer's day long ago. Ari sat in front; her little hands were buried in the Clydesdale's thick, glossy mane. Alex had one arm wrapped securely around her waist, and the other was raised in a cheerful wave.

Ari sat next to her. The bed springs creaked, and she held her breath as they studied the photo together. Alex smiled, but it was a sad smile, and her expression was too complex for Ari to read when she put the photo down and looked closely at her.

"You don't look very different," she told Ari at last. "I know it's been seven years, but you look pretty much the way you do in that photo."

Ari didn't know what to say. Alex vaguely resembled the little girl in the photo, but she was so much older. Her face had thinned, and her hair was longer and darker. Her body was different, too, in ways that made Ari tingle and blush and want to touch her. It was one of the many things that separated this grown-up Alex, this beautiful young woman, from the little tomboy in the photo. Her remoteness was also new. The old Alex, the one Ari remembered, had been cheerful and talkative, but this Alex was solemn, even guarded. What had happened to her, really, in the underworld? What had it been like for her, all those dark and lonely years? Did she secretly blame Ari for everything she'd lost?

Ari was quiet as these questions crowded her mind, and Alex didn't try to make conversation. Ari sensed Alex studying her, but she couldn't look at her old friend. The nasty sneering voice in her head, her old tormentor, was busily reciting its litany of recriminations: If you hadn't dared her, she wouldn't have died. It really is your fault. You knew about the tides. It's your fault Alex drowned. Your fault. Yours.

Alex touched her, lightly, on the shoulder. "Are you all right, Ari? What's the matter?"

Ari took a breath and tried to visualize the nasty voice as a cloud of dust she could sweep from her head, where it would evaporate, or be carried away on the wind. This technique often worked, if temporarily. She forced herself to sound cheerful. "You look the same too," she told Alex finally, "just older."

"What's this?" Alex picked up a thin paperback lying open and facedown on Ari's pillow. "*The Owl Service,*" she read. "Any good?"

"Yes," said Ari. "It's about three kids who get caught up in this ancient Welsh myth. It's a love story, but a tragic one. The girl gets sort of possessed by the spirit of a woman called Blodeuwedd. A magician makes her out of flowers, but then he turns her into an owl."

"I know that story. That's a very old story." Alex put the book down and squatted to read the titles of some of the other books jammed into Ari's low, white bookcase. "*Seaward, The Tempest, The Chrysalids, The Changeover, Art through the Ages, Greek Myth.* Have you read all of these?"

"Most of them," said Ari. "I read a lot. I guess that makes me a bit of a nerd."

"What's a nerd?"

She's serious, Ari thought. Imagine forgetting that word. Their childhood had been punctuated by kids using that word to tease both of them.

"You know," Ari said, "someone who likes to do things that other kids think are uncool, or dumb, or just, you know, boring, like reading Greek myths for instance."

"Greek myths aren't boring," said Alex, pulling the heavy volume from the shelves. May I read this?" She opened the book to the front page, which showed a beautiful engraving of Paris awarding the golden apple to Aphrodite.

"Of course. You can read any books you like. That one has some fantastic pictures. And, Alex? This goes without saying, but please help yourself to everything in the house. That means clothes, books, bathroom stuff, the fridge, whatever you need. Do you need me to show you how to use the TV? Oh, and hang on, I have something for you. It's yours, actually. I just kept it."

Ari reached up to the top shelf of her wardrobe and brought out a large shoebox. She put it on the bed. Inside were several old tubes of paint, brushes, sponges, palette knives, and other artist's paraphernalia.

Alex picked up some of the paints and ran her slender fingers along the smooth hairs of the largest brush. "My painting things," she murmured. "I don't know if I remember how to paint."

Ari rummaged in her school art folio. "Aha!" She flourished a sketchbook triumphantly. "Heaps of blank pages left in here. You should have a go. I'm sure it would come back to you. And there are lots of tins of acrylic in the toolshed, too. Nick had this brilliant idea that he was going to get a mural painted on the wall in the beer garden. He bought all this paint and then forgot about it. So, if your paints are dried up, you could use those."

Alex gazed down at her, the book of Greek myths still clutched to her chest. "Ari, thank you. I hope you understand what it means to me to be here, with you. I just hope . . ." She bit her lip then and opened the book at random. "Orpheus and Eurydice," she read. "That's such a terribly sad story, don't you think?" She looked closely at Ari then, and her expression was grave. "Ari, I know you must have read a bit about the classical underworld but I want you to know, it's not like it is in the books."

Ari, caught off guard, stammered as she replied: "Oh. Oh, okay."

Alex laughed. "Well done. And, as a reward for your restraint I will tell you that all that stuff about Tartarus and the Elysian Fields, you know about those places? About the Fields of Asphodel where the in-between souls roam around, well, that's all reasonably accurate. There is a place for good souls and bad souls and for those caught in between. But there is no three-headed dog guarding the river. There are rumors about a grim king of the dead enthroned with a wife he stole from the living, but I think they may be stories to frighten children."

"No Persephone?"

"If she exists, I have never seen her. But the underworld is vast, so who knows?" She shrugged. "I suppose what I mean is that the underworld isn't as dramatic, isn't as vibrant, as it is painted in the stories. It's actually very dreary. Not a lot happens there."

"But there is a river? You said something about the river Styx and the ferryman. How could Homer and the others have got that bit right but been wrong about the gods and goddesses?"

"Maybe they didn't get it *wrong,*" Alex said restlessly. "Maybe they just got it a bit mixed up." She lowered her voice. "Do you know what I think? I think some of the ancient writers somehow made the descent and got as far as the river. The imagination and the reality are too close for that not to be the case. But they were alive; they couldn't cross the river, and so they returned, and then they filled in the rest from their imaginations and from older stories. There are hundreds of stories about journeys to and from the underworld, and not just in Greek mythology. What about all those Scottish stories your grandma used to tell us about people crossing over? And there are Aboriginal stories, Gadubanud stories, about places right here in Stonehaven that we know nothing about, though I wish we did. Oh, and it's the *Acheron* river that new souls must cross, not the Styx. Most people get that wrong."

Alex flicked through the book, turning the pages quickly, as if she was looking for something.

Ari's skin prickled and her stomach clenched. How could they even be having this conversation? It seemed a little like one of their childhood games, but this wasn't make-believe. The underworld was real. Alex had been there, *lived there.*

Alex closed the book. "There are actually lots of gods and goddesses. But they tend to stay apart from the human shades and from those of us who look after them." Alex's voice changed from an abstracted, lecturing tone to a softer, reminiscent one. She gazed out the window and then closed her eyes, tilting her face to catch the late afternoon sunlight. "I have seen from afar the lords of the rivers riding the phantoms of horses along the high road. I have seen the lost ones wandering in the fields of white flowers. I have seen an old, old woman with serpents twined around her body, followed by a procession of white-clad girls bearing torches. Their little fires made flames leap in the darkness of the river where no light comes. But a court where a king and queen preside over the whole underworld? That I have not seen, and I was down there a long time." Alex shook her head. "Anyway…" she said. "You don't need to know about any of that. You are staying here, where you belong."

Ari occupied herself with straightening the books on her bedside table and tried not to think about how long Alex had lived in the darkness. Before the old guilt could choke her, she asked the first question that came into her head. "Did you have books to read, down there?"

"Yes." Alex frowned a little and looked away. Ari waited for her to speak, but she just opened the book again and continued to turn the pages, stopping now and then to peer intently at an illustration.

"I have to go," said Ari, catching herself before she could ask Alex any more questions. She sensed that Alex didn't like questions about how it had been for her, how she had lived down there, although she had no idea why the question about books should have upset her. Ari was overwhelmed with helplessness. What was there to say? "I'm sorry?" Had two more inadequate words ever existed? She fussed, clearing more space on her bedside table for Alex to keep her nonexistent belongings and putting a few more things of her own in a bag to take to Claire's.

"I put clean sheets on the bed," she told Alex, "and there are lots of CDs next to the CD player over there. It's actually the same one I've always had, so I'm sure you'll remember how to use it. Also, I've left you my tablet, but we still don't have any internet reception down here, which is ultra-annoying. There's music on it, though, and it's fully charged, and my password is Sally." She stopped herself, knowing she was going too fast, assuming too much. "Anyway, I'm sure you'll figure it all out." She paused, irresolute, in the doorway of her bedroom.

Alex was standing by the open window. The sea breeze made the faded yellow curtains billow around her, and the dark waves of her hair brushed the pages of the open book as she smiled briefly at Ari, then bent her head to peer again at one of the pictures.

Ari couldn't help staring at Alex's perfect lips, imagining how it would feel to touch them with her own. "Just cut it out," she whispered fiercely to herself.

She waved goodbye as nonchalantly as she could and tried not to think about how Alex would lie down on her bed later that night or about how much she wanted to lie pressed close up against her. It's a fantasy, Ari reminded herself. She doesn't think about you like that. She thinks you're still nine years old.

But, whispered a small voice from her heart, maybe Alex just can't have those kinds of feelings yet. Maybe she's never felt anything like what you're starting to feel about her. Did she meet anyone special in the underworld? Was that even possible? Maybe parts of Alex grew up, but other parts stayed childlike. But what if she could change that? What would it take, Ari allowed herself to imagine, for Alex to have some grown-up feelings for her?

○

SUMMER AT STONEHAVEN WAS USUALLY an all-or-nothing event. It was either mild, with lots of rain and disgusted tourists who left the camping area and the caravan park well before school started, or endless days of searing heat, withered crops, and swarms of blowflies. Ari could never understand why the holidaymakers seemed content to stay on in the blistering heat, but stay they did, mostly waist-deep in the calm waters of Stonehaven Bay or turning themselves regularly on the blinding sand like undercooked sausages on brightly colored serviettes.

Ari was busy. The pub was always full for lunch in hot weather, and the air conditioning wasn't the only reason this year. People were restless, and they clung together in groups. Local farmers stood uneasily at the bar beside their unfinished pots of beer, each with a soggy cardboard coaster stuck to its base. Their talk was of ruined fruit crops: apples burnt brown by the sun before they had a chance to grow, berries withered on the vines before their autumn ripening.

The dairy farmers complained of the price of feed and the fall in milk production. "It's like the bloody cows are possessed or something," grumbled old Joe Collings. "My lot seem to be anyway. Always spooked about something, even the placid ones. And when you do get 'em to stand still, they just won't let down." He lowered his voice. "And them bastard dogs was out again the other night."

Trevor Graham squinted at the TV and took a long swig of his beer. "There you are then. Bloody feral dogs. But you're not alone on the milk front, mate. My girls are refusing to come up to the sheds even. I have to get on the bike and drive them up. It's been a bad season all right. Reckon everybody's feelin' it."

The fishermen sat listening to the farmers' complaints, most of which were, after all, not unusual for a long, hot summer following a drought. But they had their own whispered conversations, and some of these Ari heard while polishing the glasses (quite legally) just around the corner from the main bar.

"Don't reckon I've seen anything like it before."

"Mate, there's some bloody weird stuff out there. You should've seen what Dave brought in last week. This squid must've been at least two yards long, and it had *fifteen* tentacles. We counted twice, just to make sure. Freak of nature, Dave reckons."

"Nah, mate, I'm not talking about bloody fifteen-legged squid."

"So, what then?"

"Well, I don't really like to say, 'specially with the little lady about."

Damn. They'd spotted her.

Ari tried to eavesdrop later, when the farmers, the fishermen, and the forestry guys had downed a few beers and forgotten to be so cautious around the boss's stepdaughter. She pretended to clean the glass doors of the drinks fridge, but she was straining to catch every word of the hushed conversation between Gary Dawson and Tommy Evans, two of the town's oldest and most respected fishermen. The others had moved on from the spooky stuff and were watching, with glazed expressions, the cricket on the widescreen TV above the bar. Dawso drained the dregs from his mug and picked up the fresh one that sat in front of him. He glanced surreptitiously over his shoulder and ran his tongue over his yellow front teeth.

Tommy rolled a cigarette and looked sidelong at Dawso. "Well, come on, mate. You might as well tell me. I've seen a lotta weird shit out there too, ya know."

"It just wasn't right," admitted Dawso at last. "I never seen nothin' like it. Nothin'."

Tommy waited. Ari scrubbed the glass as quietly as she could.

"It was just, how many of them there were, you know?" said Dawso finally. "All these faces, these bloated bodies, just bobbing up outta nowhere and floating, you know? Floating up around the boat, caught in the nets, everywhere. There was old ones and, and young ones, real young ones. I thought there musta been a plane crash or a refugee boat gone down or something." He stopped and drained his glass, then leaned closer to Tommy. "But there wasn't anything like that on the radio or the TV. There weren't any accidents at all that day or in the days beforehand. So." Dawso lit a cigarette and took a long, shaky drag.

Ari didn't even think about telling him off for smoking. Whatever Dawso happened to say next would be crucial, and he mustn't know she was there or he would censor it or more likely stop talking altogether. But it was Tommy who filled the long pause that followed. He and Dawso were old mates, so there was a touch of incredulity but mostly a lot of concern in the questions that followed.

"You reckon you saw, what? Dead bodies? Whereabouts?"

"Just past the gap, directly out from Crofts' Point."

"What did you do when you saw 'em?"

Dawso made a fist with one hand and leaned the other, still clutching his cigarette, shakily against the edge of the bar. He let out a strangled laugh. "I bloody shat myself, mate. I didn't know what to do. What would you do if you were hauling in a catch and your net came up with that sorta shit? I cut the net free and turned her around and made a run for it, that's what I did." He took another drag on his cigarette. Thin plumes of smoke snaked from his nostrils as he glanced around him.

"Did you tell the cops?"

"Of course I told the bloody cops," snorted Dawso. "Told me to stay off the piss, didn't they?" Dawso looked down at his cigarette and sighed. "Better take this outside. You comin'?"

The fishermen disappeared. Ari stropped pretending to clean the drinks fridge and crouched behind the bar. She had known Dawso and Tommy since she was a little kid, and there was no way they would invent something so frightening. Bodies? Bobbing up from under the water? It didn't make sense, especially with the currents out past Stonehaven Bay. Nobody knew better than Ari the pull and drag of those currents. So there were two possibilities: either Dawso had drowned most of his brain cells at the bar or something really, really, weird was going on.

The summer days slid by, and the more she worked at the pub, the more Ari was inclined to believe that there actually *was* a lot of strange stuff happening. Rhona, who owned a craft-and-crystal shop in Stonehaven, said that the moon was in a special phase, closer than ever before to the earth or something like that. The tides had certainly been different, not that Ari had much of a chance to go to the beach lately. What rattled her even more than Dawso's half-articulated horror story of bodies bobbing in the water was another conversation she had overheard in the bar. Liz Pearce and Sue McHenry had talked in hushed voices about Stonehaven's current obsession: things that "weren't quite right."

Sue and Liz both had adult sons who worked as clearers for the forestry department. Their job took them deep inside the pine plantation, to areas most people never saw. Ari had always thought that pine forests, especially plantation forests with their neat rows, were open, without undergrowth to trick the eye, and that it would be very hard, therefore, to get lost in one. But Sue, a glass of house red wine in her hand, was warming to her subject. She narrated, again, the unlikely story of the two bushwalkers who had recently been lost in the pine plantation. They'd only been reported missing for a day but had refused to talk to the local newspaper, and so the event had become tantalizingly mysterious.

"The state of 'em, when they got to the forestry station!" Sue lowered her voice. "My Ryan said he's never seen nobody look paler and more scared in his life. He reckons the girl was shaking like a leaf, and the bloke was actually crying. They seen something in there, all right, and Ryan couldn't get it out of 'em. But I'll tell you what I reckon scared those two."

"What?"

"Dog packs," she said, staring at Liz.

"Dog packs?" Liz looked puzzled.

"Feral dogsh, I mean, dogs. You know—the ones Matty and Hendo have been trying to get for months. Well, they've gone *really* feral now. Got into big packs an' started hunting. You know I've always loved living just outside of town, but I'm starting to wonder. We're closer than anyone else to the plantation. Our stock is suffering. At first it was just a couple of chickens, but then the whole litter of new piglets went in the night. Poor old Doris, we almost had to put her out of her misery that morning, she was that distraught. She had bite marks and deep slashes all over, where the rotten bastard dogs attacked her, but she's right as rain now. Better, now that she's pregnant again. Tell you what, though: She's in the shed full-time now. Door locked and padlocked every single night. Chooks the same. And God help me if I'm not locking our doors now too. I even got Ryan to nail a board over the cat flap. How's that for paranoid?"

Liz took a long swig of her wine. She began to fiddle with the edge of the bar mat, and her voice was unsteady as she confided, "Our stock is suffering too. But it's not losses I'm worried about. It's *wrongness*."

"Wrongness?"

"Yeah. In, in the breeding. Darryl had to destroy three goslings hatched on the weekend. They looked all right at first, but when we had a closer look..." She swallowed. "When we had a closer look, the poor little things had no legs."

"You're shitting me."

"No, 'strue. They just had these little bumps where their legs should've been." Liz shrugged. "Can't survive in the farmyard with no legs. Not nice to have to destroy things so little, though. Darryl was really upset."

Ari stopped listening. She felt sick to her stomach. What was wrong with their little corner of the world? Stonehaven was such a quiet place, a peaceful, rather boring coastal hamlet so far away from the nearest major city that hardly anything ever changed. Parts of Stonehaven itself weren't even on town water, and the tiny farms enfolded in the lush green hills between Stonehaven and the ocean were mostly hobby farms now or, like Wyndham, had long since ceased to be working farms. Tourism was the major industry, but only the Stonehaven Bay Caravan Park did well from holidaymakers. It was, on the whole, an exceptionally beautiful, but ultimately ordinary, part of the world. What dark forces would choose to infiltrate sleepy old Stonehaven? Bodies in the ocean, dog packs in the pine plantation, legless goslings... what other horrors would she hear if she hung around the bar?

Ari checked the clock. It was close enough to two o'clock to make going home a legitimate possibility. And when she got home, Ari thought grimly, it might finally be time for Alex to answer a few questions.

5.
A Painted Circle

Ari found Alex weeding the veggie garden. She had borrowed Nick's old fishing hat and she looked so ordinary on her knees among the tomatoes that Ari had to stop and remind herself that Alex wasn't ordinary, not even a little bit. Here was her lost childhood friend, grown up in the underworld and returned to her, seemingly alive but without a heartbeat.

And I nearly died too, Ari told herself. She's here because she saved me. If Alex hadn't seen my scars and figured out who I was, if she hadn't been able to carry me all the way up the road to the general store, if she hadn't broken all the rules, I wouldn't be here. She was flooded, suddenly, with gratitude and promised herself she would go easy on Alex and not pester her with questions she wasn't ready to answer. But still, some questions needed answers. It couldn't be a coincidence that all the weird, scary stuff going on had started *after* Alex's return. Alex had told her in the hospital that there might be trouble. Was it happening already? Were the feral dogs and the freaks of nature and Dawso's hallucinations warnings of some kind? And if they were, why target people like poor Mrs. McHenry or Dawso, who maybe drank too much but never hurt anybody? None of it made any sense.

Ari poured tall glasses of lime soda with lots of ice and carried the glasses out to the garden. The sun was fierce, even at this time of the day, and Ari plucked her own hat from its nail on the veranda post before she wandered over to help Alex. She held out the drink, and Alex smiled up at her from under Nick's battered old canvas hat. Ari's heart took off at a gallop. At least she could blame the afternoon heat for her flaming cheeks. All she has to do is *smile* at me, she thought, incredulously. Did it show? Could she tell?

Alex brushed some of the soil from her hands and took the wet glass. "How was work?"

"Okay, I guess. Must be the silly season, though. The locals are talking all sorts of crazy stuff." She filled Alex in, briefly, on the stories she'd overheard. Alex listened closely but offered no response. Ari glared at her in frustration. She seemed unconcerned, and her expression was serene as she put down her empty glass and resumed pulling handfuls of grass from the neglected veggie patch.

"People round here always were a little bit mad," she said at last. "It's the isolation, maybe. Gets to some of them after a while." She squinted up at Ari. "Remember old Mr. Stuart from over the creek?"

Ari remembered Mr. Stuart very well. He and his walking stick had chased a young Ari and Alex away from his raspberry canes several times during their childhood. She allowed herself to be distracted by the memory of the two of them running like the wind toward the road with their pockets stuffed with squishy raspberries, while Mr. Stuart, like an older, crankier version of Peter Rabbit's Mr. McGregor, tottered behind them waving his stick and croaking threats.

"He never picked those raspberries himself, you know," Ari said indignantly. "And he never sold them either."

Alex laughed. "He was good at protecting them, whatever he did with them." She took off Nick's hat, gently tied up a tomato stem with a bit of twine, stood up, and arched her back. Ari squatted among the rough, scented foliage and bright red cherry tomatoes and tried to pluck up the courage to ask Alex the questions that were eating away at her.

But Alex seemed to have an uncanny ability to sense when an awkward question was coming. "Want to see what I've been doing with my days?"

"What, besides transforming the garden?" Ari, glad to be diverted, looked around admiringly. Their vegetables would be terrific, despite the drought, because Alex was watering them faithfully twice a day, something Ari, Cass, and Nick often forgot to do. And she had tidied up, too, stacking dead branches by the woodpile and raking the gravel paths. "Cass and Nick are never going to believe I did all this on my own."

"Well, it's good to be able to work in a garden, in the sunshine. I'm enjoying it. But I've been busy in other ways too. Come and see."

Ari followed her across the dusty yard toward one of the smaller sheds. The warm grit sifted into her sandals, and the sticky flies clung relentlessly to her bare shoulders. Brushing them off, Ari was embarrassed to feel sweat pooling between her breasts and did her best to blot it with the neck of her singlet. Alex, of course, chose that moment to turn around. For a split second she met her gaze, and Ari's cheeks burned as she struggled to identify the emotions behind that dark stare. Was it longing she read in her eyes? Maybe desire? If so, it seemed to be for something unfathomable. And mingled with that desire was what? Sadness? Loneliness? There wasn't much left of the skinny, carefree, wild little girl who had been her best friend.

Ari couldn't meet Alex's eyes for long. Blushing, she stared fiercely at the swamp wallabies grazing the withered crops in the fields and at the blue strip of the ocean. Then, breathing shallowly, she stole another glimpse at Alex, who was now, infuriatingly, walking ahead.

"God it's hot, isn't it?" Alex stopped, and Ari thought she looked tense. "Well, here we are. This is one of my lesser efforts, but it will give you an idea."

Ari looked up. On the rusty silver of the far wall of the toolshed, a circle of color blazed and throbbed. Under the golden light of the afternoon sun, it looked out of place: a stained glass porthole in the corrugated iron wall. It was large enough that, if it had been a real window, a person could just squeeze through; but it was the intricate detailing that fascinated Ari. The circle seemed to be made up of hundreds of winding, spiraling lines in colors that reminded her of a medieval tapestry: scarlet and gold, rust and bronze, viridian and turquoise.

Ari touched the painting. It was hot, almost burning her fingertip. Lightly, she traced a long indigo line. It described an arc about half the circumference of the circle and then doubled back, took a left turn, and went straight almost to the center, where it turned left again and doubled back on itself once more. It was difficult to follow a single thread of color amid the myriad other lines and patterns, but Ari soon became distracted and stopped, her fingertip pressed to the scorching metal folds of the shed wall.

Behind her, Alex stood so close that her breasts lightly brushed Ari's back. Her heat, and the heat of the day, and the sudden heat in Ari's body became indistinguishable. She tried to slow her breathing as Alex casually reached over her shoulder, took her finger gently in her right hand, and continued to trace it along the dark blue line. With Alex's finger pressed close against hers, and her hand, firm and slender, wrapped around her own, everything else seemed to fade out of existence. Together their fingertips followed the sinuous blue curves until the line ended in a complex tangle of colors at the center of the circle.

Ari pulled her hand away and turned her face up so that she could meet Alex's gaze. "It's a labyrinth," she whispered, trying to slow her breathing.

Alex didn't move away, but whatever spell had held them close was broken. She looked sad and tired and she stared at her beautiful painting as if it really was a window and there was something beyond it that troubled her. "It's a portal, she said absently. But there are labyrinths beyond it, yes."

"You painted a portal? To the, to *down there*? Why?" Ari heard the fear in her voice as she moved back to see Alex better. Alex shuffled her feet, looking restless and guilty. Ari tried another question: "Is that . . . could we really go through it?"

"Oh, yes. It's a real portal. The underworld lies on the other side."

"But it's just a painting."

"A ring of stones, a painted circle, a hole in the earth, there are many doorways to the unlit realm."

"Can you not talk like that, please?"

"Like what?"

"Like, oh, I don't know. Why did you do it? Why would you want to paint something like that?"

"I had to," she replied. "It's . . . do you know what a compulsion is?"

"No. I mean, yes, of course I do, but I don't know what you're talking about."

"It's just something I have to do. I can't fight it. It's like these blinkers come over my eyes, and I can't see or do anything else until I've finished the paintings."

"You mean there are others? How many?"

"A dozen, maybe more. Mostly on rocks in the bush or inside the sheds, but they are all like this one. Some are a little more intricate, perhaps." She sounded detached, as if considering the merits of a collection of works in an art gallery.

Ari was furious with her. She turned swiftly away and began to storm back toward the house, swiping at her eyes and blinking away the tears that wouldn't stop welling up. She forgot that she'd intended to go easy on Alex, that she was trying to be sympathetic. She told herself she didn't care that her old friend couldn't feel emotions like a normal person. A deep ache began in her chest. Alex was going to leave. Again. The first time she lost her, she had been a child with a child's limited understanding of death. But this was different. Ari's heart hurt so much she thought great rips were running through it; she gave a gasp of pain and clutched her chest.

Alex caught up with her and tried to grab her hand, but Ari shook her off.

"Ari, what's the matter? Are you crying? What's wrong?" She sounded genuinely worried, but Ari was fed up with trying to figure out what emotions Alex could and couldn't feel. She was sick to death of feeling guilty, about Beth and Nate and the horror of Alex drowning, about the years of loneliness she must have endured in the underworld, about everything.

Alex followed her silently until they reached the shade of the veranda, and then Ari dragged one of the old cast-iron porch chairs from under their matching table and told her to sit down. Ari remained standing, her arms crossed in front of her sweaty chest. The afternoon heat had turned humid, and Ari longed for a cool shower and an icy glass of water. She leaned back on the veranda post and stared at Alex, who couldn't return her gaze and picked nervously at a patch of dried blue paint on her shorts.

Ari took a deep breath. "It's hot, and I'm sick of all of this crap. You need to tell me what's going on and stop avoiding my questions. Don't you care that poor old Gary Dawson thinks he's going mad because he saw dead bodies in the ocean or that savage dogs are killing people's animals in the middle of the night? How long do you reckon it will be before the dog packs attack someone's pet, or someone's kid? What if you knew what was happening and you didn't do anything to stop it?" Ari took a breath. "Because, Alex, I know that you must have some idea about all of this, and I reckon it's got to do with you saving me, and I want to know exactly how much trouble we're in."

Alex remained silent. She sat very still, her hands clasped and resting on the table. She seemed to be studying the white iron lace of the tabletop.

"Well?" demanded Ari.

Alex looked up at her. "We're in a hell of a lot of trouble," she whispered. "And so is Stonehaven."

O

NOW THAT ALEX HAD AGREED to tell her the truth about their situation, Ari found herself disinclined to hear it. If only, she thought wistfully, if only there was no threat, no wrongness in Stonehaven. It seemed the most natural thing in the world to have Alex around again. That's all I want, thought Ari. Just Alex, and me, and time to get to know each other properly. She didn't want to spoil whatever time they might have together talking about feral dogs and darkness and danger leaking from the underworld. So she was relieved when Alex asked if she could have a shower before they talked.

To stop herself from imagining her friend naked, Ari busied herself with assembling the ingredients for pasta sauce. She tried not to think about Alex's body while she chopped onions and rinsed cherry tomatoes from the garden. The tomatoes were delicious, ripe and firm and still warm from the sun. The garden had also yielded lush basil and spinach leaves.

Alex emerged from the bathroom, smelling fresh and looking impossibly beautiful with wet hair, and offered to stir the pasta sauce while Ari had her shower. As she passed her the wooden spoon, Ari felt the shower's heat radiate from Alex's body and she had to fight the urge to stroke her smooth, naked shoulders or remove a strand of wet hair from her cheek. Alex stood close while Ari told her what to do with the dinner, and this made it very hard to breathe properly or think clearly. Did Alex want to be close to her as much as Ari wanted it? It was impossible to tell, and Ari thought she might throw her arms around her friend and ruin everything, so she almost ran to the bathroom, leaving Alex holding the spoon.

The bathmat was wet, and faint indentations in the damp fibers marked where Alex's feet had been. As she stood under the cool water, Ari did let herself imagine, just a little, what Alex might look like in the shower. She thought, this is the same soap Alex used only ten minutes ago. She used this shampoo, and this conditioner, and maybe my razor too. If only, thought Ari longingly, if only she were really, truly, here to stay, without all the strange, scary stuff. If there was no uncertainty and no danger, they could concentrate on each other instead of worrying about a future filled with unimaginable threats.

Ari sighed, turned off the shower, and stepped from the bath. She fitted her feet into Alex's footprints as she reached for her towel.

While she dried her hair, Ari phoned Claire to beg to stay a little longer at Wyndham. She said the house was getting grubby and that she wanted to give it a thorough clean. She also, and she hoped Claire wouldn't be offended, just wanted to chill out and watch TV in her own house, maybe cook herself some dinner. Claire was fine about Ari spending the evening at home and promised to come and pick her up around nine.

So now, while the pasta sauce simmered downstairs, she and Alex sat drinking coffee on Ari's bed, cross-legged on the dark blue bedspread. Alex's shirt was missing a couple of buttons at the top, and Ari tried valiantly not to stare at the curve of her breasts that this opening revealed. Ari's yellow curtains glowed golden in the late afternoon sunshine, and a wonderfully crisp sea breeze made them flutter as it rushed through the open window. Her room was tiny, compared to the huge, high-ceilinged guest rooms and her mother and Nick's bedroom, but Ari loved it. She had wanted it because it was the only bedroom in the house that faced the ocean.

"Do you know about the three Fates?" Alex had the heavy book of Greek myth open on her lap. Alex pointed to an engraving. "The Moirai, or Fates: Clotho, Lachesis, Atropos. Clotho spins the thread of a life, Lachesis measures it, and Atropos cuts the thread."

"I've never liked that myth," said Ari. "It doesn't leave any room for free will. If the Fates decide how long we get to live, what's the point in making plans for the future?"

Alex blew gently into her coffee mug. Wreathed in steam, she looked mysterious and otherworldly.

Ari reminded herself that Alex had grown up knowing how the laws of fate measured out a human life, not reading and speculating, but knowing and experiencing death and the afterlife in ways Ari could not imagine. "Are you ready to tell me what's happening?" she asked softly.

"Are you ready to know? You might not like a lot of what I'm about to tell you and, Ari, I don't want to frighten you."

Ari gulped down her coffee and placed her mug on her bedside table. She picked up a pillow and hugged it to her chest. "Go ahead. I've already faced my own death. I don't scare that easily."

Alex took a deep breath. "I already told you that the first thing I remember is having a drink of water. I found out later it was water from *Lethe,* the River of Forgetting. After that, it was like being half-asleep. Down there, everything is either dark or very dimly lit. It's easy to imagine that you are sleepwalking or dreaming. But I was awake. I was hungry and thirsty and I needed to sleep. But that's all I knew. I didn't know my name, or what had happened to me, or where I had come from. A tall man with a gray beard was standing near me as I drank the dark water. He had a kind face. He took me to a little house in a field of golden grasses. There were lots of trees and a tiny stream, very shallow and cold, next to the house. Inside were a single bed, a table with a meal set out ready to eat, a wooden stool, some cooking things, and a tall bookshelf full of books. He left me there. I don't know how long it was, but it seemed like a long time. I read all the books, most of them twice. I fished in the stream and cooked the fish on a little fire outside the cottage. I ate the fruit that grew on the trees. I slept a lot. Then one day the kind man came back. He handed me a cloak and a new, much larger, set of clothes and he told me to get dressed for a long journey.

"He took me in a tiny boat across a shadowy river, and then we walked along a narrow road that wound its way up a steep and barren mountain. Finally, we came to a doorway cut into the rock. He drew aside a dark curtain, and we entered a large cave. Three women sat spinning, measuring, and cutting what looked to me like thousands of brightly colored threads. Each time a thread was cut, the oldest woman would look at me and place the thread carefully in a basket at her side. Some of the threads were very long, and she had to coil them up before putting them away. Some were so short they were no longer than a finger's length. When Atropos—and I knew from all the reading I'd done that it must be she—had filled her basket with cut-off threads, she beckoned me and handed the basket to me. My friend, the man with the kind face, told me that I was to pick a thread from the basket, so I did. I picked a reddish-brown one, neither long nor short.

"Then the man with the kind face pressed his fingers to my temples, and I understood what he wanted me to do, what my work would be. He put power in my body to compensate for the lack of life there and he told me the calming, reassuring words to say so that my lack of feelings and human emotions wouldn't upset the soul I was being sent to collect."

Alex stopped. She passed Ari her half-full coffee mug. "I'm sorry, it's great coffee; I just can't finish it."

Ari placed it on the bedside table next to her own. She wiggled farther down the bed toward Alex and picked up the hands that were lying limply in her lap. She felt a surge of affection for her old friend that had nothing to do with wanting to kiss her or touch her. She wanted, more than anything, to comfort her.

"If it's too hard to tell," she began, but Alex shook her head.

Alex squeezed Ari's hands and didn't let them go. "Don't worry," she told her. "It's actually a relief to talk about it." She sighed. "So I went up the endless stair to the world of the living. The light stung my eyes, and the noises and smells were incredible. I had come out of a portal into a big city.

"Cars rushed past, and buses, and there, lying on the road in front of me, was a young man, his bike all tangled up with his legs, and his shattered helmet all crushed in. But he wasn't actually there on the pavement; he was standing next to me, looking down at his body. I said the calming words that I had been taught, and the cyclist came away with me without a fuss. He followed me through the portal and down the endless stair. He stood quietly in the boat while

Charon rowed us across the river. He followed me as I led him past the Asphodel Fields and into Elysium. And then I understood why he had taken his death so calmly. In a sunny little clearing was a tree with a tire swing. A child was swinging and singing to himself on that swing, but when he saw the shade of my cyclist he jumped off and ran to him with his arms outstretched. The cyclist picked him up and held him. They walked off together, and I returned to my cottage. The basket of threads was waiting at my front door.

"And so it went on," Alex continued. "I became a Summoner of souls. I picked thread after thread from that basket and I did the work required of me. When my basket was empty, I journeyed up the mountain again so that the Moirai could fill it. They were kind to me, especially Atropos. She often smiled as she passed me the basket, and sometimes I thought she wanted to tell me something or that she would ask me a question, but she never did. I always took the basket and returned to my little house by the stream. And I would have kept on selecting threads and conducting souls to the underworld for all eternity. But then, one day, I drew a short, fine, blue-green thread. I climbed the endless stair and emerged from a portal into a forest of eucalyptus. I followed a little track through a hot and dusty field until I saw the soul I had been sent to collect. She was not going to come away so easily." Alex smiled at Ari. "And then I recognized you, and everything changed."

Ari studied Alex's face. "But why you? I mean, if I was heading for the Elysian Fields when you came to get me, and I certainly hope I was, how come you weren't taken straight there by whoever summoned your soul? After all, you were innocent, just a little girl, really. Shouldn't you have been taken somewhere nice to spend eternity, maybe with your grandparents who were waiting to welcome you or something? Why would they, whoever's in charge

I mean, why would they choose a child to be a Summoner? And why leave you alone for all those years?"

"I don't know," Alex said. "Before all this happened, I never questioned it. You have to remember, they made me drink from the River of Forgetting. I didn't know who I was or how old I was. I didn't even know my own name, and it didn't matter, because nobody called me by any name. I was just a Summoner. I don't think time passes the same way down there. It didn't seem like years that I lived on my own. And then, once I met the Moirai and started summoning souls, I was so busy that I didn't have time to think about it."

"Was it awful?" Ari asked in a small voice. "Being down there? Doing what you had to do?"

Alex shrugged. "I don't know. Some deaths were not nice to see, I suppose, and some souls did not make it to the Fields of the Blessed. They went . . . elsewhere. But, Ari, it didn't affect me in the ways you would expect. I drank the dark water. I was numbed to all of it until I saw those scars under your arm, and then it came back to me like a thunderclap. I remembered that we had been children together. I remembered, well, lots of things. I remembered your name, and I saw, clear as day, your little face, all white and scared as you clung to that cliff face. I remembered the way you clutched my hand in the doctor's room while he stitched you up. I knew, above all, that I had to save you, no matter what the consequences were."

"And the consequences?" Ari bit her lip. "They're not good, are they?" There was a long pause.

"No," admitted Alex at last. "For one thing, the strange things that keep happening around here? I think that my transgression, my messing with the rules of life and death, has caused a kind of fracture to open up between our world and the unlit realm. The feral dogs and the hallucinations, I think they are all part of an instability, a rift in the boundary that separates the world of the dead from the world of the living. Nature is finely balanced. When that balance is upset, things start to act in strange ways." She fell silent.

"And the other thing?"

"What other thing?"

"Don't play dumb with me, Alex Cohen. What's the penalty for saving someone who should have died?"

Alex slid her hands from Ari's grasp and stood up. She walked to the window and leaned against the frame with her face partly hidden by her long hair. She pressed her fingers to her eyes and then rested her fingertips on her lips. She tucked her hair behind her ears and turned around.

Ari cried out at the expression on her face. She jumped off the bed, ran to her, and clutched Alex's hands when she held them out wordlessly. Ari put her arms around Alex's neck and laid her cheek against her shoulder. Then she took Alex's arms, one by one, and wrapped them around her back. Alex tightened them and dropped her head to rest her cheek on Ari's head. They stayed like that for a long time.

Finally, when the acrid smell of burning pasta sauce floated along the hallway, Ari and Alex went back to the kitchen, where they ate plain pasta with salt and pepper and left the ruined saucepan to soak in the sink.

Ari looked at the clock. "Claire will be here in an hour," she said with a sigh. "I wish I could stay here with you." They switched on the TV and watched a mindless eighties sitcom as their hour ticked away.

"How long?" said Ari, as they stared at the flickering screen.

Alex didn't ask her what she meant or even try to evade the question. "Not long. If I can't stop painting the portals, sooner or later one of them is going to open, and I will be drawn inside."

"And then what?"

"And then I'm not sure. I suppose there will be a punishment of some kind. But you don't need to worry about that, Ari. You are safe. Your heart is beating, so you can't enter a portal, even if you wanted to."

"I'm not worried about *me*," Ari cried. "I'm worried about *you*, Alex! You're my best friend. I really, you know, I really care about you. I don't want anything bad to happen to you."

Alex smiled. "That's a kind thing to say."

Ari swallowed her frustration. "I'm not being kind," she explained patiently. "I'm telling you that if you go back to the underworld to be punished for saving my life, I won't be able to handle the grief. Not again. Not a second time. I'm telling you that if I lose you again I will probably die of a broken heart. You have to stop painting those portals, and we have to destroy the ones you've already painted. It's a shame, because they are very beautiful, but it has to be done. I don't have to work tomorrow. I'm going to come over early, and we are going to do everything we can to stop this."

Ari heard a car crunching on the gravel driveway. "Damn it, Claire's early. I have to go. Listen, Alex. We're going to fight this, you and me. After all, if we can cheat death, we can stop you from being sucked back down to Hades. Piece of cake." Ari kissed her, daringly, on the forehead. "You saved me. Now *I'm* going to find a way to save you."

As she ran out through the kitchen, Ari glanced back over her shoulder. She saw Alex touch her forehead with her fingertips and then press her fingers lightly to her lips. Ari's skin tingled with a soft electricity.

"I'm going to save you," she whispered, and shut the kitchen door behind her.

6.
In the Pines

Claire seemed a little surprised the next morning when Ari announced her intention to spend the whole day at Wyndham. She peered at Ari over the tops of her glasses, noticing, perhaps, her flushed cheeks, her bright eyes. Usually Ari slept in until at least eight o'clock, but here she was, showered and dressed and buttering toast for Oscar and Jack while Claire was still yawning and making her first cup of coffee.

"I didn't get all the cleaning done last night," Ari lied, digging her fingernails into her thumbs as penance. "I ended up flaked out on the couch watching telly. I need to weed the veggies and pick the tomatoes and basil and cucumbers before they spoil." This, at least, was true. "The birds have already had most of the strawberries."

"Why did the birds get most of the strawbies, Ari?" asked Jack.

"They just love to gobble them up, I guess," smiled Ari.

"Like me," agreed Jack and resumed eating his vegemite toast.

Claire sighed. "You're not coming down with anything, are you? You look a bit feverish to me. Are you worrying about your mum? You know she's doing great. I had a long chat with her after you two talked last night, and she asked me to keep an eye on you. She said you would be stressing." Claire narrowed her eyes and pointed her finger at Ari in half-mock suspicion. "Are you stressing? Confess now and we'll go easy on you."

"Go easy on her? No way!" Sam wandered into the sunny kitchen, kissed her wife and sons, and started to pack herself some lunch. Sally looked up hopefully from her basket under the table and thumped her tail rhythmically on the floorboards. Ari knelt down and leaned over to stroke her. Claire must have been taking Sally for her daily old-lady walk, "no more than ten minutes," as prescribed by Dana, the vet in Stonehaven. Sam zipped up her backpack. "I'm leaving in ten minutes, Ari. I overheard while I was looking for the car keys, sorry. Do you want a lift?"

"Thanks, but I think I'll walk."

"No probs. See you guys tonight." Sam kissed her family again, told her sons to behave themselves, and left. She would spend the day taking tourists out in her charter boat, pointing out the shipwreck sites and answering questions like a real maritime historian. She taught history at the tiny Catholic school in Port August, but she much preferred her summer job.

A minute later Sam poked her head around the door. "It's really overcast off to the southwest," she announced gleefully. "I might be home early if this is a proper change coming in."

"Wouldn't that be fantastic?" said Claire. "I'm so tired of this heat."

Ari found herself wishing, not for the first time, that her life was as ordinary as Claire's and Sam's. Then she gave herself a mental shake and reminded herself who was waiting for her at Wyndham. She kissed the twins on the top of each curly head, grabbed an apple from the fruit bowl, and waved goodbye.

O

"THERE." ARI STEPPED BACK TO survey the inside of the milking shed. A large patch of white paint covered Alex's most recent portal. It seemed like defacement, a form of sacrilege. But if it would save Alex from being sucked back into the underworld, then Ari was willing to do whatever it took.

Alex put the lid on the paint tin and pressed it shut. "What now?"

"Now, I distract you so that you don't go painting any more beautiful but dangerous doorways to Hades on the walls of the farm sheds," replied Ari.

Alex smiled. "There *is* something I'd love to do."

"Anything," said Ari. "Anything except painting," she clarified hastily.

"Will you take me to the pine plantation? I'd like to see if anything remains of our little castle."

Ari's heart leapt. Alex wanted to revisit her childhood. Surely that was a good sign. "Let's see if Rusty and Bob are up for it," she suggested. "They're both getting so fat. A bit of exercise would do them the world of good."

"But Bob must be in his twenties now," said Alex. "I was brushing him yesterday and I noticed that his mane had gone white. And Rusty's arthritis must be terrible."

"Alex, they're Clydesdales, remember? They do no work, and Dana has told us plenty of times that we're not doing them any favors by letting them get so out of shape. We'll take it easy. They'll love it." Ari took two halters and lead-ropes from a nail on the shed wall and handed one of each to Alex.

"Bareback and bridle-free?" she challenged.

"No problem," Alex replied stoically.

Fifteen minutes later, they rode along the track and up the ridge that led to the pine forest. The morning sun had hidden itself behind towering masses of clouds, and the humidity made their clothes cling to their bodies. Rusty tossed his mane and flicked his tail at the sticky flies, but still they settled in scores on his broad chestnut rump. Ari soon gave up trying to brush them off. Alex sat straight and proud on Bob's great gray back and looked elegant even as she swatted the flies. Though dressed in jeans and a singlet she looked, Ari thought, like a queen riding out of the mists of time and legend.

The pine plantation loomed, dark and gloomy despite its geometrically ordered openness. Without bright sunlight to cut through it, the forest looked murky, and Ari found herself pitying, rather than scorning, the tourists who had found themselves lost deep inside it.

She asked Rusty to stop and slipped off his halter. "Don't go anywhere, big guy," she told him, stroking his smooth summer coat. The big horse just snorted and dropped his head to graze.

"Won't they wander off?" asked Alex, as she unbuckled Bob's halter.

"No way," said Ari. "Look at this green grass. They haven't seen grass this lush since spring. It's all the shade and the creek. They'll just eat until we come back. Don't you remember how we used to leave Rusty here for hours? Come on." She reached for her hand, and Alex let her take it. Ari battled the urge to stop and fold herself into the circle of Alex's bare arms.

As they entered the forest, Ari stole a glance at Alex. She was still, in many ways, the little girl she remembered. But in other, more important ways, she was quite clearly a woman, and Ari found this confusing, maybe even a little bit scary. She had to admit it to herself: Whatever it was that happened when she looked at her friend was so intense, so overwhelming, that it was hard to think straight. She couldn't help thinking about what it would be like to kiss Alex, and each time she allowed this thought to flower in her mind, her body responded as if it was really happening. Ari wasn't sure how long she could conceal these feelings. Surely Alex could sense them, or at least feel the force of them. But if she did, she showed no sign.

They walked along the first row of trees, and then Ari cut in toward the center when the ground began to slope downward.

Alex looked at Ari, who was striding confidently along the fragrant, loamy avenues of pines. "Do you remember the way?"

"Of course," Ari replied. And she found that she did remember the way, even though she hadn't been here for many years.

She led Alex down the little hill to the clearing by the creek. And there, standing proudly amidst a wild tangle of pale pink roses, was their castle. Part of the roof had fallen, but the walls looked just as sturdy as they had seven years ago. Alex sat on the mossy grass that carpeted the clearing and stared silently at their little sandstone masterpiece. Ari wandered around the structure and stopped to smell one of the tiny pink roses that still bloomed along the northern wall. She straightened, tucked her hair behind her ears, and smiled at Alex.

Alex patted the grass beside her. "Come and sit with me, Ari," she said softly. "I want to remember all the times we played here. We were so proud of our castle, weren't we? Look at it; it's so much smaller than I thought it would be."

"It's not. We're just a lot bigger." Ari sat close so their shoulders and hips were nearly, but not quite, touching, and they laughed as they remembered the hours spent building their castle in the fairy-tale forest.

"I never wanted to be anywhere else, you know that?" said Ari. "I would have been happy to be right here, building our castle, forever."

"Me too." Alex smiled.

Ari was sure Alex could hear her heart thumping. Alex looked at her, and her eyes seemed to smolder as she reached out to brush a stray hair from Ari's face. Her hand trembled, Ari was sure of it, when she touched her cheek. Ari held her breath.

Then a blood-chilling snarl ripped through the forest, and Alex clutched her protectively as a huge black dog skulked toward them from behind a tree. It was an Alsatian, or something like one, and it was immense, terrifying. It stopped a couple of yards away and snarled at them. Behind the Alsatian milled a dozen other dogs of varying breeds and sizes, and they, too, growled and bared their teeth.

Ari screamed, and the black Alsatian seemed to grin at her fear as its snarl widened. Some of the dogs were drooling, and Ari was shocked by how thin they all were; their ribs moved under their hides, as if they were starving wolves.

Alex whispered in her ear, "Don't move until I do. Move with me, if you can, so we look like one person." She wrapped her arms around Ari, and Ari clung to her neck as they slowly stood up.

The black dog growled louder but it did not approach. Alex spoke to it, using a language Ari didn't recognize. Her voice was low but powerful, and Ari sensed the challenge in it and also the authority, the command. The dog heard that, too, and it growled again but more uncertainly. The other dogs stopped circling and stood immobile. Alex stood still and stared at the black dog. They held each other's gazes for a long moment, and then the dog turned its head to one side. The pack whined, obviously disappointed and hungry, but the Alsatian snapped and growled at them, and they followed it as it loped away.

Ari slowly lifted her head from where she had tried to burrow into Alex's chest. As she did, the lead dog turned its head to look back at them. It seemed to Ari that the Alsatian's black eyes sought her own, and she stared at the dog as though hypnotized. Then the dog growled again, softly, and the pack disappeared over the crest of the hill.

Ari shook so much she thought she might fall over, but Alex led her back up the slope, held her around her waist, and talked quietly about what they would do when they got back to Wyndham, about making coffee and checking the radio and television for weather updates on the extremely promising storm front that was rolling in from the southwest. Only when they left the shadow of the trees and Ari saw Bob and Rusty grazing peacefully where they had left them did Ari relax enough to ask Alex how she had done it.

"I just told him to go away." She lifted Ari effortlessly onto Rusty's back.

"Weren't you scared at all, back in there? I was so terrified I thought I might pass out or something."

"I knew there was a threat, but no, I wasn't afraid. I'm not sure I remember what fear feels like. I simply had to protect you and save us from the dogs. We will have to find a way to capture them, Ari. I didn't understand how big the pack was or how desperate they are. People in Stonehaven are right to be scared. That lead dog, he is . . ." Alex stopped as she looked up at Ari's face. She turned to lift Bob's halter and lead-rope from the fence post. "You know, I'm sure I used to be able to put a halter on a horse. Come on, Bob, cooperate with me."

Ari wrapped her hands tightly around Rusty's thick mane and peered uneasily into the gloom between the pines. Where were the dogs now? What if they had been following them all this time, silently, and were hiding behind the trees just inside the forest's edge?

"Come on," she urged. "They might come back." Alex was already sitting astride Bob when she looked back across at her.

"How on earth did you?" Ari began and then she laughed, almost hysterically. "Don't tell me. Supernatural powers, right? You can drive away ravenous feral dogs, talk in strange languages, leap onto a sixteen-hand Clydesdale in a single bound, carry me all the way uphill to the general store and then somehow walk all the way to Port August, not to mention your ability to paint real portals to the underworld—and all without a heartbeat! What's it like to be able to do stuff like that?"

Alex ran her long fingers through Bob's snowy mane. "I'd trade it this moment for a heartbeat and the chance to stay here with you," she replied quietly.

They rode homeward under clouds that roiled and swelled and turned black. The cockatoos were quiet for once and everything was still, as though the countryside was holding its breath. But no raindrops fell. Ari rode through this expectant landscape with Alex at her side and struggled with herself until they were almost home. Then, because she couldn't put it off anymore, she asked her.

"Will you come with me to the beach?"

"Of course, if you want me to."

"Alex, you don't understand. I'm asking you if you want to see the place where you died."

Ari's eyes filled with tears. She couldn't look at Alex. The sudden silence confirmed her fears. Alex didn't know what had happened. She didn't know that she had drowned and that it was all Ari's fault. She knew that her father abandoned her mother because he couldn't grieve for his daughter anymore and that her mother had been on suicide watch, and then on medication, for so long that it was unlikely she would ever leave the nursing home. What she didn't know about was the swim to the rock, or Ari's misjudgment of the tides. Alex didn't know that it was her fault that she had died, and Ari needed her to know. She needed to do penance, not to have Alex blame her, which would be terrible, but so that she could maybe, finally, accept her grievous mistake.

But Alex just looked surprised. "I know where I died *and* how I died, Ari. I remembered all of that when I first recognized you."

O

ARI AND ALEX BRUSHED DOWN the horses and fed them and then they walked in silence along the track to Seal Cove. The tide was out, and the reef lay exposed like an invitation. The southerly was blowing in now; great gusts of wind whipped across the water. The wind was chilly, but Ari's skin had absorbed all the heat of the day, and so the wind's cold fingers were deliciously welcome.

Past the sharp rocks, Alex dipped her cupped hands into a deep rock pool and splashed her face with seawater. Ari gave herself another mental scolding for having impure thoughts as she watched Alex lick the salt from her lips. But Ari's body wasn't listening. It's no use, she thought. I can't help how I feel. Even if she doesn't feel the same way, if nothing ever happens between us, I will still feel like this. I think I'm falling in love with her.

They picked their way across the reef to the flat rock where, seven years ago, they had dived into this perilous stretch of water. Alex reached for her hand. Ari looked up at her, standing tall against the stormy ocean with her dark hair blowing wildly around her face. Alex stared at the channel, at the heave and fall of the swell, and she bit her lower lip slightly.

Ari hung her head. She pulled her hand free and wrapped her arms around her shoulders. She struggled to find the words, to tell Alex what her loss had meant to her. She couldn't find the words to tell her that, even though she had been patched up and patched up fairly well, Alex's absence from her life had made a wound inside her that nobody could ever heal. She wanted to tell Alex how she had kept it together, day by day, for Cass, even though she just wanted to follow Alex. And she wanted to say, most of all, how sorry she was for making her swim to Danger Island on that day seven years ago.

But Ari suddenly felt awkward beside this tall, impossibly good-looking Alex. At Wyndham, doing the washing up or reading in the hammock or brushing Rusty, Alex seemed enough like her old self that it was easy, or easier, to forget where she'd been, what she now was. But here, where the land fell away into the sea, Alex was stronger, more powerful, and more remote. Ari thought she could detect, faintly, a flicker of that unearthly shimmer that had surrounded Alex when she'd first confronted her on the track. Ari thought wretchedly of the life that should have been Alex's: of family and friends and sunny days, and boring schoolwork, and the simple little joys of being alive in the world. She looked across the deep blue of the channel to where Danger Island stood, cold and aloof amid the swirling ocean.

She began to cry silently; tears ran down her cheeks and dripped onto her crossed arms. "I'm sorry," she murmured. "Alex, I'm so sorry. It was all my fault, my idea."

Alex put her arms around her and stroked her hair. "No, Ari."

"It was!" she sobbed. "It was my fault. If I hadn't made you do the swim that day, if I'd been more sensible about the tide, it would never have happened!"

Alex held her tight. Then she wiped the tears off Ari's cheeks and tucked her windblown hair behind her ears. "Oh, God, Ari. Is that what you think? Is that what you've *been* thinking all these years?"

Ari nodded, trying to blink away the tears that wouldn't stop.

Alex looked serious as she took Ari's face gently in her hands. "Look at me, Ari. It *wasn't* your fault. I'm older than you, remember? I could have said no. I could have refused to do it. I chose to swim to the rock that day. I wanted to. It wasn't your fault." Alex gently pressed Ari's head against her shoulder.

Ari's sobs grew more uncontrollable. She thought bitterly that this was typical of her life; here was Alex, holding her properly at last, and all she could do was cry like a baby. But these tears came from a grief that was so deep, so measureless, that it didn't seem possible she would ever run out of them.

Alex spoke softly as she let her cry. "Ari, listen. I haven't told you all that much about the afterlife, and there are good reasons for that. But I can tell you this: We don't go before our time. That may seem cruel, when it's children who die and not old people or sick people, but there is a little thread that is our life, and when it has been measured and cut, that's it. There's no point fighting against it, and there's absolutely no way my drowning that day was your fault. It was my time, that's all. One of those silken threads in Atropos' basket—that was mine, and whoever summoned me must have picked it and found me in the ocean."

Ari's sobs grew quieter as she thought about this. She wanted to ask so many questions, but instead she found herself growing angry at the injustice. What kind of twisted law decreed that an eleven-year-old girl should have lived out the span of her life?

"But that's so unfair!" she protested, speaking into Alex's bare shoulder.

"I never said it was fair," she replied mildly.

"But," said Ari, struggling with an idea that refused to crystallize, "but, if your life was supposed to end that day, what would have happened if I hadn't conned you into doing the swim? Or, what if you had just told me not to be stupid? If you had just gone back to the beach? It could have happened that way too."

"But it didn't."

"But…" Ari shook her head to clear it. "I don't understand," she said finally.

Alex still held her close and Ari had to tilt her head back to look up into those deep gray-green eyes. Alex's expression was solemn, but Ari saw, astonished, that the remoteness was gone.

"Ari, nobody knows. Do you think astronomers really understand how stars are born, or how black holes form? Doctors don't understand how our cells regenerate when we heal, not really, and physicists only think they know how gravity works. A lot of it is a mystery. And that's as it should be. I don't think we're supposed to know all the secrets of life or death. If we did…" She lowered her voice and gripped Ari's shoulders. "…if we did, that would make us like the great lords of the underworld. And that is not something I would wish for either of us."

Ari was silent as she considered this. The storm front was building low and black above them, and the first drops of fine rain made tiny wet patches on her hair. "We should go." Ari's voice was unsteady, but she tried to speak normally. "I think we're in for a soaking."

As they made their way back across the reef, Ari tried not to make too much of the fact that Alex was still holding her hand. She kept stopping to guide Ari, quite unnecessarily, over the rough patches. Ari didn't remind Alex that this reef was as familiar as her own skin. All the same, they came to a weedy stretch, and Ari slipped, stubbing her toe on the rough rocks.

"Ouch!"

"What's wrong?"

"Nothing, just my toe. I'll be fine in a minute."

Ari sat on the rocks and inspected her bleeding toe. Alex reached down to help her up, and Ari caught her breath at the expression in her eyes. Alex pulled her to her feet in one smooth motion and wrapped her arms around her in another.

Then, without thought or pause, in a gesture as natural as breathing, she bent her head to Ari's, and their lips pressed together. Fire raced through Ari's veins, but her legs turned to water. She opened her mouth slightly and Alex responded. Ari pressed her body closer, and Alex pulled her tight, until they were melded into one another; lips, hips, breasts. And then both girls froze, stunned by the seismic thump and then the steady throbbing that came from deep within Alex's chest. Alex gave a great gasp and staggered back, with her hand pressed over her heart.

"Oh my God!"

Ari sank onto the rocks. She no longer trusted her legs to hold her up. Alex stood immobile, her hand pressed against her chest. She was silent for a long time. Then, face flushed and eyes wide, she knelt and took Ari's hand in hers, placing it firmly under her left breast.

"Can you feel that?"

"Yes," whispered Ari.

"It is beating again, isn't it? I'm not just imagining it?"

"What does it mean? What happened?"

Alex looked down at their hands, still resting on her breastbone. "I'm not sure. It happened when I kissed you. There was, I don't know, all this heat, and then a sharp pain, and now everything is kind of singing inside me. I can feel the blood rushing around my veins. I can feel the goosebumps on my skin. I can feel my heart beating." She looked at Ari, and her eyes were bright with tears. "I had forgotten what it was like, to have a body that *feels*," she whispered. "You woke me up, Ari."

Ari put her hand up, shyly, to touch Alex's face. Alex caught her hand and turned it over, palm up, and then she brought it to her lips and closed her eyes as she slowly kissed Ari's palm.

Ari's heart raced. Where did it come from, this fierce sweetness, this tingling thrill all over and through her body? She was ready to do whatever Alex wanted, go as far as she wanted to go, give herself entirely without question, without restraint, and without hesitation. And Ari was astounded to discover that this was exactly what she herself wanted.

As she bent to kiss her again, Alex became more passionate and powerful, pulling Ari close and holding her hard as she kissed her. Ari closed her eyes, and as they kissed the world dissolved into nothingness around them. There was nothing but this moment, just Ari and Alex together, melting into one another as the rain came down.

O

"You're looking quite rosy-cheeked tonight, chickie," commented Claire, as she handed Ari the remote control. "There, see if you can find anything decent to watch. If I have to sit through one more weather report telling me it's raining, I think I'll throw something at the TV. Sam, honey, could you check on the boys? I thought I heard Jack crying a second ago." Once Sam had obligingly left the room, Claire looked sidelong at Ari. "Have you been talking to that girlfriend of yours on the phone or something?"

Ari was taken aback by the shrewdness of the question, and she had to stop and collect her wits before answering. Where, exactly, had she told Claire that the lovely and entirely fictional Anna had gone on her holiday?

Claire chuckled at her stricken expression. "It's okay, sweetie, you don't have to answer that. Tell me to mind my own business. I just hope you haven't caught a cold walking over here in the rain."

Ari was floating. Everything, every tree, every fencepost, every bird and wallaby and raincloud, seemed more vivid and more precious. As she'd walked to Claire's from Wyndham that evening, all the world was resonant with joy. It was as if a string had been plucked, and the vibrations of that one, beautiful, pure note made everything different. All the clichés about being in love were true. Colors seemed brighter, and the earth softer, as if she walked on clouds. The soft raindrops were millions of tiny wet kisses on her bare arms, and she splashed through the new puddles in her steel-capped boots, reveling in the miracle of the coolness, the rain, and her own transformation. If she closed her eyes, she could feel the electrical current that had coursed through her whole body when Alex kissed her. She wasn't sure if she could wait an entire night before seeing her again.

Ari smiled radiantly at Claire. "No, I don't mind telling you. I did speak to Anna. She misses me. She's arranged with her parents to come back early from their holiday so she can see me. We made plans to go to the movies in Port August when she gets back in a few days. As long as that's okay with you and Sam, of course," she added quickly.

"Ah, young love," sighed Claire. "Sometimes I wish I was sixteen again. Sorry, nearly seventeen. I'll drive you over to the Port if you like. By the way, what do you want for your birthday?"

"It's not until the end of February."

"It's a birthday. We have to do something special. And February, my fancy-free, school-holidaying friend, starts tomorrow."

Ari froze. Her birthday was on the twenty-seventh of February. School always started two weeks before her birthday. That left her with only a couple more weeks of freedom—a fortnight in which to be with Alex. The holidays had never seemed so precious or so short. What would she do when she had to go back to school? School was Port August P-12, an hour and twenty minutes each way by bus. She had to leave at seven-thirty in the morning and often didn't get home until after five. That didn't leave much daytime to be at Wyndham with Alex. In fact, Claire and Sam would probably insist on picking her up from the bus stop, which was rather a long walk from Wyndham.

Ari's freedom was finite; the walls were collapsing. She apologized to Claire, saying that she was tired and had a headache, and took herself off to the air mattress in the study that served as her bedroom at Sam and Claire's.

Lying in bed, listening to the rain pelting the tin roof, Ari tried to think practically about the future. Now that Alex had a heartbeat, was she safe from being sucked back into the underworld? Where would she stay once Cass and Nick came home with the baby? How would she explain her identity to her family and friends? Shouldn't Ari be encouraging Alex to go see her mother?

Claire had offered to drive Ari up to see Cass and was adamant that this was no trouble, even though the city was a six-and-a-half-hour drive away. They would spend the night at the hostel near the hospital where Nick was staying.

"I want to see Cass too, Ari," Claire had reassured her. "She's my friend, remember? Besides, it will feel like a little holiday for me. Sam can look after the two-foot terrors for a weekend, and I can maybe get a full night's sleep for the first time in three years."

No matter how she tried, Ari couldn't think of a way to bring Alex into this plan so that she could see her own mother. She didn't even know how to get to the Sunnymead Nursing Home, though she'd been there plenty of times. And Claire wouldn't want to drive through Port August anyway. She'd take the inland highway if they were going to the city. Ari rolled over and shut her eyes, trying to clear her mind so that she could sleep. And some time later, she did drift off, listening to the incessant downpour and the growl of thunder coming in from the sea.

7.
MISSING

"DID YOU LEAVE THE LIGHT on in your room? It's hard to see through all this rain." Claire craned her neck to see through the passenger window as she pulled her car up to the house.

Ari tried to stay calm. She pretended to look too, making a mental note to tell Alex to keep the curtains shut. "I must have. I'll be more careful when I leave this afternoon. Thanks, Claire."

She leaned over to give Claire a kiss on the cheek and felt awful all over again for deceiving her. It's not as though this is some random girl from school, her inner voice argued stubbornly. This is Alex. It's different. It's still a deception, said her other, sterner, voice reproachfully. Claire thinks you're here to clean up and do holiday homework. And you've taken all that time off from the pub. What will Jodie think? What will Nick say when he finds out? Ari told the disapproving voice to shut up.

She smiled at Claire. "Thanks so much for driving me over. I reckon it will stop later on and I'll be fine to walk."

"I'm not so sure about that." Claire peered out at the torrential sheets of rain. "Anyway, just call me when you're ready to come home. I mean, back to our place." She gave Ari a thoughtful smile. "Despite everything, and I know how badly you want Cass back, it must be nice to have Wyndham to yourself for a while. You've always been such an independent, solitary person."

Ari waved as Claire's old green Volvo splashed and rumbled away. "Not always," she murmured. "And not anymore," she added, as the front door opened silently behind her.

Alex was silent as she stood aside to let her cross the threshold. Ari gave her a long, searching look, and then floated along the hall to her bedroom, every tiny particle of her being acutely aware of Alex walking close behind her. She led her inside and shut the door. Alex stood on the seagrass rug, looking a little uncertain as Ari turned to face her. A wave of anxiety swept over Ari. What if Alex regretted kissing her? What if she wanted to tell her it was a mistake? But Alex was there, her arms around her, pushing her gently against her bedroom door as their lips found one another again.

Ari closed her eyes and let the magic of kissing Alex flood through her. The rain on the tin roof was deafening, and the summer heat had vanished. But Ari was warm, pressed closely to Alex as she caressed her hair and told her how beautiful she was. She led her to her bed.

Alex breathed in sharply. "Ari, I'm not sure, I mean, I don't know how."

"Me neither. I just want to lie here with you and watch the rain."

It was wonderful to stretch out and press her body close to Alex, to touch her face, her lips, to look as long as she wanted to into her eyes. Each iris, she concluded, was more dark green than gray, with little golden flecks that seemed to flicker when her pupils dilated. Her hair was truly black—not dark brown, or red-tinged, but black as midnight. She marveled at whatever it was that had caused Alex to kiss her, allowed Ari to touch her silky hair, and made her heart beat again. Alex was looking closely at her, too, she noticed, and not just into her eyes. Ari took her hand and placed it, lightly, on the top of her breast as they kissed.

Alex closed her eyes, and her breathing quickened. Her hand moved as gently as a moth's wings over her skin. "Ari," she whispered in her ear, "what are you doing to me? Why do I feel like this?"

"Like what?" she replied innocently, her lips stretching into a smile around their kiss.

"You know perfectly well," Alex told her, laughing. She rolled onto her back and stared at the rain crashing down in a gray sheet outside the open window. "It's all a bit overwhelming for me," she admitted at last. "And new," she added shyly.

Ari was chastened. Was she going too fast? "I'm sorry Alex, I keep forgetting. It feels like you've been back forever." She put her arm across Alex's chest, feeling its steady rise and fall and the rapid rhythm of her newly beating heart. "But this is new to me too, you know."

Alex turned her head to look into Ari's eyes. "You've never kissed a girl? Or a boy?"

"Not like this," Ari told her. She paused and then admitted, softly: "I kissed a boy once, and there have been a few girls, but I've never felt like this about anybody before."

Alex raised herself up on her elbow and rested her head on her hand. She studied Ari closely. "Have you ever, you know, done anything else?"

"If I answer that, you have to answer a question too. A hard question," replied Ari quickly.

"All right. But you have to answer first."

"Okay. Well, no, I haven't done it. I've never been all the way with anyone. I don't know why. A lot of my friends have. I'm not religious or prudish or anything. I just never found anybody special enough, somebody who . . ." Ari stopped, overwhelmed by a truth she dared not yet declare to Alex.

"It's okay," Alex cut in. "I think I understand. And, no, I never had sex with anybody while I was in the unlit realm, if that was your question."

"It wasn't. But wait, I didn't think, is that even possible?"

"Certainly. I ate, and drank, and slept. I could easily have done other physical things too, but the opportunity didn't arise." Alex gave a short, ironic laugh. She lay back down, pulling Ari's old, frayed woolen blanket over both of them as she did so. "What was your question?"

Ari, who was still trying to sort all this information, found that she couldn't, after all, ask Alex about the existence of love in the underworld. She had sort of answered it anyway. Hadn't anybody loved her while she was down there? Of course not, sneered the accusing voice in her head. What did you think the afterlife would be like? All sunshine and happiness? Why would you think it would be at all like that?

Ari writhed inwardly as the old guilt stretched and coiled around her heart. No matter what Alex had told her at the beach, it *was* Ari's fault that her best friend had lived for seven years in the darkness, without sunlight, or joy, or love. She squeezed her eyes closed and tried to chase away a sudden image in her mind.

She saw Alex, a little older than eleven, but not grown up, a child still. She was sitting alone in the doorway of a tiny cottage in the middle of a field with a book spread open on the floor next to her. There was no color in this landscape and the light was gray and dim. Alex was reading by the last dreary light of whatever day existed in that place, and Ari understood, without having to ask her, that each of these days had been the same: an endless succession of gray hours without company, without love, and without hope for the future.

Ari put her arm protectively over Alex's chest, tucked her hand under her body and rested her head gently on her heart. She listened to Alex's heartbeat and made a silent promise to her friend that she would do whatever she could to make up for the years she had lost.

Ari jolted awake at the sound of the front door opening and Claire's voice calling her name. Alex was fast asleep; her chest rose and fell under Ari's cheek.

Ari bolted from her room, slamming the door behind her. She called, "Coming, Claire!" as she thundered down the hall, hoping Alex was awake enough to hear her.

Claire stood by the open window in the kitchen. The rain was falling steadily now, and Ari heard water trickling and running outside, making new creeks and runnels through the clay and the sandy soil. Claire was silent, watching the rain cascade in a thick curtain from the lip of the bullnose veranda. She held the local newspaper folded lightly against her chest. Ari willed Alex to stay in her room. After a minute she realized that Alex must have figured out the situation, and she relaxed enough to smile warmly at Claire.

"Want a coffee?" Ari filled the kettle.

"No thanks, sweetie." Claire sat at the table and unfolded the paper. Ari watched her face as she scanned the front page. Something was wrong.

"What is it? Claire?" Ari put the kettle down and went to look over Claire's shoulder. The photograph on the front page was slightly grainy, but it was most definitely the round and freckled face of Thomas Drysdale, aged thirteen. Tom's parents were Sam and Claire's friends, and Ari had often hung out with Tom, who was a nice kid, obsessed with video games and footy. Now his photo was front-page news, looking out of place under the headline: *Local Boy Missing*.

Ari read the article with a horrible tight feeling in her chest. Tom had gone to visit the dentist in Port August. On the long drive home, he had to ask his father if they could make a toilet stop. His dad pulled the car over, and Tom climbed through the wire fence into the pine plantation. He never came out. When Craig, Tom's dad, went in to look for him, he had vanished. Craig called and called for him, but Tom didn't answer. A search party had combed the plantation through the night, but they found nothing. The police had called in rescue helicopters, and specially trained police dogs were being driven down from the city.

"It's on the TV too," said Claire, "and all over the radio. This is awful."

"They'll find him. They have to."

Claire was close to tears. "I don't know, Ari. It's such a big plantation. Look, the paper has the figures: two hundred and sixty-five hectares. That's big, Ari. That's one big bloody forest. Why they've left it unlogged for so long I don't know, but it'd be easy to lose your way in there. Think of those tourists."

"How are Erin and Craig?"

"Frantic," Claire said bleakly. "Erin called me about an hour ago. She and Craig were out all night with the police, searching for Tom. Ari, this is horrible. What could have happened to him? Erin is freaking out about that feral dog pack we keep hearing about, and Craig is terrified he might have been injured or fallen into a sinkhole or something. The police are organizing a new search party, with divers. But why would Tom have wandered off far enough to fall into a sinkhole? How could he have got far enough that he wouldn't hear Craig calling out to him?"

"Tom wouldn't go near a sinkhole. Everybody who's grown up here knows not to do that," Ari said firmly.

Claire sighed. She put down the paper and stared wearily through the window at the raindrops bouncing off the roof of the water tank. "I know. I remember your mother and Beth having a terrible argument about sinkholes when you were little. I had popped over to ride Rusty; do you remember your mum used to let me do that?

And I heard them arguing on the veranda. Your mum said she didn't want you and Alex to go into the pine plantation in case one of you fell into a sinkhole, and Beth said that neither of you would be silly enough to go near one. They kept arguing about it for ages. It was after you fell down that cliff at the beach. Cass said she wouldn't let you play at the beach anymore unless she was there. And Beth said that your Mum was being too protective. She said that you and Alex were country kids and that you needed room to explore and have adventures."

"Well, Beth was right. We would have been bored hanging around here, and Smythson's was so busy back then. The caravan park and the playground over at the bay—that was where the other kids hung out. But it was just that little bit too far to walk or ride, you know? So Alex and I used to go up to the pine forest and play there. We never went near any sinkholes, and Tom wouldn't go near them either."

Ari frowned, remembering the forbidden glamour of those subterranean pools in the forest. Some were pitch black, with an oily sheen on the dark water. Those weren't even slightly tempting. It was the big ones, the ones with clear, translucent, aqua water and waving green fronds, and fish, which were interesting. In fact, those ponds were so alluring it *had* been hard not to go near them. But, like snakes or strangers, the ponds were considered so deadly that Ari and Alex would never have gone too close. Everybody knew that the little pools of shallow-seeming water were bottomless, and that the lack of salt in the water meant you wouldn't easily float in them. The sides of each sinkhole were usually sheer, with no roots or rocks for handholds. If somebody did slip into one, it would be terribly hard, almost impossible, to climb out again. It would be like trying to climb up the slippery interior of a well.

Ari shook her head and stood up. "I'll just get my jacket and my gumboots and then I'll be ready. Is Sam in the search party too?"

"Ari, you can't go. I promised your mum and Nick I'd look after you."

"But I'll be safe with the search party! Claire, you have to let me go. I want to help."

"You would be more help to me if you watched the twins so that *I* could go with them," said Claire bluntly. Guilt clawed at Ari. She hadn't been doing nearly enough babysitting lately.

"Sure, I mean, of course I'll look after them. Is Sam already there?"

"Yes. I'll drop you at our place and go straight up to the pub, if you don't mind, Ari. That's where they're organizing from."

Ari fed the horses and the cows and tried to tell herself that they weren't bothered by the rain. The horses seemed content enough, galloping to the fence in a shower of mud and splashing water, whinnying loudly at her approach, with the cows walking sedately behind them.

As she drove away with Claire, Ari snuck a look at her bedroom window. The curtains had been pulled across, and she saw them twitch. She needed to talk to Alex, but who knew how long it would be before she could come back?

"Come to me," she willed Alex silently. "Come tonight, when everybody's asleep."

Later, as she sat watching Jack and Oscar play with their train set, Ari tried to send out little tendrils of herself, tried to visualize some of her hope and strength flowing out along each imaginary, fragile line: one to Tom and to his mum and dad; one to Alex, alone and worried at Wyndham; one to Claire and Sam, reassuring them that their babies would be safe while they were gone; and one, the strongest of them all, to her mother and her unborn sister.

She had called her mother on Claire and Sam's phone while the twins were eating their dinner, knowing that Sam and Claire wouldn't mind. Her mum and the baby were doing well. The doctors were pleased with her progress, and each day made the baby a little safer, brought her closer to being with them in the world. Cass sounded fed up with being bedridden and she was worried about Ari, but she was otherwise fine. Claire and Sam had agreed that it would be impossible to keep the story of Tom's disappearance from her, as it was all over the news, and Ari found that Cass had already heard about it. Ari told her as much as she could about what was happening at Stonehaven.

"Nick's coming back to help search," said Cass. "He'll be home tomorrow. He wants to be at the pub, to help coordinate things, you know? And the police and the SES volunteers will need accommodation. It's too much for Jodie to manage on her own, and Claire needs you to look after the twins."

"Nick's coming home tomorrow? To Wyndham?" Ari's stomach flipped over. Would she be able to warn Alex in time?

"Yes. He's planning to leave here around five in the morning, so he might even be home before lunch. He's looking forward to seeing you, Ari. I wish I could come home too. I miss you so very much. Maybe, depending on what happens, maybe you could come back with Nick. I want to see you, and Claire might be too busy now." There was a pause, and then Cass went on, with that strained maternal cheerfulness that always worried Ari. "You could stay at the hostel with Nick and go shopping in the city, maybe even go the art gallery or the movies. We could always send you home on the bus. Anyway, our priority for now is to do everything we can to help find Tom, and Claire might need you there, to watch the twins, so let's not make any firm plans. I just miss you, that's all."

Ari listened as her mother gave instructions about things that needed to be done at home and she obediently copied down a long list of clothes and other things that Cass needed Nick to bring to the hospital. But panic was starting to set in. She had to warn Alex that Nick was coming back to Wyndham. Claire and Sam were sure to come home soon and they would need her help in the morning. She toyed with the idea of sneaking out after Claire and Sam came home and everybody had gone to sleep, but that just seemed too risky. The last thing your loved ones need is for you to hurt yourself trying to get to Wyndham in the dark and the pouring rain, admonished the stern voice in her head, and Ari, for once, agreed.

She said goodbye to her mother and pushed the off button. Ari decided that calling Alex at Wyndham was worth the risk of Claire and Sam checking their phone bill and noticing the number. She could always claim that she dialed Wyndham out of habit or by mistake. But just as she finished dialing, the front door opened, and Claire and Sam came in. Ari quickly hung the phone on the wall and went to meet them.

Claire and Sam were dripping wet and exhausted after a long and unsuccessful search. Ari put the kettle on.

"So they haven't found him yet," she said quietly.

Claire began to cry, and Sam put her arm around her shoulders. "Poor Erin," sobbed Claire. "Poor Craig. Where *is* he? What's happened to him?"

"Tom's a sensible kid," said Sam, as she kissed Claire's wet hair. "They'll find him in the morning."

"We stayed on at the pub after the search had been called off for the night," said Claire. "I hope you didn't mind putting the twins to bed for us. Erin's a mess, of course. I thought I should stay with her for a while."

"So they didn't find anything? No trace at all?"

"Nothing," said Sam wearily. "The police divers searched every sinkhole they could find, and the SES crew combed the first part of the forest thoroughly. They needed to divide it up into sections, 'cause it's so big. Tomorrow they'll go even deeper in. They've got four-wheel drives that can pretty much go anywhere, and that's a lot quicker than walking."

"I'm going to have a quick shower and go to bed," announced Claire. "Ari, darling, thank you so much for watching the kids. I hope they were good for you. I know it looks heartless, me going off to bed, but we'll be better use as searchers tomorrow if we get some sleep. Do you mind looking after Jack and Ossie again tomorrow? I know it's a big ask. We could be gone all day."

"Of course I don't mind," said Ari. "But could you leave me the SES mobile number? I'm just worried about what might happen if I needed to reach one of you and you were out of range or something."

"Nick's coming home tomorrow, I hear," said Sam.

"Yes."

"Oh, Ari," cried Claire. "I just remembered: our city trip! I'm so sorry, we're going to have to cancel it, love. Erin and Craig will need us to be around this weekend, especially if—if things don't turn out well." Claire wiped fresh tears off her tired face. "Good night, honey." She kissed Ari on the top of her head. "Don't stay up too late."

Much later, when Sam and Claire were asleep, Ari tossed and turned on her air mattress and listened to the rain pouring down outside. She had been too scared to try calling Wyndham and so had gone to bed without trying to talk to Alex. Ari figured that Alex wouldn't answer the phone anyway. They had agreed in the beginning that it would be too risky, since she wouldn't know who was calling. Ari wished, not for the first time, that Stonehaven had reliable mobile coverage or internet access. It's like living in the dark ages, she thought grumpily.

Ari had stayed up for a while after Sam and Claire went to bed. She was shocked to see images of flooding on the late news. Parts of Port August were underwater, and the farms and houses along the river plain were under threat. And still the rain fell. Ari thanked heaven that Wyndham was on a hillside and not in one of the deep valleys. Still, parts of the property were low-lying, and she would have to check the horses and cows tomorrow. Then she remembered that Nick would be able to do that. What would happen if Nick saw Alex? Would Alex hide in her room if she heard a car on the drive, or would she think it was Claire dropping her off and be waiting inside the door? Apart from needing to tell her about Nick, Ari missed Alex. She had just spent most of the day without her, and it was as if someone had removed a large part of her heart and was refusing to return it.

"*Alex,*" Ari called silently. "Alex, I need you. Please come." She closed her eyes and tried to precisely recall the feeling of Alex's lips on hers, the warmth and weight of her hand on her breast, the expression in her eyes when she'd stared into them.

When somebody tapped lightly on the window, Ari jumped violently and stifled a scream. She had summoned Alex with all her strength, but she hadn't thought she would dare to come. She opened the window and clambered out over the slippery wooden sill. Alex, wet to the skin, was holding an old raincoat over her head. She spread it out so that Ari could shelter under it and kissed her forehead.

"Where can we go?" Alex asked.

"The shed, probably. It's the only dry place." They ran, splashing ankle-deep through the newly formed swamp that had been a balding, sandy lawn. Ari pulled hard on the shed door, which stuck in wet weather, and it creaked open, revealing a dark, but dry, interior.

"How did you know?" began Ari, and then she laughed, shaking the rain from her hair. "Never mind. I'm just so glad you're here."

"I'm happy to see you too," Alex murmured, her lips pressing softly against Ari's own.

As Alex tried, unsuccessfully, to dry herself with an old picnic rug, Ari told her about Tom, but she had already seen the local newspaper and the TV. Then Ari tried to explain about Nick. "He's coming home tomorrow, Alex. I don't know what to do. I want you to stay at Wyndham, but I don't know what to tell him. There's no good reason why I wouldn't have told him I had somebody staying. He'll think it's odd."

"Don't worry," said Alex. "I actually thought Nick might come home sooner or later, and I've had everything ready so that I could leave quickly. The house looks fine. I even messed it up a bit so that it would look more authentic; I left your load of washing in the clothes dryer, and some of your books lying around in the lounge room."

"But where will you go?"

"I've thought of that too. I'm going to join the search party. That's something I want to do anyway. I might be able to help, especially if the dogs decide to show themselves. If Claire or Sam recognize me from the hospital, I'll just say that I know Tom from school and that I got my parents to drive me from Port August so that I could join the search. But I don't think they'll even know I'm there. I'll get one of those orange jumpsuits and blend right in."

"Do you think they'll find Tom?"

There was a small silence. Ari couldn't see Alex's expression in the pitch dark of the tiny garden shed, but she heard the uncertainty in her voice as she stroked Ari's damp hair and tried to reassure her that everything would be fine. Ari thought of the feral dogs, about the way the pack leader had snarled, about its yellow teeth, slick with drool. She thought about sinkholes and their slippery edges. She thought about legless goslings, and bodies in the ocean, and about the grim fact that she would be dead right now if Alex hadn't saved her. Ari had to admit she'd been blocking all of it out. She'd allowed herself to become distracted, so much so that she'd almost forgotten the darkness threatening Stonehaven.

"Alex, do you think Tom's disappearance has anything to do with that rift you told me about? Is it our fault? Did we really upset the balance enough that an innocent boy might be lying dead in the pine plantation? I don't want to believe that things work that way."

Alex held her a little tighter. "Me neither. And, no, I don't exactly think poor Tom disappeared because of what we did. I'm beginning to think that the rift is just an increase, a widening out, of a fracture line between realms that has probably always existed somewhere around here. I think Tom's disappearance is a coincidence, but I also think that the longer he stays in the pine forest the more danger he'll be in. And that danger—the dogs, and the hallucinations, all the strange things that have been frightening people since I saved you—that stuff *is* partly our fault, *my* fault. I think my saving you maybe opened the rift a bit wider than usual. That dog pack is definitely unnatural and it makes the plantation extremely dangerous. I'm going to have to kiss you goodbye soon and head to the forest. I'll be able to find out where the search party got to today and I'll do a little searching on my own tonight."

Ari wanted to stop her. She wanted to cling to Alex and beg her not to leave. She immediately felt ashamed of herself. Alex was possibly the only person in Stonehaven who could help Tom. Listening to the rain pelting the shed's tin roof, Ari tried not to imagine how lonely and terrifying the pine plantation would be at night, especially in this weather. Tom would be cold, and wet, and miserable. That is, if he was still alive.

"I should go soon," Alex said, still holding Ari. "Every minute might count. I need to look for tracks before they get in there with their jeeps tomorrow and mess them up. But I want to stay with you just a little bit longer."

Alex found Ari's hand and placed it on her chest, under her shirt. Ari closed her eyes as they kissed, and it seemed as if Alex's heartbeat was trying to race her own. The now familiar electric tingle raced all through Ari's body as she wrapped her arms around Alex's neck and pressed herself hard against her. They both stopped kissing then, breathless, and Ari was certain that Alex was waiting for her to make the next move. But Ari didn't. She was spellbound by the force that seemed to be rushing them toward a change so total, so complete, that neither of them would ever be the same. Her whole body, every atom of her being, ached to be with Alex, to be with her always, without any more separation or loss or loneliness. But here was Alex, leaving. She touched Alex's face in the darkness, running her fingertips over her cheekbone and down her jaw to her lips.

Throwing away caution, she decided to tell her. After all, it was only the truth. "I love you," she whispered.

Alex put her hands on Ari's cheeks and kissed her again. "Oh, Ari," she said softly, "I love you too." She pulled her closer. "We're going to be all right, you and me. I think we were always meant to be together. I'm going to find Tom, and then I'm going to come back, and then we'll figure out what to do about my identity. I want to meet Nick. I want to see Cass and to hold your little sister when she gets here. And I want to see my mother. I want to fit in again, fit into everyday life." She laughed. "I guess I'll have to get a job or go to high school. Now there's a scary thought!" She stroked Ari's hair and gave her a final, lingering kiss. Then she opened the shed door, and the rain came in. "I have to go. Take care of yourself while I'm gone, please?"

Ari stood in the shed's crooked doorway and watched as Alex vanished into the rain and the night.

8.
A Hole in the Earth

Ari opened her eyes to find the twins sitting next to her bed. Jack was driving a Matchbox car over the green hills and valleys of her sleeping bag. Oscar was flying a toy airplane noisily above her head. Ari struggled to wake up.

Something was different. She looked at Jack's hair, his messy curls tinted gold in the morning light. The sunlight streamed in through the study window. Outside, magpies and currawongs were singing, and the twins seemed like little cherubs playing in a halo of dancing dust motes. Somewhere in the house Claire was also singing; the old Irish folk tune added to the surreal feeling of the morning. Why would Claire be singing? They must have found Tom! Or rather, Alex must have found Tom.

Ari smiled and stretched, feeling a rush of pride. She climbed out of her sleeping bag and kissed the twins. Then she ran down the hall to the kitchen.

Claire greeted her with a broad smile. "They found him! He's okay. He's in shock, but he's not hurt. Erin rang at four in the morning to tell me." She gave a huge yawn.

Ari looked out at the sunlit garden. "That's wonderful news," she said. Well done, my darling Alex, she added silently.

Claire put the kettle on as she described the brave SES volunteer who had gone back into the forest alone to hunt for Tom. "In the middle of the night, in all that rain, can you imagine? Completely against the rules, of course. But I guess you can't stop somebody who's that determined. Anyway, this volunteer, apparently she found

Tom wandering around not far away from where we were searching today. He's got mild hypothermia, but Erin said the doctors weren't concerned because the nights haven't been all that cold. It is still summer, after all. Erin said when the phone rang just after three o'clock she was too terrified to answer it. So Craig picked it up, and it was the hospital in Port August, and Tom was crying into the phone. They'll question him when he feels stronger. I reckon a lot of people will want to know how he ended up lost in a forest for two days when he only nicked in to do a wee. From what Erin told me it sounds as if those feral dogs might have chased him. Poor Tom. It must have been horrible."

Ari twisted her hands in her lap. It was clear that Claire was content to let relief and happiness carry her through the morning and that she had no real idea of the horror that Tom must have faced in the forest. For Ari, the black Alsatian was a creature of pure nightmare, and she couldn't breathe for a long moment as she tried not to imagine being chased by such a monster.

Claire put a steaming mug in front of Ari. "There you are, sweetie, extra strong this morning. Anyway, the weird thing about all of this is that the volunteer who found Tom has vanished herself! Erin and Craig called the SES this morning so that they could arrange to thank her in person, but they said she'd already left. They reckon they found her jumpsuit neatly folded on the bonnet of the truck, with a note saying she was going to get on a bus back to the city. All very mysterious. I guess that's what heroes do though, ride off into the sunset and all that. Hey, are you all right Ari? What's wrong?"

"Nothing," Ari managed. "I'm just really tired."

Claire rubbed her eyes. "God, me too. It's been a pretty intense couple of days. Anyway, you'll be wanting to get to Wyndham and be there for Nick. He's still coming down, I reckon. They'd have called us by now if he wasn't. I'll just get the twins their cereal, and then we'll go. I'll come in and give you a hand to tidy up if you like."

"You know," said Ari, trying to control the wobble in her voice. "It's already pretty tidy over there. I might just hang around here until Nick arrives, if that's okay. He'll ring when he gets to Wyndham and he can pick me up, or I can walk. You don't have to be my taxi anymore."

Ari rubbed her eyes. Why would Alex be on a bus to the city? She got up and stared out at the bright morning, trying to think instead of panic. If Alex found Tom before dawn, she should have been home by now. But where *was* home for Alex? Where would she go now that she knew Nick was coming back? Ari fought to stay calm, but panic was rising. She forced herself to smile at Claire and to make small talk about the beautiful day ahead.

"Actually, I think I need some sea air. Do you mind if I take off for a little while? I might go and put my big toe in the ocean if it's not too cold."

Claire studied her closely. "Of course I don't mind. We've all been cooped up for so long. Maybe some sun and saltwater is what you need."

The beach near Claire and Sam's was much less wild and rugged than Seal Cove. Some of the wealthier holidaymakers had found their way here, snuggled up in the bed and breakfast or in the luxury holiday cabins in the dunes. Ari counted three Audis and a Porsche parked next to the cabins and was puzzled, as always, as to why rich people spent so much money on their cars. The tiny camping area, much loved by surfers and fishermen, had become a large, shining pool of muddy water, and there were no cars in the beach car park.

Ari walked across the soggy sand, dropped her towel, kicked off her boots, and strode into the ocean. She ignored the cold and pushed through the breakers until she was standing neck deep in the sea.

"Alex," she thought desperately. "Please come back to me. Don't leave me again."

She took a deep breath and dived, letting the water hold her, becoming weightless, a piece of flotsam caught by the currents. Ari had been missing the ocean, but she couldn't relax today. The sea had lost its power to seduce her. She let herself float to the surface and lay there, face down in the water, arms outstretched. Then she rolled over, closed her eyes, and let the ocean rock her as she floated on her back. There was a game Ari played when she swam alone, but it only worked on days when the sea was flat and calm. She would float on her back with her eyes closed for as long as she dared. When she opened her eyes, she would often find that she hadn't moved, but sometimes she would open her eyes and discover that the beach was now a lot farther away than when the game began and that she faced a long, punishing swim to the shore.

It was a dangerous game, and Ari knew it. She would play it when her guilt about Alex became unbearable. She never pushed it too far and always made sure she opened her eyes in time but, even so, Ari had needed to swim scary distances on several occasions. Each time she would drag herself back onto the sand, her chest heaving and her eyes full of tears that the ocean couldn't wash away. It was penance, perhaps. But also—and this was the weird part—when she swam such a long way that she was exhausted, weakened, and gasping for breath, she felt closer to Alex.

But Ari wasn't in the mood to play the floating game today. She flipped onto her stomach and swam her fastest freestyle to shore. If Alex wouldn't, or couldn't, come to her, then she would have to go and look for her.

The sun dried her hair and her suit while Ari walked along the road to Claire and Sam's. It was still summer, Ari thought, just a bizarre one. The sun was, indeed, doing its best to dry up all the rain, as Oscar had informed her at breakfast.

"And Incy Wincy Pider goed up da spout a den!" he sang jubilantly, waving his spoon about.

Ari wished she could be so carefree. As she walked, she fought back panic and tried using reason to figure out what had happened. If Alex really had left on a bus, maybe she was trying to get to Port August to see her mother. But surely Alex would have told her if she was planning to do that. Or she might simply have been trying to avoid discovery. Maybe she intended to get off the bus at the next stop and cut back across the hills or through the bush.

As the morning wore on, Ari had to admit that this scenario was becoming less likely. Even without her ghostly aura, and with an undeniably healthy heartbeat, Alex still had her unearthly powers. She could easily have made it back to Claire and Sam's and back to Ari before dawn. Why would she wait around to catch the bus at eight in the morning? If she planned to go to the city to see Beth, why hadn't Alex told Ari about it? And surely she would have called her at Claire and Sam's if she was leaving for a long time? That went beyond worrying about having to explain who she was.

There was one other possibility, and Ari didn't want to face it. But it came creeping back into her mind every minute or so until she couldn't ignore it. Alex hadn't painted any more portals, she was sure of it. But that didn't mean anything. What if a portal had opened in the pine forest and Alex had been sucked into it? She had said that might happen. Or, worse still, what if she had tried to take on the dog pack alone? Ari's heart sank as she realized this was something Alex would be likely to do. She pictured her leading poor, terrified

Tom from the forest and waiting, talking softly to him, until the ambulance came. She saw her fold her borrowed orange jumpsuit and leave it, with a note attached, on the bonnet of the SES truck. Once she was certain nobody would follow her, she would have made her way back into the forest, her face grim and determined, to hunt the dog pack alone.

Ari shuddered as she imagined the slavering jaws of the lead dog snapping at Alex's heels. Tom must have been terrified. Why, though, didn't the dogs attack him? Why had Alex managed to find him, alive and unhurt, if the dogs had been after him? Ari was puzzled and could find no answer to this question.

Ari checked the clock in Claire and Sam's kitchen when she got back. It was almost ten-thirty. Nobody was home, and Ari supposed Claire must be out with the twins, taking advantage of the good weather. The phone rang, sounding too loud in the empty kitchen. She picked it up, hoping it might be Cass, but it was Erin, calling from the hospital in Port August. She sounded exhausted and bewildered as she explained that Tom was awake and asking to speak to Claire and Sam.

"It's all he's been saying since he woke up," said Erin anxiously. "Wait a minute. What is it, honey? Oh. Now he's saying he needs to speak to you, Ari. He says he has a message for you, and that it's really important. What are you kids up to? I didn't think you and Tom were that close."

"We're not," Ari replied, flustered. "I mean, Tom's a great kid, but he's a lot younger than me."

Erin sighed and Ari heard her fussing over Tom as she passed him the phone. There was a small argument between mother and son as Tom demanded privacy for his phone call and Ari heard the relief in Tom's voice when he spoke into the phone.

"Ari," he gabbled, "I don't know if I should tell you this, but I reckon it's something you'd want to know." He told her about the young SES woman who drove away the wild dogs and led him out of the forest, and Ari's pulse quickened; her guess had been correct. "She said she was going back in to look for the dogs, and that, if I wanted to do one thing to thank her, it would be to ring Claire and Sam and make them promise not to let you out of their sight. She said that you were her girlfriend and that you'd try to follow her and you mustn't. Ari, you can't. Those dogs . . ." Ari heard the deep horror in his voice and in his ragged breathing. "Mum's coming back. Listen, I've been trying to ring Claire and Sam all morning. You won't go looking for her, will you? She didn't want anybody to know that she'd gone back in. She made me promise not to tell. But I reckon somebody needs to know, so that's why I told you. Call the cops, Ari. Your girlfriend, she shouldn't be in that forest on her own. Nobody should." He hung up.

Ari pushed the off button on Sam and Claire's cordless phone. She stared at it for several seconds, trying to think clearly. Should she call the police? What would she tell them, exactly? She thought about grumpy old Sergeant Donaldson, and imagined the silence on his end of the phone and the expression on his face, as she explained that her girlfriend had gone into the pine forest to hunt for the feral dogs, and would the police please go in after her?

"What's the young lass's name?" Sergeant Donaldson would reply. "And where are her parents?"

She was wasting time even considering it. Glancing at the clock again, Ari judged that she would have just enough time to leave a note for Nick at Wyndham and catch the bus if she ran there. Nick couldn't hope to arrive before twelve, not if he was driving at his usual grandfatherly pace. The Stonehaven bus left the stop just up the road from Wyndham at a quarter to twelve.

Ari hurriedly packed a change of clothes, a bottle of water, and some apples. She found her old beach hat, pulled it down over her ears, and was comforted by its presence, though she didn't quite know why. She left a note for Claire, explaining that she had gone home to wait for Nick. After a minute, she bit her lip and added: *Thanks so much for everything* and a row of kisses.

As she left the cottage, she thought how inadequate that sentence was, but it was too late to go back. She would miss the bus if she didn't hurry.

The sun was scorching hot now, and the landscape was eerily atmospheric; great plumes of steam rose from the water that lay everywhere on the ground, shafts of white sunlight pierced the foggy air, and Ari's skin grew slippery as she splashed along the muddy track through the bush. Her backpack chafed her sweaty shoulders, and she thought briefly about discarding some of the heavier things, like her jacket.

At Wyndham, Ari hurriedly fed the animals and then wrote a letter to her mother and Nick. She explained that she missed her new girlfriend Anna so much that she had run away to the city to be with her. The two of them intended to spend a long camping holiday somewhere in the bush up north. They wouldn't be in mobile range, but Ari would call when she could. She finished by apologizing profusely for her imminent bad behavior and begged her mother not to worry. *I'm nearly seventeen,* she wrote, hating herself, *and I need to be a normal teenager who does normal teenage things. I love Anna, and she loves me. We need to be together. I hope both of you can understand. All my love, Ari.*

She put the letter in an envelope and rested it against the fruit bowl. Then she paused, remembering Nick's hastily scrawled note to her that had been left in the same place. She asked herself, for the hundredth time, how worried her mother would be, and got the same answer: not as worried as if you just disappeared. At least she can be angry at you, and that's better than worrying.

Ari sighed and looked up at the sundrenched kitchen. This was her home. She was miserable about leaving it, and completely wretched about leaving her family. "But I have to find Alex," she told the empty kitchen.

As she closed the door behind her, Ari had a cold, prescient feeling that she would not open it again for a long time.

O

ARI STOOD UNDER THE DRIPPING trees at the forest's edge. The day had clouded over. She felt conspicuous getting off at the remote stop near the crossroad, and she told herself nobody she knew was on the bus. Nobody had seen her. Ari thought the bus driver gave her a suspicious look as she thanked him, and no wonder. It certainly looked like she was up to no good: a teenage girl, getting off at a bus stop in the middle of nowhere, wearing dark glasses and a beach hat under a rain-filled sky.

As the bus pulled away, Ari wondered how many seconds it would take the driver to forget about her altogether. The pine plantation loomed, an immense dark wall. Now, as she furtively entered the rows of pines, Ari thought longingly of the warmth and normality of the Port August bus. Its passengers would be chatting, or dozing, or listening to music as the old bus labored over the hills, while she fearfully prepared to search the dark forest for a person that everybody thought had died long ago. And nobody, not one person, had any idea where she was.

Ari armed herself with a strong stick. It felt comforting, though it would be little use against the dogs if they happened to appear. She tightened the straps on her backpack and wished that she had thought to pack a raincoat. In the chinks of late afternoon sky that flickered and wavered between the creaking treetops, Ari caught glimpses of storm clouds building. A fine mist gathered on her hair, and she put her hat back on, squared her shoulders, and walked on. She smiled grimly as she thought about the ridiculous fragility of her defenses. She had a stick to ward off a pack of starving feral dogs, a terry-towel hat against the rain, and only a desperate, fragile stubbornness to sustain her.

As she walked farther into the forest, Ari began to notice evidence of the hunt for Tom: a red ribbon left tied around a slender tree trunk, a plastic water bottle crushed and caught under a piece of bracken, even a woolen scarf half trodden into the spongy earth. This part of the forest was silent, spookily so, but the part of the pine plantation near her house was quiet too. The trees here had smoother trunks and fewer needles. There were no birds, no signs of life apart from the endless rows of trees.

The part of the plantation that backed onto her family's property hadn't been cleared in a long time. Ari had never thought to ask why. The trees there were over a hundred years old, and their trunks were rough and wrinkled and spotted with bright orange fungi. Fallen trees had been left to rot and saplings to grow at will. Bracken and other undergrowth had managed to insinuate their way underneath the trees in Ari's pine forest, and the forest floor was cushioned by decades of fallen needles and patches of moist, spongy moss. Alex and Ari had bounced on it as kids. Birds, wallabies, and rabbits inhabited Ari's patch of forest, and it was beautiful, though the pine trees didn't really belong where the mountain ash and the beech trees should be growing. This forest, though, looked exactly what it was, a commercial plantation that grew trees only to cut them as soon as they were big enough, and the naked earth under these bare trunks had become a slippery, rank-smelling clay.

Ari tightened the straps on her backpack. She had been avoiding the gloom of the deep forest by walking parallel to the road along the first avenue of trees. "Coward," she told herself and turned resolutely into the darkness of the interior.

The ground began to slope steeply away. Ari slipped and had to pick herself up several times as the clay grew slick with rain. Here, where the trees were only a few years old, was a huge clearing. The trees still loomed overhead, but they were baby trees—tall and straight and whippy—and there were more stretches of darkening sky between them.

Ari was tired. She stopped and had a drink of water while she considered her next move. Hunting for Alex in over two hundred hectares of forest was insane. But there might be clues, thought Ari. There might be *something*.

The clouds that blotted out the sun were much darker now, and Ari shivered as she thought about being lost in the plantation after dark. This search might be pointless, but the alternative—walking out and catching a bus home—was unthinkable.

Ari sighed and adjusted her clothing. Her jacket was damp, but her T-shirt was still dry underneath. The cuffs of her jeans were splattered with mud and caked in ochre-colored clay, and she scraped her boots on a fallen branch to remove some of the mud. As she zipped up her backpack, Ari thought she saw a flicker of movement through the trees on the far side of the clearing. The skin on the back of her neck tingled, as if somebody had snuck up behind her and breathed softly there.

"Alex?" she called softly. Then, cursing her own fear, she cupped her hands around her mouth and screamed: "*Alex! Where are you?*" as loudly as she could. The forest rang with the pale echo of her yell, but nobody answered, and it seemed, if anything, even quieter than before.

Ari began to run, her backpack thumping on her spine. She charged downhill across the clearing and plunged into the denser forest on the other side. Her foot caught on something, and she fell, lying winded for a few seconds on the cold earth. She slipped again and again on the steep decline and finally resorted to a crab-like slide to reach the bottom. The valley floor was freezing, and there were pools of oily, brackish water everywhere. In this sun-forsaken place, it seemed already night.

Ari stopped to catch her breath and was struck with paralyzing fear. She scrambled from the edge of the nearest pool, realizing with a sick feeling that she had nearly slipped into a huge sinkhole. She stared at the smooth, white clay sides of the hole where the water had receded slightly.

Of course, she thought wildly, they would fill up with all the rain! They would look just like puddles. She forced herself to face the worst. Did Alex accidently fall into one? Nobody would walk through a puddle that size on purpose, but if she was running? Or, she thought miserably, if she was being chased. She gripped her stick tightly. The pool gaped, its black mouth so shadowed by the trees and the hills that it reflected nothing, not even a glimpse of the darkening sky. All the fear, all the strangeness, all the wrongness that had been seeping out into the world seemed to come from this valley, from this particular sinkhole.

Ari suddenly remembered what Alex had told her about portals: "A ring of stones, a painted circle, a hole in the earth; there are many doorways to the unlit realm." A hole in the earth.

She stared at the black water as though hypnotized, and so she didn't see the dogs until it was too late to run. When she looked up, the black Alsatian was staring at her with its mouth open in a leering grin and its salmon-colored tongue lolling out between its teeth. The dog sat down beside the sinkhole and panted, and the other dogs whined and ran in and out among the trees.

"It was a trap," Ari said, her mind slowly fitting the pieces together. "You knew Alex would come looking for Tom." Her stick was slippery with sweat. Ari adjusted her grip and raised her stick like a sword. "You waited for her to rescue Tom and to hear about what you did to him when he was lost in here. You knew Alex would come back and hunt for you. Did you lead her into a sinkhole? Was that your job? What do you get out of it?"

"My gratitude, and the right to hunt all who enter this forest," growled a low voice behind her.

Ari froze. The dog whined and lowered its head submissively. Ari whirled around, clutching her stick. There was a man on the hillside. He was dressed all in black, and the hood of his long cloak was drawn up, shadowing his face.

As he came down the hill toward her, he said, conversationally, "You are correct. The dogs, the missing girl, it was a trap. But I have no personal interest in the fate of Alexandra Cohen. Her trial will be diverting, I suppose. Perhaps I will attend it."

He came closer. Ari was so terrified it was as though she was standing outside her body, watching objectively as the dark figure took her stick and her backpack and tossed them carelessly into one of the puddles.

"You won't be needing any of that again." The man pushed back his hood. At once, Ari was hit by a hideous smell of decay that seemed to come from his skin. She vomited violently at his feet.

"How charming," commented the man coldly. "Now that I know you intimately, Arielle, allow me to introduce myself. I am Lord Acheron, ruler of the river that bears my name and second only to Hades himself in the kingdom of the dead."

Ari made herself look at him. She wiped her mouth with the back of her hand and stared. He was skeleton-skinny, with gaunt, aristocratic features. He had pallid, waxy skin, and his long hair was an ugly shade of blond. His eyes were a light, almost colorless, blue and they were red-rimmed, with black shadows under them like the ones under Alex's eyes before she'd lost her unearthly glow. Acheron was surrounded by the same ghostly aura, and Ari recognized the power that this uncanny force field seemed to muffle and contain. He towered over her, and she saw that he had a huge sword belted to his back. From him emanated a stench that was faint and yet so vile that she gagged and had to hold both hands over her mouth to keep from vomiting again.

She didn't bother asking him what he wanted from her or where Alex was. She just stood and tried to hold herself upright as she waited for him to kill her. But he did something worse. He reached out, took her hat off, touched her wet hair, and then held a limp strand between his long pale fingers. Then he bent his head over hers and smelled her hair.

Something in Ari snapped. She screamed as if her lungs would burst and began to run, mindlessly, toward the far side of the valley. She slipped almost at once and fell on her stomach.

He laughed then, a chilling, mirthless noise. He called, "Don't run, little rabbit; it only makes the dogs more eager for the chase!"

Then she was running blindly, and the dogs loped alongside her, behind her, circling her, panting and barking and biting at her heels. The lead dog growled deep in its throat as the pack began to drive her back toward Acheron. Ari stopped just short of the sinkhole and spun around; her boots sent up a spray of muddy water as she fought to stay upright. But it was no use. The last thing Ari saw as she fell backward into the black water was the pale, jeering face of Acheron bending over the pool.

9. Into the Dark

Ari was sinking, falling into darkness. The water closed over her head, shutting out all sound. The copper-colored light that filtered through the brown water receded as she was sucked down into the sinkhole's black depths. Her chest burned.

So this is what drowning is like, she thought. I'm drowning. Alex, was it like this for you? She kicked strongly and tried to swim toward the surface, but a current pulled her down and water began to fill her nostrils, then her throat, and finally her lungs. Ari closed her eyes. There was a rushing noise, and then a moment of stillness. Ari's lungs had just enough oxygen to sustain her for a few more seconds. Then, just when she thought her chest would burst, Ari was sucked further down, falling suddenly through air, not water.

Ari landed hard on a cold, wet surface. She rolled onto her side and coughed and vomited muddy water until she could breathe properly. Then she sat up, slowly. Where was she? Was she dead?

Ari pressed both palms against her chest, feeling for her heart. It was there, still thumping heroically against her ribs, but she couldn't understand how, or why, she was still alive. She heard water rushing overhead and she groped around with her right hand until her fingertips met a smooth, wet surface, like hard-packed clay. It was so dark that the blackness seemed solid, and Ari sat up straighter, reaching fearfully above her head with both hands in case she was in a small tunnel or hole. But there didn't seem to be anything immediately above her, nor, when she explored a little more, anything behind her, in front of her or to her left. To her right, the cold wall seemed to go on forever.

Keeping her wall close, Ari inched forward on her hands and knees. Her knees were soon aching and bruised, so she risked standing up and, by holding the wall with both hands, she soon gathered enough courage to take faltering steps through the blackness.

The wall came to an abrupt end. Ari took her hands away and felt around in the dark. There was another wall in front of her, as smooth and as damp as the one she'd been following. But this one had a door. Eagerly she traced its outline. Whatever was behind this door had to be better than the terror of walking blindly in the dark. There was no door handle, but Ari pushed hard, and the door moved, swinging silently inward. She held her breath.

It was still dark, but Ari could just make out the shape of a steep, narrow staircase leading sharply down. There were no walls and no handrails on either side, just darkness and a feeling of immense, empty space.

The stairs were made of stone, which seemed solid enough. Ari clenched her fists, breathed in deeply, and took a step down. She didn't topple off the stairs into the void, so she took another step, and another, and soon she found herself picking her way painstakingly down a staircase that sloped downward so sharply that she had to put a foot lightly on each step before she felt safe enough to stand on it.

She had been going down for several minutes when she stopped dead, caught in the grip of vertigo so paralyzing that she thought she might never move again. There was no wind and no sense of movement, just an emptiness that seemed to magnify the darkness.

Ari whimpered, and the sound echoed in the stillness. She told herself not to panic. As she stood there she began to sense, rather than see, a wan glow coming from the stairs themselves. It was ghostly green and so faint that it hardly made any difference, but at least she could see where her feet should go. She stood, trembling, for what seemed like forever. Finally, Ari gritted her teeth and tried to take a step down, but she was shaking so much that she had to sit and take each step on her bottom, like a toddler. Soon, even this was too hard, so terrified was she of falling sideways into the darkness. She turned herself around and went down backward on her stomach, slithering little by little, like a baby.

For a long while, Ari was focused only on the narrow stairs and so didn't notice how far she had descended. It seemed as if she had been worming her way downward forever, and yet she could not have said whether it was hours or days that she spent clinging to the ghostly steps. By now, her feet automatically groped for the next step, so when she didn't find one she stopped, wondering what new terrors awaited her. Then Ari realized that the stairs had finally ended and she stood stiffly upright, rubbing her lower back with one hand as she recoiled at the barrenness around her.

She stood on a wide, flat plain. Everything was the same brownish green color, like mud or army uniforms. The sky, if it was a sky, was dirty gray, and the staircase wound improbably out of this featureless landscape up into the murky darkness. It wasn't exactly cold, but Ari shivered and rubbed her upper arms, which were covered in goosebumps.

As she tried to peer into the distance, she thought she could hear, faintly, the sound of water, and so she went toward it. As she walked, feet sinking slightly into the dust that blanketed the plain, Ari tried to breathe calmly and deeply. She kept her mouth closed and breathed through her nose, in and out, reminding herself that she could control her fear, that she didn't have to let it swallow her.

"I think I'm in the underworld," Ari told herself. Because, really, where else might she be?

That terrifying spectral stairway was evidence enough that this was no ordinary subterranean cave system, and Ari had been herded into the sinkhole on purpose. But if Acheron had wanted her dead, he would be disappointed. She was alive, very much alive, in the underworld.

As Ari walked, she tried to make this seem real, testing her surroundings with her senses. But there was only meager light and no sound except the distant rush and hiss of running water. Even her footsteps were muffled by the thick gray dust. The air was thick, like fog, and it was uncomfortable, but it wasn't a discomfort that could be understood with any physical sense. It was more, Ari thought, like the desolate atmosphere around an abandoned house or the uncanny emptiness of the school corridor when everyone had gone home. It would be easy to forget all the senses down here, including any sense of self.

Ari pinched herself hard on the arm and was relieved to find that it hurt. She was hungry and horribly thirsty. Her chest was tight and sore with fear and longing for Alex, and this was oddly reassuring, reminding her that she was still herself, still Ari. She stared at the vastness of the gray, dusty plain. She had no idea where to start looking for Alex, but she had to start walking and keep on walking.

The trick, Ari thought a little later, was to keep a cool head and not let the eeriness of this place get to you. Although the plain was still an empty wasteland, Ari was beginning to see things as she walked. She passed a solitary tree growing out of the dust and told herself sternly that it made no difference to her that a tree could grow here, away from the sunlight and the rain. She would not question anything she saw and, that way, she could maybe keep the panic at bay a little longer.

All along the horizon, a dark line of hills or mountains rose like a black wall, and the sound of the river became louder as she grew closer.

"It's almost like the real world," Ari whispered. She looked over her shoulder, but nobody was following her. "I'll keep talking to myself," she said softly, "and that's fine. It's totally fine, Ari. I think people probably do that down here. It's not so different from the world up there. There are mountains, and there's a river. I can see it now, a big river, and I'm sure I'll see people soon. Oh, look. There they are."

Ari watched, skin crawling, as a group of figures took shape along the riverbank. They were too far away for her to see their faces, but she heard their voices, faintly. They seemed to be crying and calling out to something, or somebody, in the river or on its farther shore.

Ari stopped. She didn't want to approach the ghostly throng. The figures were all gray and indistinct, like the landscape. She did not want to see their faces. But the ghosts, if that's what they were, stood between her and the river, and Ari knew instinctively that she had to cross that river. It cut the landscape in two, running in both directions as far as she could see before disappearing into the gloom. She could just make out the pale line of the bank on the opposite shore and, beyond that, the blackness of the mountain range. The river flowed swiftly, and Ari saw gigantic toothy boulders sticking up from the water. The thunder of the water rushing around these rocks was magnified by the silence and the emptiness of the landscape.

Ari took a few cautious steps forward, trying to choose a path that would lead her away from the wailers on the riverbank. As she padded softly through the dust, she began to feel as if she was being watched. It was an uncanny feeling, and it grew stronger with each step she took. Ari remembered Acheron's pallid skin and red-rimmed eyes and the stench of decay that had made her vomit. Would he find her down here? What did a god of the underworld want with her, anyway?

"I have to find Alex," she told herself desperately and began to run. Her sudden movement attracted the attention of the ghostly figures upriver, and they pointed their wasted fingers at her and shouted in voices too faint to hear. Their mouths were big black holes in the whiteness of their faces, and Ari saw that their eyes were red-rimmed, like Acheron's. All the terror she had been fighting rose up against her and inside her and made her nauseous.

She struggled to breathe, and her legs wobbled as she ran, stumbling and gasping, through the dirty brown spume and tiny wavelets that washed the riverbank and into its fast-flowing waters. Ari didn't bother wading out. She dived into the great river, and the waters closed over her head. She surfaced, swimming strongly with the current, and saw the ghosts shrinking with distance, their mouths still gaping as they spoke to each other and performed their obscure gesticulations.

The river carried her swiftly along, and Ari concentrated on staying afloat in its black and saltless waters. The water was like the atmosphere, neither warm nor cold, but at least it was fast-flowing water, which was preferable to the dismal nothingness of the landscape. It was relatively easy to avoid the boulders that occasionally pierced the river, but Ari was worried about the current. Would she be able to swim against it to reach the other shore? She had to try, and try soon, or she wouldn't be able to keep herself afloat. Ari had always disliked swimming in fresh water. She missed the buoyancy of the ocean, the gentle pressure of its embrace. Fresh water always made Ari anxious, as if she could fall through it, and the constant struggle against sinking was exhausting.

"I can swim," Ari told herself. "That's one thing I know how to do well. I can swim this saltless river." And so that is what she did, stroke by stroke, swimming diagonally with the current.

As she pulled her arms through the water and kicked her legs, Ari tried to remember her classical mythology. Was this the river Styx? Weren't there other rivers in the underworld? Alex had said something about another river, the Acheron river. Ari shuddered as she recalled Acheron's cruel, pale face leering at her and told herself that she should have done more reading. She knew many stories, but not much at all about the topography or the gods of the underworld. If she made it safely to the other side of this river, she still had no idea where to go next.

Where should she start looking for Alex? Ari was convinced that she had been taken, probably through the same sinkhole portal that had sucked Ari down. If they, whoever "they" were, wanted to punish Alex, she might be awaiting her retribution in an underworld prison. Would there be a trial? Did it work like that? Acheron had mentioned a trial, and so perhaps there was still a chance to rescue Alex before a trial could take place.

Thinking about her next move made the distance she had to swim seem less immense, but Ari knew she was fooling herself. Her arms and legs began to ache and then to feel heavy as she ploughed through the water. She tried not to look at the other side of the river, but occasionally she had to look up, and it was a long, long way away. Meanwhile, the current had become stronger, and Ari was swimming as much with it as she was across it, knowing that she was being borne downstream at a frightening rate. The grim landscape began to flash past, but there wasn't much to see, just an endless flow of empty, dusty plain, a few stunted bushes, and the long, low mountain range holding up the gray vault of the sky.

She let the river carry her along, saving her strength for what she knew would be her last attempt at reaching the shore. Ari was so terribly thirsty, but she kept her mouth tightly closed. What would happen if she drank this water? She closed her eyes and pictured Alex lying on her bed at Wyndham with her dark hair spread across Ari's pillow. She conjured up the warmth of Alex's arms, the softness of her lips, and the tingle when their bodies were pressed close together. If she had to swim this vast underworld river for a chance of seeing Alex again, then that is what she would do.

Ari opened her eyes. She kicked strongly and pushed her way through the dark water. As she swam, she found a little place deep inside her that held a reserve of strength, a small cache of hidden power. She drew on it now; her breath came in broken gasps as she flailed and dog-paddled across the endless yards to the riverbank. When at last her feet found the soft mud of the shore, Ari staggered through the calm waters of the river's shallows and lay where she fell in the mud on the far side of the river.

10. The Hunter

Ari surfaced from a tangle of nightmares and opened her eyes. She was lying on her back on something soft yet prickly, like dried grass. It was dark, but a pale glow came from somewhere to her right and she turned her head to find it. She saw a candle burning with a clear white flame atop a roughly made stone bench.

She sat up, ignoring the stiffness in her muscles, and stared cautiously at her surroundings. She seemed to be sitting on a pile of hay or straw. A woolen rug was tucked over her legs, and Ari wriggled out of this as quietly as she could. The room was tiny, much smaller than her bedroom at Wyndham, and there were no windows, but the air was fresh. Ari creaked slowly to her feet, then stood bent over for a few seconds, trying to rub life back into her aching legs.

Once she'd steadied herself, Ari went to the bench, lifted the candle from the sticky pool of wax that supported it, and examined all the walls. A small grate was set high up on one wall, and the fresh air came from there, but it was much too small for her to squeeze through. The door seemed to be made of some dark metal. It did not yield when she pushed on it. Ari retreated to her bed of straw and crouched, waiting.

Soon enough, the door creaked open, and a tall, cloaked figure entered carrying a bowl in one hand and a bottle in the other. Ari squatted with her fists clenched, ready to spring and fight if necessary, but her jailer (if that was what he was) merely put back his hood and gestured at the bench, where he had placed the bowl and bottle. "Eat and drink some water," he said simply.

Ari was starving, and her throat was tight and dry. She took a few steps toward the table, studying the man as she did so. He stood impassively in the dark doorway, watching her. He seemed to be old, or at least middle-aged, with graying hair and beard and a high forehead creased with wrinkles. His eyes had a proud, aloof expression that reminded her uncomfortably of Acheron, though his brown skin made his face look much healthier, and more human. He wore a long leather shirt, belted at the waist, over gray trousers and long boots. The long cloak completed what reminded Ari of a Robin Hood costume Nick had once hired for a party, and she laughed defiantly as she poked the hard bread in the bowl and inspected the bottle by sniffing it.

"Whistling in the dark?" the man enquired.

"Maybe," Ari replied, as insolently as she could. She refused to be cowed by the underworld and its creepy inhabitants. "Are you going to tell me who you are and why I'm a prisoner?" She put the bottle down. "I'm not going to drink that water, by the way, or eat anything. I might not know much about this place, but I know enough not to do that."

"As you wish."

The man clicked his fingers, and a servant scurried in to remove the bowl and bottle. She was a pretty, dark-haired girl, about fourteen or fifteen, and she stared at Ari as she picked up the things. The man made a low noise in his throat and waved her away, and the girl hurried out again, giving Ari a sidelong glance as she did so. The man gestured toward the doorway. Ari hesitated. The tiny candlelit cell suddenly seemed safer than the unknown dangers outside in the dark. The man smiled, but there was no pity in it.

"Come now," he taunted. "Is this the brave mortal who dared to swim the great river?" He lowered his voice and stared intently at her.

"No one has ever done that and lived. No one. Many souls have tried, but the river merely swallows them. When I found you I thought you were a shade." He shook his head. "How is it that you are still alive? Where did you find the strength? You're not even fully grown."

"I'm looking for somebody," Ari told him.

The man laughed, but Ari thought she caught a glint of approval in his dark eyes. "So, you have come to this place of eternal night seeking your lover? Few have made it so far on such a journey, especially alone and unassisted. And those who came before were ferried across the river. How did you do it? How did you swim such a distance without drowning?"

He was waiting for an answer. She swallowed, trying to moisten her parched mouth. "I let the water carry me," she whispered.

The man fiddled idly with a lump of soft wax at the base of the candle. Then he looked at her and nodded as if he had made his mind up about something. "You must leave this place if you wish to continue searching. I cannot help you except to let you go free, and that is granting a great favor. I am a hunter of shades. You may call me the Hunter if you like. My task is to collect all those who wander far from their appointed place and return them. But I will let you go. Go swiftly."

He stood next to the open doorway and once more gestured for Ari to precede him. She walked past him as quickly as she could and plunged into the blackness beyond the doorframe. It was like going blind in an instant, and she stopped, uncertain. As the darkness settled around her, Ari heard the Hunter clear his throat.

He took her hand and pressed three cold, round shapes into it. "These are coins," he said gruffly. "You may need them down here."

"Why are you helping me?"

He was silent a moment. "Because once, long ago, I, too, was courageous among my people. My Mara was a brave girl. I think she might have done extraordinary things if she had lived."

"Was that your daughter? The girl with the dark hair?"

"Yes. Now go, before I change my mind and drag you in chains to the Plain of Judgment."

Ari shivered as she tried to peer through the gloom. Now that her eyes no longer missed the light of the candle, she found that she could see, but there wasn't much to look at. Ahead of her, mountains stretched black and menacing along the horizon, and the river thundered at her back. Ari stood irresolute in the darkness. She had no idea what to do next or which way she should go. Crossing the river had been terrible, but swimming it had at least given her a purpose. Now Ari was truly lost.

She turned back toward the river, intending, perhaps, to find the Hunter and beg him for directions. But there was no sign of any building or dwelling place, not even a hill or mound that might conceal a cave. A few small, choking sobs escaped as Ari began to walk upstream, retracing on foot the unknown distances the river had borne her. The gray dust of the river plain had given way to dry black earth scattered with rocks and boulders. It reminded Ari of pictures she had seen of the surface of the moon, but without the moon's glamour. The absence of life was appalling.

Ari's stomach twisted with hunger. She thought about the apples she'd put in her backpack, which was now lying in a puddle in the forest. She tried not to think about her water flask. She had never been so thirsty. The sound of running water was a torment. But worse than thirst or hunger was the slow creep of despair that dogged her. Each step she took seemed more pointless than the last. Ari tried to hold onto thoughts of Alex: her smooth shoulders glistening with sweat as she worked in the garden at Wyndham, the way her lips curved when she smiled. She made herself go over all the sunny days, the kisses, all the precious moments with Alex she had preserved in her memory, but it was no use. She was alone and lost in the underworld. Alex must be imprisoned somewhere in all this vast darkness, but Ari was no match for this place, not matter how desperately she wanted to find Alex. Sooner or later she would be captured. And in the meantime, she would die of thirst.

Ari tried putting her fingers in her ears to block out the sound of all that delicious fresh water so close at hand. She told herself sternly that Persephone ate the pomegranate seeds because she didn't know any better, and that she should learn from her mistake. But, she argued with herself, if I'm going to die down here anyway, what does it matter if I eat or drink? I'm not likely to find my way back.

As the truth of this broke like a dark wave upon her, Ari ran the few yards to the river, cupped her hands in its fast-flowing waters and drank and drank and drank.

So intent was she on quenching her thirst that Ari didn't notice him until he was close behind her. Her face flushed with fear as a cold voice enquired, "And who gave you permission to drink from my river?"

Ari stood up and turned around. It was, unmistakably, Acheron, though he looked different down here. He was clad in bright chain mail, with a dark red cloak over the top. A thin silver band held back his yellow hair, and his fingers were covered in rings of silver with red stones. A huge sword was belted to his waist. He didn't stink, and she was oddly, ridiculously, relieved by this. At least she wouldn't have to add nausea to her list of troubles.

Acheron walked a little way along the river's edge and stood staring pensively over its vast expanse of fast-flowing water.

"I underestimated you, Arielle," he said at last. "I thought to find you drowned and a shade, wailing on the riverbank near the crossing place. That sinkhole is deep, and I saw it swallow you. I was planning to escort your shade to the trial of Alex Cohen myself. It would have amused me. But you are still living. That complicates matters. And you have aroused some interest among certain acquaintances of mine because you swam my river."

There was a note of incredulity, an outraged disbelief in his tone. "Do you *know* who I am? Have you any idea of the forces contained in the water that still drips down your silly little chin? How did you dare to immerse yourself in the river of woe?" He looked at her then, and Ari felt her skin creep under the cold power of his gaze.

"How else was I supposed to get across?" she stammered.

"Stupid girl. You were never supposed to get across. Especially not while your heart still beats inside your breast. This is the underworld. This is the realm of the dead. You have cheated death once already, and now you thumb your nose at me by daring to swim across the mighty and immortal waters of the Acheron, a river that only the dead may cross. Have you never heard of Charon? The dead must pay the ferryman who takes them across the river. They must then linger on the far side of the river to learn their fate on the Plain of Judgment. That is the order of things and has been since before the world began."

"But I'm not dead," whispered Ari.

Acheron glared at her. "It is an outrage that you are not. But that is not my decision, though it is something I hope to amend very soon. You will follow me now to my house. Soon, I will escort you to the trial of Alex Cohen, and there you will learn that the laws of the underworld are implacable. You may not flout them nor escape the decrees of fate."

He made a small gesture with his left hand, and Ari stifled a scream as several dark figures on horses seemed to materialize out of the darkness around them. They were tall, grim-faced men, but they didn't look rough or mean. They reminded Ari of the old black and white etchings in her battered copy of *The Odyssey*, of warriors with long, straight noses and flowing hair springing from their high, proud foreheads. The black horses were silent and still. They all, men and horses, had the dull, insubstantial glow that Ari was learning to associate with the dead.

They're shades, she told herself, like ghosts, but more solid seeming, more real. Alex was the same, until her heart started beating again. Suddenly, Ari understood that Alex's heartbeat, like her own, was unique and more precious down here than light or air or sunshine. That small, steady rhythm, that thump thump thump, stood for hope. It meant, "I'm not a ghost, not a shade. I don't belong here." But what happened to living people in the underworld? What would happen to Alex? Would her heart still beat? What if they had already killed her?

One of Acheron's henchmen took her arm, and though she could almost see her arm through his phantom's hand, she couldn't break free.

Ari's control snapped. She screamed as loudly as she could, hearing her voice ring out across the arid landscape: "Alex! Where are you? I'm here! I'm down here too!"

She heard it only faintly, like the echo of a whisper. It seemed to be coming from far ahead, lost in the immeasurable distance: "Ari, can you hear me? Ari? *Ari*?"

Ari covered her face, and her eyes filled with tears as Acheron's silent shades lifted her onto the back of one of the horses. She gripped the front of the saddle, and she noticed despairingly, even through her tears, that the horse wore no bridle. One of the shades called out words of command, and the horses broke into a canter.

Ari held onto the saddle. Acheron saw her face and gave a cruel laugh as he whipped his own unearthly mount into a gallop, but Ari was crying tears of joy and relief. The voice inside her head belonged, unmistakably, to Alex. She was reaching out, somewhere in this abhorrent netherworld, calling to Ari as Ari herself had called to Alex on that rainy night at Claire and Sam's.

She squeezed her eyes shut and tried to visualize a golden thread spiraling boldly through the darkness from her heart to Alex's. As the horse moved swiftly and soundlessly under her, she formed a question in her mind and let it sing wordlessly along the imaginary golden line: "Where are you?"

The reply came immediately, and Ari heard dread mixed with relief in Alex's answer. "I'm in prison. Oh, Ari, where are *you*? What are you doing here? Are you all right? Try to send me a picture of where you are, and I'll see if I recognize it."

Ari looked around her. There was nothing to see but the blur of long black manes and necks outstretched as the phantom horses bore their riders swiftly across the ruined landscape. Far out in front, she could just make out a red flicker that was Acheron's cloak. The mountains still stretched endlessly in both directions on her right, and the river flowed swiftly away to her left. Ari squeezed her eyes closed and tried to send as much of this image as she could.

Alex's reply was confused. "You're riding? Who are you riding with? Do you know where they're taking you?"

"To Acheron's palace," replied Ari, mouthing the silent, dreadful words as she projected the force of them.

Alex didn't reply for several long moments. The horse tossed its head as they galloped, and Ari clutched at its mane, aware as she did so that her fingers were trying to grab a handful of hair on an animal without warmth or substance or life.

"Ari?" Alex came through strongly, her voice almost audible along their invisible connection. "Ari, listen. You have to escape. Do it now, while you're riding. Once you are in his keep, he will not release you, and not even Hades himself has the power to command a lord of the five rivers once he is in his own house. Do you understand? Can you do it? Jump from the horse or do something, anything. Just don't let Acheron shut his front door behind you. Promise me. Ari? I can't help you. They've chained me, and I can't see." Alex's silent voice was panicked, and Ari thought she might be crying. Something broke inside Ari.

"Alex?" Like a child in a nightmare, Ari cried her name aloud, calling, unthinking, into the void.

One of Acheron's shadow men turned his head to stare at her from large, empty, eyes. Then he turned away and continued to ride impassively alongside her. Ari tried to think. She forced her brain, exhausted and sluggish from hunger and terror, to confront the problem of an escape, but it was no use. She was surrounded on all sides by Acheron's henchmen, and, if she were to jump or feign a fall from her horse, she would, she was sure, be picked up and placed straight back on with a minimum of fuss. Even if I did manage to get away, Ari thought miserably, I'd still be lost down here, with no hope of finding Alex or getting home. What am I going to do?

The dull landscape blurred as Ari began to cry again, silently and helplessly, from terror. Tears splashed onto her horse's mane, but the horse paid her no attention. She may as well have been riding on top of a speeding train; she would have as little chance of escape.

Ari watched bleakly as her escort of gray-clad riders rapidly approached a small group of figures walking along the river's edge.

They were the first shades Ari had seen since the wailers upriver, and she didn't want to look at their faces. These shades were dressed in clothes of varying styles, but the colors seemed faded into a uniform drabness that suited the miserable landscape. All wore long cloaks with hoods. Some of the shades turned to face them as Ari and the riders drew alongside, and their faces were different too. Ari glimpsed an old woman with long black plaits, a man with a pointed beard, and a young boy with hair so white it looked like a tiny lamp glowing against the dark river. A tall figure at the back turned to look at the riders, and Ari gasped. It was the Hunter.

As her horse bore her swiftly past the people on the riverbank, Ari called out as loudly as she dared: "Hunter! Please help me!"

Alex's voice came in, urgent and frightened, asking what Ari was doing. She told her, holding her breath as she beamed the image of the Hunter along their invisible telephone line.

The response held a wary excitement. "Try jumping off the horse now. The Hunter will pick you up and bring you to the Plain of Judgment. I am being held in a prison near there, I think. At least you'll be away from Acheron. Don't be scared! Swing your leg over the horse's neck and jump clear. Bend your knees when you hit the ground."

"Alex, we're galloping flat out, and I've got no reins."

There was a small silence inside her mind, and then Alex's voice came, shaky with a terror she couldn't hide. "Ari, I don't know what to tell you."

"I'm going to jump anyway," Ari told her, and she did.

11.
Walking with the Dead

There wasn't any good way to fall. Ari heard a tiny splintering crunch as her right shoulder hit the rocky earth. After such a small noise, the pain was unbelievable. She lay where she fell, dimly aware that the horses had disappeared into the distance and that she was once again alone by the great river. Then she heard footsteps and waited with her eyes closed as they got closer. When she opened her eyes again, the Hunter's gray-bearded face was bent over her. She thought, suddenly: He's not as transparent as the other shades. I wonder why?

"Not you again," he growled. The Hunter lifted her gently and paused to examine the unnatural bulge in Ari's shoulder as he helped her to stand. "First you swim the forbidden river, then you leap from a galloping horse." He sighed. "And it seems to be my fate to rescue you."

Ari was aware of Alex trying to reach her, but she was in too much pain to maintain the connection. She closed her eyes and bit her lip, trying not to make any noise.

The Hunter took off his cloak and placed it as gently as he could around Ari's shoulders. She cried out as the fabric brushed her injured shoulder, and the Hunter apologized as he raised the hood of the cloak so that it partly concealed her face.

"Acheron will come back for you soon," he explained. "We have to hurry." He raised his arm, and Ari watched, grinding her teeth with pain, as the dark-haired girl from the cell by the river emerged from behind a large rock. The Hunter beckoned her impatiently. "This is Mara, my daughter. Where are the shades, Mara?"

"Behind the boulder."

"Keep them there a while." The Hunter turned back to Ari. "What is your name?"

"I'm Ari."

"Well, Ari, it seems that you are now in my charge. I am leading a group of lost souls to the Plain of Judgment. If you travel with us, you must look like a shade and you must be completely silent. I cannot protect you otherwise. Mara will fetch you some different clothing. I will do what I can to mend your shoulder. The joint is dislocated and must be forced back into alignment. It will hurt you. I've no need to ask whether you are brave, but you will need to stay completely still. And drink this first."

He passed her a small glass bottle and she took a sip. The liquid was golden and tasted vaguely like honey. The pain eased a little. Then the Hunter asked Ari to lie down, and he folded a corner of the dusty cloak and wedged it between her teeth. Ari saw Mara standing a little to one side with her arms full of folded gray fabric, her dark eyes wide with what looked like fear. She squeezed her own eyes tightly closed.

The Hunter unzipped her jacket and pulled her right arm from its sleeve. The sudden movement hurt so much that Ari couldn't help screaming and thrashing. She spat out the cloth gag and whimpered.

The Hunter put his finger to his lips and shushed her, putting the wadded cloak back in her mouth as he did so. Then he slipped one hand behind her shoulder and gripped her arm with the other. This time, instead of spitting out the cloth, she bit down on it as hard as she could, and her whole body went rigid as the Hunter brought his hands together in a swift, brutal movement. Through the blinding pain, Ari could hear the Hunter asking Mara for bandages and water. He bound her shoulder tightly and then helped her to sit up. Mara held a stone bottle to her lips. She drank thirstily and whispered her thanks. The Hunter just nodded, briefly, and strode off toward the large rock to check on his prisoners.

When he left, Mara helped Ari take off her filthy T-shirt and jeans and slipped a loose beige dress and cloak over her head. While Mara was bundling up her clothes, Ari remembered her coins, and Mara showed her a hidden pocket in the cloak where she could keep them.

"Now you look more like a shade," she said, fastening the ugly, bone-colored cloak at Ari's throat. Suddenly, she scrambled to her feet and stared fearfully over Ari's head. "Quickly! Acheron is coming! Put your hood up and stay here. Father!"

The Hunter appeared, walking unhurriedly with his group of lost shades. "Remain calm," he ordered. "I will talk to him. Ari, you need to stand up and mingle with the group. The rest of you put your hoods up. The Lord Acheron approaches. Do not look at him! He is fearful to behold."

Ari stood quietly in the middle of the little throng with her eyes fixed on the ground. Her shoulder was on fire, but she clenched her teeth and concentrated on staying still. She heard Acheron's horse snort and stamp and kick up the gravel as he reined it in. Her skin crawled when she heard the quiet fury in his voice.

"Hunter. I am missing a prisoner. She jumped from the horse that was carrying her, and my men, who, alas, do not possess any wits, failed to notice until we were well advanced. Have you seen a girl, not quite full grown, with fair hair? She is a foolish, ill-mannered wretch, and she is still living."

The Hunter shook his head. "I do not deal with the living, my Lord."

Acheron was silent. Ari went cold all over.

When he spoke again, each word was edged with ice. “Be careful, Hunter,” he warned. “Most would agree that the great lords have been *most* generous in allowing you to keep your daughter with you. She should have passed the last gate long ago. It would be a small matter for me to persuade the Unseen One himself that these special privileges are . . . unmerited.”

Ari held her breath. Surely the Hunter would give her up now?

When he spoke again, he merely repeated what he had said before, adding, “I have my own prisoners to conduct. If your Lordship will permit me, I will continue on my way.”

Ari heard Acheron give a great hiss of barely controlled rage, and then she heard the metallic rattle of stones as he kicked his mount into a furious gallop.

The Hunter didn’t look at Ari or at his daughter. He merely raised his arm and started walking upriver. The shades shuffled forward with Mara and Ari at the rear of the group. Ari snuck a quick glance at her companion as they walked, but she didn’t know what to say. Would Acheron really try to separate Mara from her father? Mara didn’t appear to be concerned, but her pretty face seemed thoughtful as she strode along the river’s edge.

Alex reached out again, her voice panicked and desperate inside Ari’s head.

“I’m okay,” Ari told her. I’m with the Hunter and his daughter.” And she tried to send an image of the Hunter’s face, concentrating on his beard and the gruff kindness in his dark eyes.

Alex seemed to relax a little at this image, and then Ari received a beam of love and hope so strong she could almost touch it. “I love you, Ari. We have hope now. The Hunter—he will take care of you, you’ll see.”

O

ARI WAS NEVER SURE, AFTERWARD, how long she walked through the dark wastes of the underworld or what distance they traveled. Her shoulder burned and throbbed, and pain clouded everything else. Her legs moved automatically, and she closed her eyes for long stretches of time as she trudged along the river's edge in the midst of the group of shades. When she opened her eyes, the landscape looked no different. She talked silently with Alex, but it was hard to maintain the intensity and the energy needed for speaking without words, and more than once Ari had to break the connection.

At one of their infrequent rest stops, the Hunter gave Ari another sip of the golden liquid from the glass bottle. She drank eagerly, desperate for any respite from the agony in her shoulder. Mara broke a small loaf of dark bread and passed half to Ari, who tore it into chunks and swallowed it without chewing. Mara watched her sedately and ate her dry bread with apparent enthusiasm.

Ari watched her, perplexed. Then she asked a question she'd meant to ask Alex. "Why do the dead need to eat and drink?" Ari's cheeks reddened as she heard how bluntly she'd phrased her question, but neither the Hunter nor Mara seemed to mind.

"I don't know," Mara answered. "I suppose we don't really need to. I think perhaps it is because we made a habit of eating and drinking while we were alive, and so we continue to do these things, even in the underworld. It brings comfort, perhaps." She brushed the crumbs from her skirt and stood up. Then she reached down to give Ari her arm so that Ari could pull herself up too.

Ari was still puzzled. "But," she said, wincing as the movement made her shoulder throb, "but surely nothing grows down here. Where does the food come from?"

The Hunter told her that some food could be grown even in the underworld, and that the rivers contained fish. "Other foodstuffs are brought from the world above. The great lords have feasts where the tables groan with food and drink, and in Elysium there are trees that bear fruit. Much of it is illusion, but not all."

As Ari pondered this, the Hunter rallied his ragged band of prisoners and set them to walking the river's edge once more. He seemed anxious, insisting that all the shades wear their hoods pulled up to help conceal their faces. He warned Ari not to take her own hood off for any reason in case Acheron returned.

Ari soon became accustomed to seeing the world through the narrow oval of her hood, and the pain in her shoulder and neck quickly taught her that she must turn her whole body if she wanted to see in any direction other than straight ahead. Mara walked silently beside her.

Ari was a little afraid of this inscrutable underworld girl, but she needed answers to so many questions. Eventually she found the courage to ask, in a shaky voice, the question that was tormenting her. "Mara, what will happen to me at the Plain of Judgment?"

Mara replied, hesitantly, "I cannot tell. For a shade, there are only three possible judgments. But you are alive. Your path is hidden."

"If I was dead, what would happen? Would I go to the Elysian Fields?"

"If you had lived a good life, and broken no laws, then yes, almost certainly you would be sent to the Blessed Isle. All of these..." She gestured at the shuffling shades that surrounded them. "...have lived good lives. Their paths are certain. But it is not always thus. Once, not long ago, Father and I had to escort one who had committed a crime; not a large crime, perhaps, but a crime nonetheless. He was sent to the Fields of Asphodel."

Ari heard the quaver in her voice as she asked: "Is it—is it terrible there?"

"No, not terrible. Not good nor bad nor hot nor cold nor happy nor unhappy. Those who dwell there forget everything, so they need nothing. They cannot feel, so they crave nothing. Is that terrible?"

"Of course it's terrible!" Ari cried loudly, and saw the Hunter turn his shaggy head to frown at her. "Not to feel anything would be awful," she said, more quietly. Then she put her hood back so she could see Mara's face more clearly. Ignoring the girl's gasp and before she could speak, Ari whispered, "What if somebody committed a crime when they were a child? What if was an accident—a, a mistake? Would that count as a crime? Would they still have to go to the Asphodel Fields?"

Mara gently pulled Ari's hood over her face. "I am not a judge, Ari. I do not know the answer to your question. I am just a shade, like my father, and like these poor souls that have wandered. But I have been to the fields where the white flowers grow. I can tell you about it if you like. Sometimes," Mara gave her a sidelong glance, "sometimes it helps, if you are frightened of something, to know as much about that thing as possible. Would you like me to tell you?"

12.
Mara's Tale

"Once," began Mara, "long ago, I lived with my mother and my father by the edge of a great, dark forest. I loved that forest. I knew it leaf and stone, from the youngest sapling to the strongest tree to the oldest branch crumbling into loam on the forest floor. My father was a lawman. He went to town each day to speak for those whom the court had accused. His days were long, and so my mother and I did all the work around our little house. Our friends in the town used to worry that we would be lonely, living on our own so far from the town. You see, the townspeople were afraid of the forest. They had stories about wolves, and worse, that would come out at night and eat us up.

"One day, when I was chopping firewood, I heard my mother scream. It was not a wolf. It was a man and he had not come from the forest, but from the road. I must have been about ten or eleven years old. I saw my mother struggling with this man and I remember thinking, 'Oh, he's so dirty, he will muddy her dress and Mama will have to wash it.'" Mara looked at Ari. "Do you want to hear the rest?"

"Yes. I mean, if you want to tell me," whispered Ari.

"I was still holding the little axe my father had had bought for me. I came up behind them. The man had his back to me. He was holding my mother by her hair, and she was screaming. I swung my axe and chopped him. I chopped him in the back, and my axe stuck in his flesh. He fell on top of my mother, and she had to wiggle out from underneath him. He was stone cold dead. We dragged him to the bonfire and burned his corpse, just in case.

"Later, when my father came home, we showed him what was left. He spat on the smoking bones and swore he would never leave us alone again, and so we sold the house and moved into town. My mother was happier there, I think. She made friends quickly, and our new house was always full of people. She had another child, my little brother. I missed the forest. I was angry with my father for making us move into town and I used to sneak back there when I could.

"As I was walking home from one of my visits to my forest, I saw an old beggar woman on the road. She was shuffling along, shivering in the autumn chill. I took her home with me. We nursed her, my mother and I, but she died. It was a fever, but nobody knew what it was. Then I caught the fever. I don't remember much after that. I know that I was somewhere dark, and that my mother cried all the time.

"Then a lady came to me. She was pretty, like you, Ari, with coppery hair and lovely kind eyes. She told me it was time to leave the world and she brought me down to the river. We crossed in Charon's boat." Mara gave Ari a solemn little smile. "That's the usual way to cross, you know. Well, when we reached the Plain of Judgment my lady kissed me and told me not to worry. But I was worried. She looked sad, and I didn't know why. Then an old, old, man came out of the shadows and stared down at me. He placed his hand on my head and spoke to me. He told me that I couldn't go to the Blessed Isle because I had killed somebody."

"But you had to kill him! He would have hurt your mother."

"He acknowledged that. He said that he was sorry, but the law was unbreakable. I had killed in defense, not in rage or revenge or evil pleasure, and so I didn't deserve to go down to Tartarus. But I had killed nonetheless. He told the copper-haired lady to take me to the fields where the white flowers grow, and to give me the water of forgetfulness. I don't know how long I wandered there. It's hard to describe that place. Everything seems gray, or blurry white, and there is no feeling, no sensation. The asphodel grows thickly on the ground, and its white flowers are the only color. Shades drift in and out of the clumps of asphodel, but their faces are all the same. I didn't recognize my father when he came for me. I do not know what bargain he made, or how he did it, but he came and found me in the fields and he led me out. I woke up by the great river and I have been with him ever since."

Ari drew her hood back a little so she could study Mara's face. Mara was definitely a couple of years younger than Ari, and yet she seemed so much older. She had large dark eyes and warm brown skin. Her hair was thick and black and shiny and fell in waves past her hips. She must have been astonishingly beautiful when she was alive.

"How long have you been down here?"

Mara looked confused. "I, I cannot tell. A long time? No, it was only a little while ago that I wandered lost in the white lands. But surely . . ." She looked up at her father, who had stopped and was waiting for them to catch up.

"Mara has been with me since I retrieved her from the white meadows." It was not a statement that encouraged further questioning. The Hunter patted Mara on the shoulder, and she smiled up at him.

Ari watched them enviously. She missed her mother, and Nick, and her real father who she hardly knew. But she pushed these feelings down deep inside her where they couldn't rise up and choke her. There was no time to sit down and cry. She had to concentrate on survival and finding Alex. Once she found her, they would return home, and then she would go straight to her mother's hospital bed with Alex and never let either of them out of her sight again. Ari squeezed her eyes shut and swallowed hard.

She sensed Alex trying to reach her and tried to reassure her that she wasn't hurt, just lonely.

"I just miss you," she told Alex miserably. "I miss you and I miss my mother and Nick and Claire and Sam and the twins. I miss the horses and Sally and weeding the veggie patch and walking with you in the sunshine. I miss the sun. Alex, I want to see the sun! How am I going to find you? How are we going to get out of here?"

"I don't know. But we're not going to give up, okay? Promise me, Ari. Promise you won't give up? I'm being held near the Plain of Judgment, I know that now for certain. I heard the guards talking about it. And that's where the Hunter is taking you. Ask him to help you find my prison. He is a good man, Ari, and you can trust him with your life."

"How do you know?" She sensed Alex hesitate before her answer came through.

"He was my guide when I first came down here. I recognized him from the picture in your mind. I didn't know, then, that he was a hunter. He was more like a teacher to me."

"The man with the kind face? The one who took you to the Fates?"

"Yes. And I know he will help us if you ask him."

"You didn't mention Mara in your story."

"He didn't have her with him when I knew him, and that's strange, because from what you've told me it seems like they have been together for a long time."

Ari was sick of trying to work it all out. "I just want to see you," she said, feeling her longing sing along the thread that bound them.

"You will. Have faith."

"In what, exactly?"

"In us, Ari. Have faith in my love for you and yours for me. That's stronger than anything they have down here, even death. Why do you think I'm locked up? Why do you think Acheron is so desperate to capture you? There's immense power in a love that can overcome death. Stay strong and stay safe. We *will* be together soon. Trust in that, as I do. I love you."

"I love you too," said Ari aloud, and her eyes filled with tears.

The Hunter left his daughter's side to walk next to Ari. He gave her another sip of the numbing medicine and asked her to stop so he could examine her shoulder. As she stood, trying not to flinch, the Hunter unwrapped the bandages, gave a satisfied grunt, and then said conversationally, "time does not mean the same thing down here as it does in the world above, Ari. Mara has been here a long, long time. That is why she cannot remember. That, and the draught of Lethe they gave her in the Asphodel Fields." He was watching her closely. "What did you think of Mara's story?"

"I think she was brave," said Ari, "and kind," she added thoughtfully.

The Hunter passed Ari the stone water bottle. "She was both and still is. It's ironic," he said, wiping drops of water from his beard, "that it was kindness that killed her, in the end. If she hadn't brought that old woman home… But then, who knows? Maybe she would have died some other way. All I knew, when she died, was that I had to follow her. Her mother's heart was broken, but she had our son to care for. When the fever began to consume me, she wept, knowing that I wouldn't survive it. Her last words to me were a mother's plea to find our daughter, at any cost." The Hunter sighed. "And so that is what I did. I went deep into the forest, so that she wouldn't have to watch another loved one die. When the time came, I descended."

He seemed about to tell her more and then stopped, replaced Ari's cloak, and drew her hood over her face. "We are nearly there, Ari. The Plain of Judgment is close. How do you feel?"

"Terrified."

"Do not fear. The judges are not like Acheron. They are stern, ageless, and implacable, but they are just. I have never known them to make an unfair or ill-considered judgment, and I have brought many, many souls before the judges."

"But you haven't ever taken a living person, have you? Mara said she didn't know what they would decide because I'm not dead. What will happen to me?"

"I can't tell you that." He hesitated, and again Ari thought he was about to tell her something, but he changed his mind. He put his hand on her good shoulder. "There have been others who stood on the plain and awaited judgment while still living. They are rare, those ones. And never in my time have I seen any so determined as you."

"Who are the judges?"

"They were men once. Wise and great kings. You will likely see only Rhadamanthys, for he is the judge of the Elysian Fields."

Ari couldn't speak. She couldn't tell him about the fear that was eating her. Ari was certain the judges wouldn't send her to the Elysian Fields, not because she was still alive, but because she had caused a death. Mara had said the law was unbreakable. What matter if Alex's death had been an accident? The thing about accidents was that somebody always caused them. Ari knew this, knew it in her bones, her flesh, and her soul. She heard the hollow ring to the phrases no matter who spoke them: *It wasn't your fault, Ari. It was an accident, Ari. You were only a child, Ari.*

Without looking at her, the Hunter said in a hushed voice, "There isn't much time left. When I set you free from my cell by the river,

I feared that Acheron would pursue you. Swimming his river was bound to enrage him. If he appears at your judgment, do not look at him. He cannot take you once you are seated before Rhadamanthys, and he may not interfere with the judgment, but he may try more subtle ways to ensnare you."

Ari tried to read his expression, but the Hunter's face was impassive behind his gray-streaked beard. "Did Acheron mean what he said, back there? Would he really try to separate you and Mara?"

"Very likely. He bears me a grudge and he would relish the thought of causing me pain."

"Do you think," Ari stammered, "do you think he knows you're protecting me?"

"Yes. He is not a fool, Ari. You would have been unlikely to run far after leaping from that horse. And where would you hide?" The Hunter gestured at the empty landscape. "Down here, we have the river, the mountains, the Plain of Judgment, and that is all. The other places, like the Blessed Isle, are inaccessible to anyone, living or shade, unless the judges decide they may venture there."

He beckoned Mara, who was standing watching them. "Mara knows my thoughts. She agrees that you have but two choices: to stand before the judges without knowing what they might decide or to escape once again and continue your search. Remember, we do not know what your judgment might be, given that you are not supposed to be here."

"So, you think I should try to get away?"

Mara nodded.

"I do," said the Hunter. "I think you need to keep searching. You will not have to look far beyond the Plain of Judgment for what you seek." The Hunter lowered his voice and bent his shaggy head so that he could whisper in her ear. Ari felt his beard tickle her cheek. "There is a prison, well-guarded. You cannot enter by the main door, but there is another way, a hidden way into the jail. If you can rely on your courage one more time, I believe that is where you will find your Alex."

Ari stared at him. "Have you known all along that it was Alex I was looking for?"

"No. But I can sometimes hear the silent speech. Mara and I talk like that when the need arises. I recognized her voice. Alex is right. I will do what I can to help you."

Ari bit her lip. She wanted to take him at his word, but something just didn't feel right. She decided to ask the Hunter a question that had been gnawing at her heart. "But why would you want to help me? What if Acheron does talk to the gods in charge, and they take Mara from you?"

The Hunter looked at her. "The Lord Hades does not do Acheron's bidding. I do not fear Acheron's empty threats. Yet he is dangerous to you. I dragged you half-drowned from the riverbank and I let you leave the cell because I thought you might have a chance to escape him. When I found you again and discovered it was Alex Cohen you were searching for, I knew I needed to keep you close and protect you, for your sake, but also for Alex's. She has the right to claim my assistance."

"She said you helped her when she was a child down here. She called you 'the man with the kind face.'"

The Hunter gave a bitter, mirthless laugh. "With the kind face," he repeated softly. "Oh, gods, I am not fit to brush the dust from her feet." And Ari watched, aghast, as the Hunter buried his face in his hands.

Mara put her slender arm around her father's broad shoulder. "Father," she whispered, "Father?" Ari put her hand on his other shoulder.

The Hunter looked up at them and the faintest of smiles creased his face. "No man should be unhappy with two such kind girls to look after him. I am sorry, Ari. I wish there was more time to tell you everything. And Mara?" He gripped her hand. "Mara, I have much to tell you too. There is so much you still do not know. Alex Cohen was a child when they brought her to the underworld and gave her to me."

Ari gasped. "You? But why?"

"I still don't know," the Hunter said simply. "But the judges did not send her on to Elysium. They gave her to me. I was a Summoner, and she was to learn from me. I wanted to argue with them. I wanted to tell them, 'No. She is too young, choose another,' but I did not. They would not have listened anyway. But there was another reason. You see," he whispered, and Ari recoiled from the anguished plea she heard in his voice, "they promised to give me my child. They showed me an image of my Mara wandering among the white flowers and they told me I could go and bring her out, that I could keep her with me, if I trained the girl Alex to do everything I did. She was to be my successor."

Mara looked at Ari, and then at her father, standing with his proud head bent and his eyes fixed on the gray earth. "It was a hard choice, Father," she said at last.

"It was the only choice you had," said Ari. "What father wouldn't do the same?"

The Hunter looked at her, and his eyes were clouded with guilt. "I wonder if Alex would be so forgiving if she knew the bargain I made. She could have passed the last gate long since and been reborn into a new life."

The Hunter put his head in his hands once more. Mara and Ari looked silently at one another. Ari thought about Alex and the cottage by the creek where the Hunter had left her alone. If underworld time was different from time in the world above, how long had Alex lived alone down here? And what did Mara think of her father now that she'd discovered the hand he'd played for her freedom? And was it freedom? What was the "last gate," and what was all this business about being reborn? Ari wondered if Mara was considering this part, too, and making the same connections in her mind. Mara's face was as unreadable as ever, but Ari looked thoughtfully at the Hunter as he shook himself, took a deep breath, and put his shoulders back.

"Come now. These shades need to be guided to the Palace of Judgment and you, Ari, need to stay hidden among them for now. We will speak more of this when we have time."

Alex's voice came through then, asking her where she was. Ari told her, and Alex seemed cautiously hopeful about the possibility of finding the prison. Ari left out the part about her sneaking in alone.

Alex sounded exhausted. "Ari," said the voice in her mind, "I need to sleep. I haven't eaten or drunk anything, and sending messages to you like this takes a lot of energy. If you can't reach me for a while, don't worry. I just need to rest."

"They haven't fed you? Alex, you must be starving. I didn't know. Why didn't you tell me?"

"I'll be fine," came the faintest of replies. "I'll be waiting for you."

13.
The Secret Prison

The Hunter's little band of shades shuffled through the dust as though nothing had changed. But Ari kept her head down and tried to ignore the sudden throng, the sea of shades waiting to absorb her. In the awful closeness of all those hooded figures, Ari was grateful that her own hood concealed her face.

I don't look like one of them, she thought, panicking. They're going to find me.

The crowd seemed to thicken toward the mountain range, and Ari saw a high stone wall enclosing what looked like a cluster of buildings: the first large structures she had seen down here.

The Hunter whispered in her ear, "The Palace of Judgment. They all go in by the narrow door. Those who are destined for Elysium emerge on the far side and will travel by boat into the West."

Ari nodded, but her chest was tight with fear. And those who aren't destined for Elysium, she thought, where do they go?

She took a deep breath and wiped her eyes surreptitiously with her cloak. The Hunter pointed to a large rocky outcrop a short distance to her left. The rocks were unusually high and flat and they gleamed eerily in the darkness. Ari shuddered.

"The prison is there. You will need to be swift and silent. Keep your face covered. Soon I will lead our shades toward the judging place. Do not linger here. As soon as we start moving, slip away and weave your way through the throng. Make your way toward the pale rock face. The main entrance is well guarded. You must avoid it at all costs. But there is another way, as I told you. At the back of the prison, where two walls meet, there is an opening at the base of the rock. It is narrow, little more than a cleft. You must crawl inside." The Hunter paused, his face grim. "Your shoulder," he said uncertainly.

"It will be fine," Ari told him. "But could I maybe have some more of that medicine? It really helps with the pain."

The Hunter handed her the bottle. "This is special, this liquid. A small sip will quench your thirst and ease your pain. Do not lose it." He looked as though he wanted to say something else but changed his mind. "You must take some food also. For you, but also for Alex. I am certain they will not have fed her. Mara?"

Mara wordlessly handed her a small loaf of the hard brown bread, and Ari tucked it gratefully into the inside pocket of her cloak.

The Hunter's weathered face was creased with worry. "Ari, please be careful. The secret prison is a dangerous place. There are beings in there who have committed terrible crimes while alive. They await their retribution in chains, most of them. But I have heard it said that some prisoners roam the tunnels at will. It is dark, and the passageways are narrow. If your courage should fail you in there, I cannot follow you."

Mara placed her hands on Ari's forearms and squeezed them gently. "Be safe, Ari. I hope you find the one you seek."

The Hunter raised his hand in a brief farewell, and then strode away to rally his shades. Mara grabbed Ari's hand and pressed something heavy and hard into it. Ari looked down. It was a knife with a long silver blade.

"Keep it hidden," whispered the underworld girl. "You may need it where you're going."

Ari thanked her, but the knife filled her with dread. What new terrors awaited her in the underworld prison?

O

ARI CROUCHED BEHIND THE PRISON, holding her breath. It had been easy to work her way through the milling shades, and nobody had seemed to pay her any attention as she veered off from the crowd and stole to one side of the large, pale rock, which turned out to be a stone building, rough and squat and fortress-like. The front of the prison was a sheer rock wall, with a narrow, barred door set deep and flanked by row upon row of grim-looking guards. They reminded her of Acheron's henchmen, and she crept as quietly as she could toward the rear of the building.

At first Ari couldn't see anything that even vaguely looked like an opening, and she felt a pang of doubt as she scrabbled among the rocks at the base of the wall.

On her hands and knees, Ari made her way slowly and painfully along the edge of the wall, bruising her bare knees on the jagged rocks. Her shoulder ached, but the pain was bearable now, and the new pain in her knees gave her something else to think about. She stopped frequently, squatting on the sharp rocks that lay in heaps, as if they'd been blown by an invisible wind to batter against the walls of the fortress. She found nothing, no opening, no dark entranceway.

Then, as her courage was beginning to fail, she saw it: a tiny crack, no wider than a handsbreadth, where the wall turned the corner. She pushed aside the rocks that concealed it, but the cleft was still ridiculously narrow, and Ari didn't think she would be able to squeeze through. She peered into the crack, but it was so dark that it was impossible to see what lay inside.

Ari unpinned her cloak and bundled it around her bread and medicine and knife. She pushed the bundle into the opening, and then lay flat on her stomach and began to wiggle her way through backward. Like a worm, she thought unhappily, going blindly into the ground. Her head and shoulders were still outside when she heard the voices.

"It came around the back here."

"Are you sure?"

"Yes. It was a woman or a girl, I think. Light-colored cloak."

"Just find her and chain her, and let's get back to the front. You know they don't like it when we leave our posts."

"Well, where is she then?"

Ari lay like the stone that was pressing into her back. Peering out of the cleft she saw the dusty boots and the cloak hems hanging only inches from her face. She tried to hold her breath, but her shoulder hurt so badly from the wrenching it had just received that she couldn't help exhaling just a tiny puff of air.

"What was that?"

"What was what?"

"Thought I heard something."

"Too many shades all at once, that's what it is. Addles the brain. But there's nothing here."

"Oh, well. Nowhere for it to go anyway, even if it did break away."

"That's right. Chasing shades is the Hunter's job, not ours. Let's go."

Ari, breathing shallowly and unclenching her fists, watched the boots recede. She tried to get her bearings in the cramped space of the little rocky crevice. She had no idea if the cleft would widen into open space or if she would have to drag herself backward on her stomach for miles through the flattened, coffin-like space. Ari hated small, enclosed spaces. She tried not to think about what lay ahead and focused instead on trying to reach the bottle of numbing medicine tucked away in the pocket of her cloak.

Unwrapping the bundle of her cloak was a useful distraction and so, when she finally uncorked it, was the medicine. It dulled the pain and helped to calm her so that she was able to inch her way backward, using her good arm and shoulder as much as possible.

As she wiggled away from the entrance, Ari realized that even the weird twilight of the underworld was better than no light at all and that she would soon be in total darkness. The tunnel was so tight that Ari froze, seized by panic so terrible she started to breathe in little gasps. Cold sweat ran into her eyes. It will close in on me, she thought frantically. I will be crushed by this stone or buried alive. I will be stuck and not be able to breathe and I will die in this tunnel, alone, with no light.

She stopped herself from giving in to the panic by closing her eyes and trying to picture Alex waiting in a cell just a little farther down this loathsome tunnel. But then, just as she got her fear under control, Ari was plagued by a sudden doubt of the Hunter. Had he sent her to her doom? Were he and Mara laughing now, picturing her trapped and helpless in some little-used prison burrow? For some dark minutes Ari turned this nasty thought over and over in her mind, before realizing that it was only a phantasm conjured from her fear, her pain, and her exhaustion.

She tried to reach Alex but got no reply. She told herself Alex was still sleeping.

Ari gritted her teeth and kept going and was relieved to find that the tunnel was becoming gradually larger, so that she was able, at last, to sit up and turn around. She was so grateful to be moving forward instead of backward, and crawling on her hands and knees was such a relief after dragging herself along on her belly, that Ari soon forgot to look ahead. It was pitch black anyway, so she kept her head down and pushed blindly on through the widening tunnel.

When she next raised her head, Ari thought she saw a pale light filtering through the darkness.

The light grew stronger as she inched toward it. Ari thought bitterly that it was typical of the underworld that darkness should mean safety while any light represented an unknown danger. The tunnel was horrible, but at least it was familiar. Ari knew that the outside and relative freedom were on the other end of the tunnel, while in front of her the prison, with all its unknown horrors, was just a lantern's flicker away. The tunnel began to slope downward, and the light grew stronger. And then, without warning, the passage came to an abrupt end.

Ari crawled out of the tunnel and into a broad, stone-paved corridor. The light came from small lamps set in dull metal holders attached to the walls. They gave a bluish light, without warmth.

She stood up, stiffly, and took another sip of her medicine. The pain in her shoulder had come back and it was competing for her attention with the pain in her knees, which were bruised and bloodied. Ari was curious, briefly, about what her medicine was made from, but she didn't really care. Whatever it was, it was wonderful at subduing the pain. The corridor stretched endlessly away behind her but turned a sharp corner just ahead.

As she stood, irresolute, Ari heard footsteps coming toward her from around this corner. It was too late to run. Instead, she planted her feet and pulled out the little knife that Mara had given her. Its thin blade gleamed in the lamplight. Shadows danced on the grim stone walls.

Ari's stomach lurched and her skin prickled as a squat, goblin-like guard came around the corner. He stopped and stared at her.

"You're not supposed to be here. Who are you?"

"I'm looking for a prisoner. Will you help me?"

The guard sneered at her. "Now why would I do that?" He grabbed her arm and shook it. The little knife fell with a musical clatter on the flagstones, and he kicked it aside. Then he twisted her arm so that Ari cried out.

"Stop, you're hurting me!"

The guard dropped her arm and backed away a little. His ugly face was confused. "You're living? How can that be? Who sent you?"

"Please," Ari begged him. "I have money. Look!" She pulled one of the Hunter's coins from the pocket in her cloak and held it out warily. He leaned toward her hand, eyes narrowed suspiciously, and then grabbed the coin and stuffed it in his jacket. Ari breathed out, slowly. "The prisoner I'm looking for hasn't been here long. Just show me any new prisoners you have. And I want my knife back."

She bent over to retrieve it, keeping her eyes on the guard as she did so. She put her cloak on and fastened it tightly at the throat. She didn't like the way the guard watched her. She checked to make sure the bread and the medicine and the other coins were safely stowed in her pockets, but she kept her knife drawn.

The guard grunted and shuffled back around the corner, warning Ari to remain silent. Ari followed him along the dimly lit hallway; her pulse raced as she thought about Alex. Surely this was it? Surely she would see Alex soon?

"There is only one new prisoner," the guard stated flatly. "Came in a few nights ago." Ari followed him down a long flight of steps and into another narrow corridor. Her heart was in her mouth. It had to be Alex. If only they were together, everything would be easier. They would find a way to escape and return to the world above. Alex had lived in the underworld; she would know how to take them both home. But where was Alex? What had happened to that invisible connection that allowed them to speak to one another? Surely she wasn't still asleep?

The guard stopped in front of a heavy iron door. He pushed a long key into the lock and turned it. Then he stepped back and gestured for Ari to go inside. "In there," he said shortly.

A figure sat hunched in the corner. Its arms were wrapped around its head, and a thin shaft of light from the guard's lantern touched its head and shoulders.

"Alex?" she said falteringly, "Alex, it's me. Are you all right?"

The figure looked up at her, and Ari clapped both hands over her mouth to stop herself from screaming.

It was a young man with blond, straggly hair. The pale light showed her a face raked with long bloody gashes that oozed yellowish liquid where they were cut most deeply. His eyes were bruised and hollow, and he opened his mouth to speak, revealing two jagged rows of broken teeth.

"I'm not Alex," he rasped. "But I could be. I could be Alex for you. I could be anybody you like, my pretty lady."

Ari stood and stared at him, aghast. She turned to the jailer, who watched, leering at her, from the doorway.

"Are you sure there are no other prisoners?" she asked desperately, "no one who might be being held somewhere else? They might not have told you."

The guard shrugged. "He is the only one. And *I* would know. Nobody comes or leaves this place without my knowledge. Now you must pay me again to let you out of here." He held out his hand, palm outstretched.

Ari shook her head. "Not so fast." She pointed to the prisoner, who was leaning listlessly against the wall. His eyes were staring and empty. He reached up to scratch one of his wounds, and Ari closed her eyes.

"What happened to his face?"

"Oh, he does that to himself." The guard gave a short, brutal laugh. "Sometimes I think he will tear all his skin off."

"But he's a shade, isn't he?"

"They still bleed. Might not feel it as much, but they still bleed." He gave a repulsive cackle.

"Why? Why would anybody do that to themselves?"

"Ask him yourself," growled the guard.

The prisoner looked at Ari, groaned horribly, and began to crawl toward her over the rough stone floor, dragging a rusty chain attached to the manacle on his ankle until it became taut. The prisoner strained at his chain a little, then sighed and sank down onto his stomach.

"You'll not get anything out of him now," said the guard blandly. "He's gone off to sleep."

And the man on the floor did, indeed, appear to be asleep. Ari thought quickly. "If I pay you double will you promise to tell me if there are any other places you know where a prisoner might be taken?"

The guard looked at her suspiciously. "All right," he agreed at last.

Ari put her hand into the inside pocket of her cloak and took out the other two coins. She gave them to the guard, and his mouth went slack with greed. "Is it enough?" Ari asked anxiously.

The guard put the coins away hastily in one of his many pockets and nodded. "For that price, overlander, I'll take you to the forbidden cells myself. Follow me and don't make any noise."

Ari followed him back up the stone stairs to a narrow door set deeply in a niche. It had no handle or lock, but the guard seemed to know some trick of opening it. Ari didn't care how the door opened if Alex was somewhere behind it. But this was not at all certain. How could she trust the guard? What would he do when he discovered she had no more coins?

The guard pushed open the door to reveal a narrow tunnel snaking away into blackness. Ari shrank back in horror. The passage was so narrow it seemed little more than a crack in the rock.

"No," she whispered. "Not again."

The guard grinned and waved his lantern toward the opening. "Hidden prison's at the end of that tunnel. Still want me to take you?"

Ari lifted her chin defiantly and agreed, but her heart sank. Was this a trap? If it was, she had no choice but to walk into it. She followed the guard into the horrible little tunnel, watching his wan lantern light bob and sway on the end of its chain. She kept her arms close by her sides, trying not to touch the cold stone of the walls. Mercifully, the tunnel was shorter than Ari had expected and it soon widened into a corridor much like the one they'd just left. Ari tried not to think about what might happen if she became lost in this labyrinthine system of corridors and tunnels. She tried sending another message to Alex, but still there was no reply.

The guard stopped at another narrow door. He opened it, again without a key or any other means that Ari could see. He swung his ghostly lantern, and its rays lit the interior of the little cell.

Ari gave a strangled cry and lurched forward. Alex lay curled up on the stone floor.

She was asleep. Ari thanked the guard, who grunted and begrudgingly lit the candle in Alex's cell from his lantern.

Ari decided to push her luck. "Will you show us the way out?"

"More money."

"I don't have any more money," admitted Ari.

"Then find your own way out." And the guard left, taking his lantern with him.

Ari didn't care. She sank to the cold stone floor beside Alex and lay down close to her, drinking her in. She was here, and alive, and she belonged to Ari. She watched Alex's eyelids flicker as she slept.

And then, as though she sensed Ari was there, Alex slowly opened her eyes. Ari's own eyes filled with tears as she reached wordlessly for her, pulling her close until her face was pressed hard against the warmth of her throat. She only stopped kissing her hair to whisper Alex's name, over and over again.

"I'm here," Ari told her, laughing now. How could she have ever doubted that she would find her? As if reading her mind, Alex shook her head in disbelief.

"How did you do it? How did you find me here?"

"The Hunter told me about the secret entrance, and then I bribed the guard. It doesn't matter. What matters is that I've found you. Are you really okay?" Ari peered at her. Alex's face was pale and gaunt in the candlelight.

"Not bad. A little thirsty and hungry, maybe."

"Oh, God, here. I forgot. Drink this." Ari passed her the little flask of medicine. "And here's some bread. It's hard and dry, but it's food." Alex gulped some of the medicine and turned away from Ari so she could wolf the bread. Ari got up and explored the tiny stone cell, searching for any crack or crevice that might be a way out.

Alex finished eating and told Ari what she already knew. There were no windows, no secret passages. There was no visible means of escape. Ari gave up and sat down next to Alex on the cold stones of the prison floor. Alex reached for her, and Ari leaned in to kiss her. Filled with the joy of being with Alex again, Ari forgot where they were and the problem of their escape. Their lips met, and then she was drowning in that tingling feeling that flooded her, and Alex's breath was hot against her neck as she kissed her throat. Ari pulled her closer.

"We can't do this here," Alex said. Ari paused, her fingers still stroking the back of Alex's neck. Alex kissed her again and she gave a little moan, but then she pulled away and shook her head. "It's not right, Ari. Look at where we are. Do you want to make out here? In a prison cell in the underworld?"

Ari laughed and took a deep breath. "It has a certain gothic charm," she said, looking around at the horrible windowless cell. "But you're right. Let's get out of here." She sprang to her feet and gathered up her cloak, checking that her bottle of medicine and her knife were safely tucked away in their little pocket. Alex didn't move. "What's the matter? Come on!"

Alex shook her head. "I can't. They did this while I was sleeping." She pointed to her right leg. An ugly iron manacle bit deep into the flesh around her ankle, which was swollen and bruised around the restraint. She shook her leg, and Ari saw the heavy dark chain that tethered Alex to the wall of her cell.

"It's not fair," she whispered, as rage and despair fought within her. "After everything, after searching and running and crawling on my guts through stone, I find you chained to a bloody wall. And now we can't escape!" Ari burst into angry tears.

"Ari, don't."

"No. It's not fair, and I've had enough of this, this *disgusting* place! I want to go home. I want to see the sky. I want to feel wind in my hair and rain on my skin. And you have to come with me." She looked down at Alex, whose eyes widened in alarm.

"Actually," said a dry voice behind her, "Both of you have to come with me."

14. The Trial

The Palace of Judgment was cold and cavernous, and all its halls were empty. As their silent guard led them through the echoing spaces, their footsteps sounded like thunderclaps amid the tempest of their ragged breathing.

"There aren't any shades in here," Ari said, glancing fearfully around. "Where are they all? I saw so many go in, hundreds and hundreds of them. Where did they all go?

"I don't know," whispered Alex. She was limping, and Ari saw her flinch every time her injured foot hit the ground.

The new guard had unlocked the manacle around Alex's ankle, but then Alex and Ari had to work the sharp-edged metal free from the bruised and swollen flesh. Alex had borne it stoically, with the help of the Hunter's medicine, but now her ankle and foot were black and puffy, and she couldn't walk properly. She had refused to lean on Ari when the guard escorted them from the prison and across the Plain of Judgment, but as they entered the palace Ari grabbed Alex's hand and pulled her arm around her neck to support as much of her weight as she could. Ari's shoulder burned under the sudden pressure, and she had to face the reality, miserably, that neither of them would be able to run should escape become possible.

Some deep, ingrained stubbornness insisted this wasn't the end, that they could still escape, that there had to be a way. But Ari saw they had little chance of escaping this enormous, heavily fortified palace. The guard who came to collect them was no gap-toothed ugly who could be bribed, even if they had more coins. He carried no weapons, but the authority in his voice, the heavy gold chains he wore over his robes, and the miasma of power that surrounded him were visible warnings to both of them that he must be obeyed.

Alex squeezed her hand. "It's the trial, Ari. I hoped for a while that I might be able to escape before they came to collect me, but I think that was just a dream, something to cling to in the dark. I never thought you'd be here with me. I'm sorry."

"What will happen? What will they do to us?"

"I don't know. But we're going to be brave. Both of us." She kissed her cheek. "They will judge me. Judgment, down here, usually means being sent to the Asphodel Fields or…" Her voice cracked a little. "…or down to Tartarus. If that happens, Ari, there's nothing we can do about it. But let's not give up all hope. I don't know what they will do with either of us. We're both alive, and that complicates things."

The guard stopped before a huge set of iron doors worked in bas-relief with pictures of men and horses and intricately detailed landscapes. Ari felt numb. She was so terrified that the enormity of what lay ahead refused to seem real. She was about to stand before the ancient beings who passed judgment on the dead. They would judge Alex and judge her too.

Beside her, Alex was grim and silent, but her hand trembled in Ari's. Ari turned so that she could look into Alex's eyes. Alex removed her arm from Ari's shoulders and stroked her cheek. Her eyes filled with tears. "Ari, my love. I'm so sorry. It's my fault you're here."

Ari shook her head and wiped the tears from her own cheeks. She kissed Alex and pressed her face into her neck, ignoring the sudden movement of the guard behind them. "It's *not* your fault. And no matter what happens next, I want you to know that I love you and I wouldn't change anything. I would do it all over again:

swim every river in the underworld, crawl through a million dark tunnels, whatever it took, just to be with you."

Alex kissed her as the doors swung open and she lifted her chin as the court turned to stare at them. Ari copied her, feigning as much courage as she could. They walked together along an aisle flanked by ghostly, dark-hooded figures holding swords.

Alex squeezed her hand. "Whatever happens next," she whispered, "wherever they send me, my soul belongs with you, to you, forever."

They marched Ari into a cage-like box, high up and to the left of the judges' bench, and they put Alex in a similar structure on the right. Each box was a cross between a prisoner's dock and a pulpit, and Ari had to climb a steep flight of stairs, with a sword at her back, to enter hers. Behind the judges' bench, which seemed to stretch forever, were three empty iron thrones. The room was so vast that Ari doubted if Alex would hear her if she shouted.

Ari could see Alex's face, but she was too far away for Ari to read her expression. She tried sending her a thought message, but it was the psychic equivalent of trying to talk with a mouthful of cotton wool. She closed her eyes and tried again. For a moment she thought she detected a faint whisper along their line of connection, but it was too faint. Either Alex was too worn out to receive messages or something about the courtroom was blocking their signals.

There was a rough bench made of the first wood Ari had seen down here, and she sank onto it, exhausted. The judges still hadn't arrived, and Ari peered through the bars of her cage at the throng of hooded figures below. She saw row upon row of grim faces, mostly men. To her right was a long bank of seats, tiered slightly so that its cloaked and hooded occupants had an unobstructed view of the prisoners, the judges, and the audience. This must be a jury, thought Ari, and a whole series of TV courtroom dramas flashed through her mind. Would there also be a prosecutor and a defense lawyer? Who would speak on their behalf? Not the Hunter; he had too much to lose. Did Alex have any other friends down here?

Somewhere below, a deep voice commanded the court to rise, and Ari scrambled to her feet, holding her breath. The judges entered in silence with their heads bowed and their hands hidden in the sleeves of their robes. As each judge sat, he put back his hood. The judge in the middle seemed the oldest as well as the tallest. His cheeks drooped on either side of his dour mouth, as if dripping into his beard. The judge on the right, closest to Ari, was gray-haired and stern, with a long beard. The judge on Alex's side was short and bald, but she couldn't see his face. All three shared that underworld pallor, yet they seemed more substantial than the shades, different somehow. The judge in the middle raised a bony hand, and the court sat. There was no commotion of scraping chairs, or rustling clothes, or whispering, the way there would be in a living courtroom. This congregation of shades was silent and expressionless.

In the front row, one figure was still standing, and he seemed to be one of the court officials, with a slightly different, more ornamental, robe. His face, like those of the shades around him, was deathly pale, and his eyes were heavily shadowed.

He turned slightly so that he could address the audience and the jury. "I speak for the court. This is the trial and judgment of Alexandra Louise Cohen, Summoner. She stands accused of the following crimes: Firstly, as a Summoner, Alexandra Cohen failed to bring a soul to the underworld at its appointed time. Secondly, she has, by her actions, disrupted the balance of life and death, and finally, she has defied the gods and the Fates, whose words are law. For these crimes she will be judged."

"And is this not also the trial and judgment of Arielle Wyndham?" called a horribly familiar voice. Heads turned, and the armed guards that flanked the aisle bowed their heads as a tall blond figure strode toward the judges.

"Lord Acheron." The court official nodded in curt acknowledgement. "Her case will also be heard. But in the proper time, my Lord, in the proper time."

"She is alive," growled Acheron. "She swam my river and then she drank of *my* river and yet she lives! It is an outrage. I demand a trial now. In this court, before these judges."

Ari gripped the iron bars of her cage and held on tight. She looked from Acheron, resplendent in robes of scarlet and gold, to the court official, who was conferring with the judges, to Alex, slumped and silent in her cage.

The judges spoke to one another in hushed voices, and then the middle judge said something to the court official, who nodded and turned to address the court. "The younger girl shall be judged also."

Alex stood, bowed low to the judges, and stared down at Acheron. Even from so far away Ari could see how terrified Alex was as she gripped the bars of her cage. Ari's own fear was strangely muted. She remembered a documentary she'd seen in science class, about people who had suffered extreme pain or fear. One of them, a plane crash survivor, had talked about the body's natural morphine, which kicked in, apparently, when a situation was so extreme that all the body's normal coping mechanisms shut down. Whatever it was that made her numb now, Ari was deeply grateful for it.

"My Lords, the Lord Acheron is too harsh." Alex's voice rang out clearly in the hushed courtroom. "Do not judge this girl, I beg you. She is blameless. I am the one who broke the rules. Let her go and guide her back to the world of the living. She has committed no crime."

Ari cried out as a guard, moving quickly at a gesture from the court official, strode up the stairs into Alex's cage and struck her ceremoniously but viciously across the face.

The middle judge spoke then, and his voice was as hollow and bleak as the eyes of the shades in front of him. "You are already on trial for your hubris, Alex Cohen. Do not add insolence to the list of your offences."

When Ari saw Alex dab at her bleeding mouth with the sleeve of her jacket, she also saw for the first time that she was still wearing the same clothes she had worn the night Ari left her in Claire and Sam's garden shed. How long ago had that been? As the court official began to drone on about the responsibilities of Summoners and the importance of their role, Ari looked down at her body. The court was better lit than the underworld itself, and so Ari could take in the details: her own filthy fingernails, matted hair, and strange outfit. The underworld dress was like a medieval smock, laced at the breast and free-flowing to her ankles. Her robe and hood were the color of old bones. I look like I belong here, she thought. Except that I'm not dead. What am I doing here? What is Alex doing here? This is ridiculous.

Ari stood, heedless of the guard who dug the point of his sword into her back. The court official stopped mid-sentence and raised his pale face to stare up at her.

The judges' heads turned slightly, and the gray-haired judge raised his hand as the court official opened his mouth to speak. "Be quiet, all of you. I will hear the girl. She is interesting. She has done what no other, living or shade, has ever done. I would like to hear how she swam the mighty river Acheron."

He gave Acheron himself a brief, ironic nod. Acheron lunged forward, all fury and indignation, but the gray-haired judge ignored him.

"The girl has a right to be heard. She has not broken any laws. If she has angered Lord Acheron by swimming his river, then let the lord make a submission of complaint to the court and let him wait until she is a shade and her fate is in our hands."

The court official held up a long pale hand to stop Acheron as he began to shout. The gray-haired judge gave Acheron a hard stare, and then turned his head to address the other judges. "I say the girl Arielle should be allowed to speak, and I also say that she should *not* be tried before this court. It is not the proper time."

The middle judge frowned and drummed his skeletal fingers on the bench for a long time. Finally he nodded. "Let it be thus. She shall not be tried at this time. But she shall be brief in her testimony. Are we in agreement?"

The gray-haired judge nodded and looked up at Ari. He reminded her of the Hunter. The judge closest to Alex said nothing, but his bald head tipped forward slightly.

Ari took a shaky breath. "Thank you, my lords." She smiled gratefully at the gray-haired judge, who was watching her closely. "Please don't judge Alex for saving my life. I refused to go with her when she came to collect my soul. I, I begged her for help, my lords. When she recognized me and wanted to save me, she was being merciful. Shouldn't all Summoners be able to show mercy? It would be horrible for the souls they come to collect if all Summoners were cold and heartless. Surely, my lords, you can show mercy to Alex? After all, she saved me out of kindness, not from any desire to do the wrong thing."

The gray-haired judge looked at her. He seemed to be considering something. "You have spoken for Alex Cohen, and your plea is noted. But you have not spoken on your own behalf. You have told us nothing about how you came to be here. How is it that you are still alive in this place? And how did you swim the river?"

Ari told him, briefly, about Acheron and the dogs and the sinkhole. She tried to remember what happened when she fell into the dark water and the little air-filled cave that had saved her from drowning. "When I got to the river, my lords, I only jumped into the water to get away from the shades on the riverbank. They frightened me. Then I just… I don't know. I swam across it bit by bit. I knew I had to get to the other side."

"And what happened when you reached the other shore? Ask her that!" The middle judge frowned at Acheron but did nothing to stop him as he shoved the court official to one side and glared up at Ari. The courtroom was silent, and Ari was sure that they could all hear her heart pounding guiltily inside her living body.

Acheron sneered at the judges and flung a string of questions at her: "Come now, girl. Did you find the secret prison all by yourself? How did you come by food to sustain your living flesh? Who helped you to vanish when you jumped from my horse? Don't bother trying to lie to me. I *know* who helped you. I know who should be punished. It seems, however, that my word, the word of Lord Acheron himself, is not valued here. And it also seems that a brazen mortal girl, a creature of no importance, may say what she likes and be heard." He turned to the jury, pointed at Ari, and stabbed the air with his long, white forefinger. "She was my prisoner, but she escaped."

He took a few steps toward Ari and looked up at her. She found that she could not look away. His eyes were two pits of pale fire. He spread his arms and raised his hands theatrically. "Now, how *did* you escape, I wonder?"

"Leave her alone, Acheron, you brute." Ari closed her eyes. The Hunter was here.

The Hunter's deep voice echoed across the courtroom. Ari looked down to see him, standing broad-shouldered and proud near the far wall, with Mara at his side. He looked up at Alex, and then he raised his hand in the briefest of waves and smiled at Ari. Warmth and hope flooded Ari, and she stood a little straighter. They had a friend here after all, she and Alex. The Hunter's smile was like a life jacket that would hold her up, keep her from drowning in the terror of this place. But he shouldn't be here, she told herself. They will take Mara away from him and punish him for hiding me and helping me. She gripped the bars of her cage until they became slick with sweat.

The judges sat silent and impassive on their iron thrones, but the court stirred uneasily, and Acheron's face was livid with rage. Ari thought she would burn to dust if he glared at her like that.

His voice was strangled with violence as he spat his venom across the court. "How dare you?"

But the Hunter stood like a rock and let Acheron's furious words beat and crash against him. The court official gestured to the guards, who surrounded Acheron with drawn swords.

From his cage of blades Acheron continued his tirade. "It's always *you*, isn't it, Hunter? They would have given her to me. She was promised to me, but you, with your treachery and your guile, you stole her from me!" Guards restrained him as he fought to break free of the wall of swords.

Alex was on her feet now, shaking the bars of her cage, heedless of the guards. Anger roughened her voice as she screamed: "Ari was never meant for you! She wasn't meant to be here at all. You trapped her. You pushed her into a sinkhole! But you didn't count on her being alive, did you? That put a hole in your plans. Gods, let me *out* of here!" Alex pounded on the bars. The court was restless; muted voices swelled and mingled with the rustling of robes.

The Hunter held up his hand. "Be still, Alex," he shouted. "He isn't talking about Ari."

The court fell silent at the sound of Mara's clear, lilting voice. "He means me. He's talking about me." She stood proudly, with her pointed chin raised high, but Ari could see the naked terror hidden behind her defiant gaze. The Hunter clutched her protectively, one arm around her slim shoulders and the other gripping her hand.

Ari closed her eyes and wished desperately that the courtroom and the judges and the menacing guards and Acheron would simply disappear. She wanted nothing more than to be somewhere safe, to feel Alex's arms around her and not be afraid. Ari wanted no part in the intrigues and private dramas that played themselves out in the underworld. But, like it or not, she was caught up in them now. By accepting the Hunter's help and Mara's companionship, she had tied herself to them with stronger bonds than any the guards could use on her. Now she saw clearly and for the first time that Mara wasn't merely pretty, but extraordinarily beautiful. And there was some indefinable quality about her beauty, something tantalizing and addictive. Of course Acheron had wanted her. Mara's courage and spirit, plus this kind of beauty, were qualities Acheron would be eager to own and control. But why hadn't Mara told Ari about it? Why hadn't the Hunter mentioned that part when he told her about rescuing Mara from the Asphodel Fields?

The court was alive with whispers and the judges were conferring at the bench. The guards surrounding Acheron stepped back and lowered their swords, but they kept him within their circle.

"Explain yourself, Hunter," the middle judge intoned.

Holding Mara tightly by the hand, the Hunter walked up to the bench. He stopped in front of the middle judge and bowed to him. "My Lord Minos." He bowed to the gray-haired judge. "My Lord Rhadamanthys." Then he turned to the bald judge and bowed again. "My Lord Aeacus." The judges nodded solemnly in return.

They respect him, thought Ari. And they don't like Acheron, or they're afraid of him. Who is the Hunter? The Hunter turned to face the court, and Mara stood proudly beside him. She tilted her head back to smile at Ari, and Ari, marveling at her composure and her courage, managed a small smile in return.

The Hunter cleared his throat. "My Lords and people of the court of Hades. The Lord Acheron wanted my Mara for his wife. The Unseen One himself told me this. He offered me a choice, a bargain." The Hunter looked uneasily at Alex before continuing; his voice was rough-edged with guilt. "He said . . . he said I could have my child with me and that she would be safe from Acheron, but that I would have to agree to train a young shade, the youngest ever, to be a Summoner in my place." The Hunter swallowed. "He told me he wanted a Summoner who would never go against the decrees of the Fates, who would accept the laws of life and death without question. He said that the older Summoners, like me, were becoming tired and quarrelsome, and that the time was nigh for many of them to pass the last gate. He said the next Summoner to be trained would be a very young shade, a child's shade."

The Hunter twisted his hands together. "I didn't want to do it." He looked up at Alex and then turned to the jury. "I didn't want to train a child to summon the souls of the dead, especially since I knew from experience the horror, the pain, and the misery that child would have to witness. I also know the loneliness of a Summoner's existence. Old people and old shades value solitude, my Lords. They crave it. But the young need constant company. Alex Cohen should have been sent to Elysium to join the shades of her forebears." He paused and ran his hand distractedly through his hair. "I almost said no. I almost turned away." The Hunter hung his head, then he mumbled, without looking up again. "But Mara is my *child*. My daughter. How could I let her be taken by a loathsome beast like Acheron?"

Acheron flailed in his prison of swords. "How dare you? My Lords, how can you let him speak in that way about me? Am I not a lord of the five rivers and second only to the Unseen One in power and privilege? And why should this, this common *hunter*, have been given a choice in the matter of his daughter's marriage? She was a shade, and in the Fields of Asphodel. She was mine to claim!"

The Hunter stood close to the jury and included them in his reply. Suddenly, it looked as though the Hunter was cross-examining Acheron, who was being held securely in the ring of raised swords. And the jury was listening, and the judges were listening.

Ari held her breath. Maybe the Hunter could get them all out of this. He had saved her twice already.

The Hunter's voice was calm and scornful, but Ari thought she understood the effort it took for him to stay calm as he answered: "By what right did you claim her, Acheron? She was judged and sent to roam the white flowers. Are all maidens who dwell in the Asphodel Fields your rightful prey? She belongs to no man and certainly not to an animal like you."

Ari flinched. Surely Acheron would fight his way free of the guards and attack the Hunter.

But Acheron only laughed scornfully at him. "So you say. But you are of no importance. A Summoner who couldn't perform his duties anymore. A failed Summoner who became a hunter of shades. Did it sting when they gave your job to a child? Does it smart still, that terrible wound to your pride? Tell the truth to this court, Hunter. Tell them that you hated Alex Cohen. You would have hated whomever they sent to replace you, because it would mean that eventually you would no longer see the sun. Hunters of shades do not climb the endless stair, do they, Hunter? Only Summoners do that. Only Summoners see the world above in all its filth and glory. It's worth the trouble of a recalcitrant soul clinging to the hem of your robe, isn't it? That glimpse of the world you lost? You didn't want to face an eternity of chasing shades in the dark. When they brought out your girl, you put the child Alex in a hovel and left her there. I used to ride by sometimes for amusement. The child was alone for a long, long time."

Ari closed her eyes. She couldn't look at the Hunter's face or at Alex, who had slumped in her cage again, her head resting listlessly against the bars.

"Enough!" The gray-haired judge, the one called Rhadamanthys, stood and raised his left hand in stern command. "This is not the place or the time to debate the deeds of the Hunter or your deeds, Lord Acheron. Wrong has been done on both sides. And the judgment for each will be dealt in the proper time and the proper place. But this is the trial of Alex Cohen. We are here to decide what the punishment should be for breaking the laws of life and death. When we have done that, the girl Ari will be sent back to the world above, there to live out the span of her life as the Fates decree. Our business is not with the living, but with the dead."

The court was silent as Rhadamanthys sat. He conferred quietly with Minos and Aeacus and then bent to listen when the court official, gesturing excitedly, whispered something in his ear. Ari saw

Rhadamanthys look up at Alex, and then the whole court became completely still.

A cold wind washed over the room, a strange sensation in the underworld's numbing, atmospheric nothingness. The hundreds of hooded figures fell forward onto their knees, like a dark wave. Even the judges bowed their heads. Acheron alone stood, his ring of swords now flat on the floor with the guards who wielded them.

Ari looked fearfully toward the back of the courtroom. Three figures stood silhouetted against the dim light that shone through the open doors. They advanced, slowly, and Ari knew without question who they were. The first was a slender young woman with curly brown hair that fell past her knees. She held a little wooden cone wrapped in a greenish thread that she turned over and over in her hands. The second was older and full-figured. Her greying hair was twisted up on top of her head. She carried a large basket on her rounded hip. The third woman was white-haired and bent with age and leaned on a wooden staff. All three were electric with veiled power. They made their way to the judge's bench, and the judges stood and led them solicitously to their own thrones. Minos, bowing low, helped the old woman into his seat, and Rhadamanthys gave his throne to the young woman, who sat winding her spool of thread and twisting it between her fingers. The middle-aged woman took Aeacus' seat.

The judges stood behind the thrones, and the shades of the court slowly stood and then crept back to their seats, all in silence. Ari tried to catch Alex's eye, but she was staring fixedly at the three Fates.

The court official shuffled about, uncertain, in front of the bench, and it was the dour middle judge, Minos, who finally broke the silence. "We honor the Fates. Their word is law. Lady Atropos, Lady Lachesis, Lady Clotho, we salute thee." The whole court repeated his words, even Acheron, although Ari observed that he did so with a scornful expression. The old woman, Atropos, held up a long, bony hand. Her voice shook with unmeasurable age.

How horrible, Ari thought, to be eternally old and to know that death would never come. Was there any humanity in Atropos? Did she feel the weight of the old age she had borne since the beginning of time? And did she ever question her own role as the one who cut the thread, who snuffed out each tiny human life again and again? How could such a being show any mercy at all?

The old woman cleared her throat, and the court waited in deathly silence to hear her speak. "We have come to settle this matter. It is our judgment that Arielle Wyndham be escorted from this place and returned to her rightful place in the world of the living. She was supposed to die, it is true, but she was returned to life and to life she must return. A new thread has been spun for her, and she must live if she is to honor it."

Ari looked at Alex. She still stared as if hypnotized at the Fates, and terror flushed through her as she heard the old woman say, "Alex Cohen has broken the laws of life and death. She failed to conduct a soul at the proper time and, unlike this younger girl, she has been told the penalty for breaking our laws. She knew that there would be a price to pay for her actions. But I am told that she also has been returned to life. Her heart beats and so she cannot exist either in Elysium or in the dark country. What, then, shall we do with such a one?"

The old woman looked out across the rows of shades. "There is also the matter of Lord Acheron's complaint against the girl and the Hunter's supposed transgressions. I say these matters, which are small in comparison, shall be dealt with at another time. Until that time..." She gave Acheron a direct stare. "...let no one disturb this judgment again."

Acheron made a loud noise, but Atropos ignored him. She stood up, and the other women stood too. They looked just like the etching in her book of myths, and Ari sensed the terrible power that bound them and would always bind them.

Atropos raised her voice, and there was no cronish quiver in it now. "*This* trial was to decide the appropriate punishment for Alex Cohen, and it has been interrupted and diverted from its course. Alex Cohen was a Summoner. A Summoner knows the laws. To break these laws, even for a loved one, is to upset the balance between life and death. Dark things trouble the places where such a breach has occurred, and now the girl Arielle must return to a place that has been marred by such a rupture. And it is getting worse up there. Arielle will see, when she returns, that the darkness has crept farther over the place where she lives. What she will do about the dark forces she and Alex Cohen have set free, I do not know. But they must be contained, or that place and all the living who dwell there will be mired in darkness and despair. Indeed, if that darkness is not contained it will spread farther, eating away like a disease at the world above."

Atropos stopped and whispered something to Lachesis. When she straightened up, Ari froze. This was it, this was the verdict. She closed her eyes.

Atropos' voice was clear and cold. "Hear our Judgment. Alex Cohen will also return to Stonehaven to heal the rift. She must, with Arielle, destroy the forces of darkness unleashed by her irresponsible decisions." She paused and consulted with Clotho and Lachesis. She nodded briefly and continued: "And she must achieve this without the aid of any Summoner's special abilities. Alex Cohen has forfeited the right to use those powers and they are henceforth removed." Atropos raised her hand and mumbled something under her breath. Ari saw Alex shake her head, as though she had water in her ears.

Atropos continued. "Alex has a heartbeat, and so she belongs more to the world of the living than to this world. She must rid Stonehaven of the threat from the wild dogs and she must find a way to mend the rift. If she achieves this, a new thread will be spun for her and she will continue to live. If, however, she does not succeed, then her heart will stop beating and she will be taken to the Asphodel Fields to await rebirth like any other mortal soul. Listen now, as I pronounce the final part of the judgment. It is customary for disobedient servants of the realm of Hades to be dealt severe and eternal punishments. But we have considered the age and inexperience of Alex Cohen, and the fact that she was, perhaps unwisely, made a Summoner while so young. Here, then, is our judgment, which is as lenient a judgment as has ever been given in this court. She will have one half-month. The moon is waxing to full in the world above. If Alex cannot heal the breach before the moon becomes dark, then she will die for a second time and for all time. This is our judgment."

A murmur rippled through the court. The judges stood with bowed heads behind the Fates. Acheron turned on his heel and tried to snatch his sword from the hand of the nearest guard.

"Let him go," ordered Atropos curtly.

The guard released Acheron's sword, the other guards lowered theirs, and Acheron strode haughtily from the chamber. Ari looked down at the Hunter. He and Mara were still standing near the judges' bench, but they were not looking at her. They were watching Alex. Two guards gripped her wrists, and another held her up. She staggered and almost fell as they led her down the steps to the courtroom floor.

Atropos stepped unhurriedly from behind the judges' bench, flanked by Clotho and Lachesis. The three women stood close to Alex, and Atropos gestured toward Ari. Guards were already tugging at her, pushing her down the narrow staircase.

When her feet hit the floor, Ari started running. Nobody stopped her. She ran to Alex, who opened her arms to enfold her. Ari clung to Alex, her face buried in the softness of her neck.

When she opened her eyes, the Moirai were watching her. A chill crept up Ari's back. Atropos stared at Alex, then turned her gaze upon Ari. Ari saw that her eyes were different colors: one greenish brown, the other pale blue, the color of blindness.

The crone lowered her voice. "Three things I will tell you. They may help both of you if you remember them. The first is a warning. Do not underestimate Acheron. He does not like to be crossed, and you have greatly angered him. What he will do when you are returned to the living and he is brooding in his keep, I cannot tell. Be wary. He can enter the world above when he chooses, at least until the rift is closed. If his fury should lead him back to you, Arielle, there will be little we can do to prevent him, unless we are called to intervene in another trial." Atropos lowered her voice. "And he would not let you anywhere near the Palace of Judgment, my girl, not once he had you in his palace and bound to him."

The old woman seemed to want to say something else, but the youngest fate, Clotho, placed a slender hand on her shoulder and whispered, "Not yet, sister. Tell them the second thing instead."

Atropos nodded. "The second is a reminder: There is power in all the old tales, which are always more than merely stories. You would do well to pay heed to the elements that recur, in such tales. They may be weapons for you when other weapons fail. And the last is simply some advice for you, Ari. Only you can defeat that which you fear the most. In the end, that task will be yours alone."

Atropos sighed, and Ari thought her old eyes were sad as she looked away. She turned to look up at Alex. "These words are all I have. I cannot help you further. The law forbids it. You have made this new path together, and together you must follow it. But we wish you well, Alex Cohen, Arielle Wyndham; my sisters and I wish you well."

Ari was only half aware of what happened next. It seemed that the courtroom slipped away like a wave, and she suddenly remembered the Hunter and Mara. She looked up at Alex, who had her eyes closed. They seemed to be standing still, while the rest of the world rolled and spun and swirled.

"I didn't say goodbye," she said, stricken. "What will happen to the Hunter? Will they take Mara away from him?"

"I don't know. But there's nothing we can do for them now. Hold on to me, Ari."

"I didn't even say goodbye!" Ari pulled away from Alex's chest and tried to focus on the courtroom and its shadowy figures, who were blurred and shifting, like reflections on the surface of a windswept pool. It was impossible to focus on individual faces, but Ari thought she could just make out two figures: one tall, the other smaller and delicately built. They seemed to be smiling at her. "Hunter!" she called desperately. "Hunter! I'm sorry. Thank you."

The world tipped and swam. Alex clutched her and together they were lifted off their feet by some enormous invisible force.

Alex pressed her lips to Ari's forehead. "Hold on to me," she said again, fiercely. Something very like a sob escaped her. "I think they're sending us home."

15. Seal Cove

Ari woke to the rush and whisper of little waves. She was lying facedown in very shallow, icy cold water, and the waves seemed to be tugging at her ankles. It was dark.

She sat up, panicking, and reached around in the darkness, but Alex was lying close by. She lay on her back, and her eyes were open. She was smiling. Ari watched, confused, as a tear trickled over the ridge of Alex's cheekbone. A wave crept under her and lifted the dark strands of her hair. She laughed, reached for Ari, and pulled her down beside her into the water.

"Look! Oh, gods, Ari, look up."

She lay in the water beside Alex and stared at the blackness above them. It was awash with stars. They lay still, pinned to the beach by the immensity of the Milky Way. A meteor raced across the sky, and blue-tinged clouds drifted across the bright full moon. A bird called somewhere in the night, and the night was so clear and so still that its song filled the whole world. It sounded as if the water was singing. The little waves hissed on the sand and sighed away again, and Ari had never been so happy to be cold and wet and uncomfortable.

Soon, though, she had to persuade Alex that the water was freezing, and they stood up shakily, hugging each other for warmth and laughing at how cold they were, and how strange, how ridiculous and wonderful it was to be cold and wet and shivery under the night sky.

Ari looked around her. "It's Seal Cove," she murmured.

Alex clutched her arm and pointed to the reef. "And there are the seals, look, just there by the rocks."

Ari stared at the shiny black heads bobbing in the sea. "I don't believe it," she whispered. They watched, breathing in the cold air and the stars and the sea spray while the seals played in the moonlit water.

Alex's shivering turned to shaking, and Ari tried to hug her, but a hug wasn't much use given the cold and their wet clothes. "Come on, we'll be warmer in the cave."

She had to support Alex all the way along the beach. Alex fell once, stifling a groan as her foot gave way beneath her. Ari was so weak herself with hunger and thirst and exhaustion that she thought she would never get her back on her feet. But they managed it eventually, though Alex had to crawl the last few yards to the cave. Ari tried to think, though her chattering teeth made this difficult. What should they do?

The best thing would be to get Alex back to Wyndham and hope nobody was there, so that they could figure out what to do next without also having to tackle Nick or worry about her mother. But Ari needed to rest as much as Alex did.

She made Alex lie down and then lay behind her, pressed up as close as she could get for warmth. Moonlight washed over them, cold and bright. She tried not to worry about what she would say to Nick, if he happened to be at Wyndham, or what she would tell her mother or Claire. How long had she been in the underworld? Ari tried to count the days since she had gone looking for Alex in the forest, but it was too difficult. Had she spent hours or days descending that endless staircase? How long had it been, that journey with the Hunter and his shades to the Plain of Judgment? She had rested often and had shared a meal with Mara many, many times. The long marches on foot between these rests had seemed interminable. She remembered wrapping herself in her cloak and sleeping many times on a pile of spare clothes next to Mara. But were these naps, or were they sleeps that had lasted the length of a whole night? If so, there had been many, many nights. Then there was the horrible tunnel and the prison and the time they spent at the trial. How long had that all been?

Ari gave up. Without the sun, there was no way to measure time in the underworld, but it had felt like weeks and weeks. She had probably turned seventeen in the land of the dead. Missing her birthday would have upset Cass, and Ari hoped desperately that her absence hadn't caused her mother too much grief or jeopardized the safety of her baby sister.

Ari tried to stop worrying. She concentrated on nuzzling into the soft, salty warmth of Alex's neck. Laughing, Alex rolled over and cradled Ari's face in her hands. She stared at her for a long time in the soft moonlight. Ari wanted Alex to kiss her, but she knew Alex was trying to find words to tell her something. Ari waited, drinking Alex in, unwilling to look away. She was half afraid Alex might vanish suddenly, or that she might open her eyes to find herself in some dark underworld place, alone.

Alex stroked Ari's cheek and touched her lips with a salty fingertip. Her eyes were bright with tears. "You saved me," Alex whispered. "You found a way into the underworld, and you swam the great river, and you found me in the secret prison. There's never been anybody in the world like you, Ari. And you are here with me. What did I do to deserve that?" Alex brushed Ari's lips with hers in the softest of all kisses. Ari tasted more salt on her lips.

Ari struggled to find the right words. How could she tell Alex what she really meant to her? She thought, and then, feeling the inadequacy of her words, she told her that when she had died, it didn't feel as though she'd lost a best friend or even a sister.

"It was like somebody had cut me in half and told me to live like that. Sliced down the middle, you know? Maybe twins feel that way when one twin dies. I don't know. But when you came back, I knew that I wanted to hold you so tightly that you would become a part of me again. And it's different now. A very different kind of closeness." Ari smiled and closed her eyes as Alex kissed her, not quite as softly as before. "Besides," she said, breathlessly, "if I saved you from anything, and I'm not sure that I did, we could call it square. I'd be dead from snakebite and probably fetching Acheron's slippers if you hadn't brought me back to life."

Alex frowned. "Don't joke about it, Ari. I've never wanted to kill anybody before. But I would have killed him with my hands, my teeth, whatever I had, if he tried to take you. You are mine, Ari. Forever and forever." She paused, laughing a little at her own vehemence. Then she lowered her eyes. "I mean, I'm yours forever. If you'll have me."

Ari pulled her closer. "Forever won't be long enough."

Neither of them said anything about portals, or wild dogs, or the moon.

Even holding each other tightly, they were freezing. Ari began to worry all over again about Alex and her injured foot. If she no longer had any of her Summoner's abilities, did that mean she could get really sick? The farm girl in Ari knew what happened when wounds like Alex's were left untreated. "We need to get you somewhere warm and find some food and water."

"I'm fine," Alex said stoically. "Let's go."

Ari shook her head. "We can't walk the beach track in the dark, Alex. At least, you can't."

She tried to peer through the darkness at Alex's foot. She was very weak, and Ari could feel, even if she couldn't see, that her ankle was swollen and hot. Alex protested, but Ari knew she didn't have the strength to walk all the way to Wyndham. Better to let her rest and to wait for dawn, however far off that might be.

Ari suddenly remembered her little bottle of medicine. At first she thought it must be gone, snatched from the pocket of her cloak during whatever tempest had carried them home. But it was wedged deep in the pocket, and she pulled it out and offered it to Alex.

She drank a few drops herself and felt a little warmer, though no less hungry. Her knife was still in her pocket, too, and she was comforted by its solid weight, as if she'd brought a piece of the Hunter's and Mara's kindness back with her. Ari considered the almost empty medicine bottle. It was a beautiful thing: dark, knobby green glass with a sharply tapered end. It would never stand upright. In the underworld, its contents had seemed magically inexhaustible, and Ari realized she'd never questioned this. Now, though, only half an inch of the precious fluid remained, and something told Ari to save it.

Alex watched as she put the bottle away and peeled off her dripping cloak. Ari saw her shivering, and her own body was tense with cold. Wordlessly, she began to unlace the bodice of her gown; her fingers were stiff and clumsy.

"Help me," she said, teeth chattering.

Together they stripped off the wet dress, and then Ari helped Alex remove her shirt and jeans, flinching with her as they eased the soaking denim over her swollen foot. They sat close, still trembling, only now it wasn't just because of the cold. Finding herself shy and unsure, Ari waited, hoping that Alex would lean over to kiss her. All they needed to do was turn toward one another.

Finally, as if she was following steps set out for her, moving without thinking, guided by some ancient, wordless script, Ari turned and wrapped her arms around Alex, rising to her knees and pulling Alex onto hers so they could press their bodies close. Alex kissed Ari's throat and trailed her fingers from the nape of her neck all the way down her spine. Ari smiled as she felt Alex's heart galloping next to hers.

"You know," Ari said breathlessly, "we'd be warmer skin to skin. These wet clothes..."

"Let's get rid of all of them then," Alex whispered, reaching around Ari's back to unclip her bra.

There was a moment, a pause, where the world stood very still. Was it in the moment Ari's bare skin pressed wholly against Alex's? When she lay back and pulled her gently down on top of her? Was it that moment when, awestruck, they entered that boundary space that divides a life from childhood and adulthood? Ari heard, as if from far away, the sound of birdsong and the dawn wind ran its icy fingers along her back. But the cold could not claim her now. The electric current that tingled through her when she was close to Alex had become a fire that neither of them wanted to control.

O

Ari woke. Alex was asleep, pressed close behind her. The sun streamed through the mouth of the cave, and she shook Alex, very gently. There was no need to say anything. Ari stretched her arms out until the sunlight caught them. The light was like a hug from an old friend. Ari turned her arms this way and that and was dazzled by the tiny rainbows that the sun's light made in a grain of sand on her skin. Alex sighed happily and gave her goosebumps by placing the lightest of fairy kisses on her bare shoulders. They lay still, watching the play of sunlight on the water and listening to the magpies warbling in the bush not far away.

Finally, Ari stretched and sat up, looking for her clothes. They lay where she had tossed them, cold, soaking wet, and horribly sandy. Alex's were the same, and they looked at each other and laughed.

"We can't walk back to Wyndham naked."

"No."

Ari tried to brush some of the sand off her dress. The next part of their homecoming still lay ahead, and Ari was anxious about her mother. Alex was still lying stretched out on the sand and she was smiling at Ari in a way that made her want to lie back down with her and forget her mother, forget Wyndham, forget the terrible ultimatum they'd been given. She felt a flush of love and desire so intense that she had to close her eyes and take a deep, shuddering breath.

Refusing to meet Alex's gaze, she shook her head, pulled the clammy dress over her head, and did her best to make the sodden laces respectably tight over her chest. She couldn't face putting her wet, sandy bra or knickers back on, so she buried them in a corner of the cave. Then she picked up Alex's clothes and shook some of the sand off them.

"Come on. It's not that bad. Put your shirt on. I'll help you get the jeans over your foot."

"Not until I get a kiss," she said, reaching up for Ari.

Quite some time later, Ari and Alex walked together along the track toward Wyndham. Alex said her foot was a little better, and it did, perhaps, look a little less swollen. But she still limped, and their progress was slow. Ari tried to give her anxieties the attention they deserved. Apart from anything else—the time she'd been gone, the terrible lie about Anna and the camping trip, and the worry she'd caused her loved ones—it was Alex herself who would be the most difficult to explain.

"We're just going to have to tell them who you are."

"They won't believe us. They'll think we're crazy. Well, they'll think *I'm* crazy. They probably wrote you off a long time ago." She laughed and dodged when Ari swatted at her.

"Can you please be serious? We might be back, but we're not out of danger yet. And I wish I knew how much time has gone by while we were underground. You know, if it's been more than two weeks, then my birthday has come and gone. I've never had a birthday without my mum. She'll be really upset."

Alex stopped. "You had a birthday? Down there?"

"If it's after the twenty-seventh of February, yes. And oh no!" Ari paused, struck by a horrible thought. "Alex, I must have missed at least two weeks of school already! How am I going to explain that?" Ari looked at Alex, who was bending over as though hunting for something in the long grass. "What are doing? Have you been listening to me? I'm in big trouble. The world has been turning while we've been gone, and I need to know how many times. I need to know how long I've been away."

Alex straightened up and handed her a bunch of tiny yellow sea-daisies. She smiled. "Happy birthday, Ari." She shook her dark, sand-matted hair and laughed at Ari's stricken expression. "Come on. You haven't journeyed through the darkness and terror of the underworld to start worrying about high school. That sort of thing will sort itself out, you'll see."

The beach track usually seemed to stretch forever, but now it seemed too short. Ari wanted to keep walking hand in hand with Alex. It seemed each step she took was carrying her farther from their precious night in the cave; each yard of sandy track that slipped away behind them was eroding that moment of perfect, enchanted closeness and steering them closer to the unknown dangers ahead. The bush looked different. The weather was certainly much less summery. There was a chill in the air that usually meant the coming of autumn, but surely they hadn't spent that long in the underworld? It had been midsummer when they'd left. It wasn't unusual, Ari reasoned, to have a run of colder weather after a hot spell. And it wasn't all that unusual, in summer, to see early apples ripening, although how they'd managed to grow and ripen during the drought was a bit of a mystery. It must have been all the recent rain. But the storms and flooding weren't recent at all, but weeks ago.

Ari's stomach growled violently when she saw the shiny red apples hanging from the old tree near the fence. As they got closer, she could smell their sweetness like a heavy cloud in the frosty air. Ari couldn't tell how long it had been since she'd last tasted anything fresh. The last meal she'd eaten had been hard bread and lukewarm underworld water. She bit blissfully into her sun-warmed apple and let her gratitude spill out like the juice that trickled down her chin.

Thank you, apple tree, she thought passionately. Thank you, sun, and earth, and air and water.

Watching Alex bite into her own apple, Ari marveled at her all over again: at her smooth skin and dark hair, all tangled with sand and seawater, at her curves and her angles concealed under the stained and dirty T-shirt and jeans. Ari's body longed for the warmth and strength and softness of Alex's body. Images from the cave sent a delicious tingle through Ari's veins, but the real miracle was not their lovemaking. Alex was here. Really here. Alive, with a heartbeat and a whole new life stretched out before her.

Ari didn't allow herself the "if" that attended that thought. They would find a way to do what the Fates demanded of them. Everything would be fine. Ari chose another apple for herself and jammed four more into the pocket of her cloak. It was possible that nobody had been at Wyndham for a while. Until they could get to the general store, they might have to make do with whatever food was left in the cupboard and whatever the garden and the countryside could provide.

In spite of her gladness, a renewed wave of exhaustion made Ari's knees wobble, and Alex gripped her shoulders tightly as she slumped against her.

"Come on," she said. "Let's get you home. Don't worry about what you'll find when you get there, or about the future. Just think about that one thing, Ari. You are going *home*. Not to some stinking underworld prison or courtroom and not to some new terror. Home. Come on."

They scrambled down the grassy bank, away from the apple tree and back onto the track. Holding hands, they walked in silence.

As they rounded the last bend in the track and Wyndham came into view, Ari clutched Alex's hand, her heart racing. "What if Nick's there and he yells at me? What if something's happened to Mum or the baby? Or what if nobody's there, and they've given up on me ever coming back?"

Entering the farmhouse gate, Ari looked for Nick's white four-wheel drive, but there were no cars parked in the circular driveway. Everything looked pretty much the way she had left it except the veggie garden, which was sprawling and unkempt, choked with weeds. The lantana bush, which Cass had always kept ruthlessly clipped, had spread and grown wild against the veranda. The wisteria vine, though, was dry and dead. The cows pulled peacefully at a round bale of hay in the paddock, and Ari glimpsed, far off toward the forest fence, two horse-shaped dots, one gray and one chestnut.

"Thank goodness somebody's been feeding the animals," said Alex. Ari ran up the front steps, leaving Alex to pull herself up, painfully, by holding onto the veranda posts.

As she flung open the front door, there was a familiar crunching of gravel from the driveway. Ari turned, slowly, as the Land Cruiser rolled toward the house. Ari saw Nick at the wheel and, in the passenger seat, a familiar, beloved figure with wavy blond hair. Before Nick had switched off the ignition, Cass was out of the car. She looked at Ari and opened her arms wide. Ari ran to them.

There was no yelling after all, no tears or recriminations. Cass kissed her and held her close for a long, long time. Then she let Ari go while she opened the back door of the car. Ari watched, speechlessly, as Cass unbuckled a tiny bundle and lifted it from a padded baby capsule. The bundle began to cry, and Cass put the baby on her shoulder and gently rubbed her back.

"She's just woken up," she explained. Then she cradled the baby in her arms so that Ari could look at her properly, though she had to wipe her eyes with her sleeve before she could see anything.

"She's so beautiful," said Ari, reaching out to touch one of the tightly curled little hands that waved above the blanket.

Cass smiled radiantly. "Isn't she? We chose the name Miranda ages ago, but we've already shortened it to Andi, can you believe it? Ari and Andi. People will think we're crazy. She came a little early, but she's perfectly healthy and well. I wish you could have seen her when she was just born, Ari. She was so tiny. There's nothing quite so special as a newborn baby. Luckily, they just get cuter the bigger they get."

Ari was hardly listening. Tears slipped down her cheeks as she stared at her baby sister. "I missed it," she said miserably. "I missed her birth and I missed being there with you." Little Miranda grabbed her finger.

Ari gulped. Everything was all mixed up: joy and relief at seeing her baby sister safely here in the world and distress because she missed the birth and hurt her mother. She looked at her little sister and then at her mother, and her tears blurred both of them and made their outlines wobbly. Cass gently disengaged the baby's fingers and passed her to Nick, whose own tears were fogging his glasses. Nick smiled and patted Ari's cheek as he took Miranda inside.

Then Cass hugged Ari so hard that she thought her ribs might snap. "Don't you ever, ever, run off like that again, okay?"

Ari nodded, surfacing from her mother's embrace to find her staring at Alex, who was watching from a tactful distance.

"Hello," she said. Then she blinked. "Don't I know you already?"

Ari left her mother's side and put her arm around Alex's waist. "Mum, Alex has a badly infected foot. She needs a doctor."

Cass shook her head. She didn't speak for a long moment, then she shook her head again. "Sorry, I must be a little confused. I thought you said your girlfriend's name was Anna." She looked closely at Ari. "You look different. Older or something. Not to mention like you've been through a hedge backward. And what in God's name are you wearing? You're a little old for dress-ups, Ari, don't you think?"

She took a few steps toward them and studied Alex's face up close. Ari waited, holding her breath.

"I see," Cass said finally. Her voice had that tight, controlled quality that it often had when she was confronting a crisis. There was a pause, and then Cass drew a deep breath. "I don't know what's going on here. I don't know where you've been all this time, Ari, or why you look so thin and pale and tired. But I do know one thing for sure. I know that this couldn't be anyone else but Alex Cohen."

She shook her head again, in wonder. "Little Alex, all grown up. So we didn't lose you after all."

They both heard the whisper of accusation behind the astonishment.

Ari watched Alex's face. She could sense her mind searching for the right words. "I *was* lost," said Alex simply. "Lost for a very long time and almost for all time. But Ari found me and she saved me." She smiled. "It's wonderful to see you again, Cass." Ari tightened her grip on Alex as she swayed slightly on her feet.

Cass put her hand on Alex's forehead. "You have a fever." She wrapped her arm around Alex from the other side, and she and Ari helped her limp up the last couple of veranda steps.

"Come inside and lie down. We have a lot of talking to do, but it can wait until you're better. Ari, call Doctor Walker. He still makes house calls out this way. Claire had him over a little while ago when Jack fell and banged his head on the coffee table. Oh, and we need to call Claire and tell her you're safe, and I'd better ring the school too, at some stage." Cass talked at her usual breathless rate while she helped Ari half-carry Alex inside.

They put her to bed in Ari's room. It looked exactly the same as when she'd left. Ari curled up in her old cane chair and watched as Cass rolled up the leg of Alex's jeans to inspect her foot. She tried to calculate, for the hundredth time, exactly how long she'd been away. Months. Not weeks, months. But her mother was busy dabbing iodine on Alex's ankle and hissing with concern, and she knew all such questions could wait. Alex lay with her eyes closed, breathing quickly. Her face was flushed and damp with perspiration. Ari tried to keep her own eyes open, but it was a struggle she was losing. She leaned her head against the chair and gave in. I'm home, she told herself silently. Home.

16.
HOME

ARI OPENED HER EYES. SHE was warm and cozy and comfortable. She almost snuggled back down to sleep but remembered, with a rush of gladness, where she was. They'd put her in the guest room because Alex was in her bed. The curtains were drawn, but warm, golden light filtered through them. Not nighttime, then. What time was it?

Staring at the patterns on the old-fashioned plaster ceiling, Ari breathed in the smells of home. The sheets and quilt smelled like the lavender oil her mother always put in the wash, and somewhere in the house somebody was making toast. Ari breathed deeply, reveling in the peace and the silence.

Then, like a car alarm or a police siren, baby Miranda gave a piercing cry. Ari jumped. The crying got louder and didn't stop. Ari smiled. The twins were getting so grown up, she had forgotten what a tiny baby sounded like. And this wasn't just any baby. This was her little sister, marking her presence in the world with the universal, wordless language of babies. It was appallingly loud.

Ari heard her mother's voice soothe the baby, and soon the crying stopped. Ari found that she'd been awake for some minutes and not yet worried about Alex. Was she asleep? How was her ankle?

Ari threw back the quilt and sat on the edge of the bed. Her feet cringed away from the chill of the floorboards, but someone had put her slippers next to the bed. Her ruby-red, sequined slippers, like Dorothy's from *The Wizard of Oz*. Ari hardly remembered them, but her feet settled into the same indentations that they always had. Her dressing gown was draped over the end of the bed, and Ari wrapped it around herself. Why was it so cold?

As she opened the door, Ari nearly tripped over something warm and hairy lying across the threshold. Sally looked up at her and thumped her tail on the floorboards. Ari crouched to hug and stroke her, to breathe in all her old dogginess. Sally smelt like home, just like the smell of lavender in the linen and the smell of burnt toast, which meant Nick was operating the toaster. Ari allowed herself one more minute of patting Sally and wondered happily whether she should check on Alex first or hunt out her mother and little Andi. But Alex found her. She came slowly out of Ari's bedroom, holding on to the wall as she shuffled toward her. She was wearing Ari's pajamas, which were a little too tight. She looked exhausted, but better than she had when they'd put her into Ari's bed.

Ari stood and hugged her, feeling a rush of love and warmth as Alex wrapped her arms tightly around her.

"I'm sure you should be in bed," Ari told her sternly. "Come on. Back you go."

Ari made Alex lie down, laughed as she saw all the sand in the bed, and then remembered the guest room bed probably looked the same. All of a sudden, she wanted nothing more complicated than a long, hot shower and the chance to wash her hair. She felt gritty and dirty and cold. Ari sighed as she realized she wouldn't be able to slide into bed and snuggle up next to Alex. The house no longer belonged to them the way it had before. So she settled for the cane chair and closed her eyes.

Sleep seemed to want her, and it claimed her every time she sat still. But this time she slept fitfully, troubled by images of the underworld that flickered across her consciousness like a slideshow. She saw the Hunter most often, striding across the barren gray plain with his horde of ragged shades. She saw Mara, cloaked and hooded, walking proudly beside her father. She saw the river, the black rocks that littered the dusty earth, the towering walls of the prison, and the black despair of the tunnel; each image was a snapshot of the dark places she'd left behind. Ari woke with a shiver and saw her mother watching her from the doorway with baby Miranda in her arms.

Ari found jeans and a woolen sweater tucked away at the top of her wardrobe where she stored all her winter clothes. The jeans seemed at least a size too big, and Ari was a little shocked at how much weight she'd lost. She pulled her sweater down over her waist, hoping Cass hadn't noticed. Alex was still asleep.

Ari watched as Cass turned up the heater and put another blanket on top of her. There was a packet of antibiotics and a glass of water on her bedside table, which meant the doctor had come while she'd slept. Was that the first time or the second time? That nap in the chair seemed like minutes but could have been hours. It was dark outside. Ari thought maybe she'd lost all sense of time, and it was an unnerving feeling. She kept her eyes on her mother, the way she used to do when she was a child and something had frightened her.

Ari perched on the edge of her bed. Cass sat down with the baby in Ari's cane chair and began to feed her. She smiled at Ari and told her the doctor had been very concerned about Alex's foot, but suggested trying strong penicillin and bed rest instead of the long and disruptive trip to the Port August hospital.

"What time is it?" asked Ari sleepily.

"About eight-thirty."

"At night?" Ari heard the squeak of disbelief in her voice. "I can't have slept all that time!" Cass smiled again.

"I guess you were worn out. I wanted to move you into bed, but the doctor said to leave you, so we just covered you up. Alex has slept even longer. Ari, we need to talk, obviously, but not until you've had more rest. I got Dr. Walker to examine you while you slept. He said you looked dehydrated and malnourished and that you needed lots of rest and fattening up. So here, you hold your sister while I go and make you something to eat."

Ari held her breath as her mother put the baby into her outstretched arms. Then she let her breath out in a wondering "oh" as she felt the warmth and weight of the precious bundle in her arms. Miranda smelled milky and sweet, and her little eyelids fluttered in her sleep. She made a few kitten-like noises, then settled back to sleep.

Ari was mesmerized by her tiny features. "Oh, Mum. She's so beautiful. Look at her perfect little nose and her little lips! She looks like you. Or does she look like Nick? No, definitely like you. Oh, I can't decide. It's like a dream. I'm not dreaming, am I?" And Ari looked around her room, half afraid that she might indeed be conjuring this homecoming.

Cass put her hand on Ari's forehead. "Back to bed," she ordered, taking baby Andi gently from her arms. "Come on. You can cuddle Andi again when you've had more rest and something substantial to eat."

Ari ate her toast and drank the hot chocolate her mother brought her. She fell asleep in the guest room as soon as she lay down. Ari dreamed. She dreamed she was standing once again by the sinkhole in the forest. It was night. The wild dogs sat in a half-moon in front of her, trapping her between them and the hole. The lead dog stood on its hind legs and took a step toward her.

And then, suddenly, it wasn't a dog anymore. Acheron stood before her. He was dressed in black, just as he had been that afternoon under the dripping pines. Ari turned to gaze at the pool, wondering if perhaps she could swim across it and escape. But as she gazed at the dark water she saw, with horror, two pale faces staring up at her through the black glass of the pool's surface. The Hunter and Mara were alive but trapped under the water. Ari saw Mara's fragile fingers pressed against the underside of the water, as if she was trying to find a hole in sheet ice.

Ari reached into the pool, and her hand passed through the water and found nothing. When the ripples cleared, the Hunter and his daughter were gone, and Acheron was laughing at her. He didn't speak but made a slight movement with his hand. It seemed to Ari that the treetops parted, and the clouds scuttled away from the moon. She could see it shining full against the darkness. But it wasn't completely round. The moon was ever so slightly flattened on the left-hand side.

Acheron laughed at her again. "The moon wanes, Arielle. What will you do when she dwindles and darkens? The old woman has tricked you. You cannot possibly defeat my hellhounds and close this portal in a half-month. *Less* than a half-month." He held her gaze, and Ari's skin prickled with a familiar cold sweat. "But try, by all means. It will be amusing. Then, when the days and nights are gone and Alex Cohen lies dying in your arms, you can at least comfort yourself with the thought that *this* time the fault is not entirely your own. Oh, but hold on a moment. If you think about it, it *is* actually your fault. Everything can be traced back to the day you made Alex swim to that rock, can't it? If she hadn't died and been made a Summoner, somebody else would have come to collect you after the serpent's bite, and then the rift would not have opened, and the dogs would not be gathering their strength. *My* strength." His thin lips stretched to release his cruel, mocking laugh.

Ari put her hands over her ears and closed her eyes. It seemed as though Acheron was speaking with her own voice. The words were hers. They were the same words that nagged and gnawed in her mind when she forgot to block them out.

"You're not real," she told him. "You don't exist. This is a dream."

She awoke, shaking and sweating, but found little comfort in being awake. Against all the rules of logic and reason, Acheron did exist, the dog pack still roamed the pine forest, and the moon was wearing away, little by little, each night.

O

IN THE SHOWER, ARI STRETCHED her arms above her head and closed her eyes, giving herself up to the glory of the warm water and the feeling of strength and life returning to her body. She pondered the happy question of what she might make for breakfast—or was it lunch? Her nightmare nibbled at the edges of her mind, but she wouldn't let it in, not quite yet. One more little bit of home, Ari promised herself. One more day of happiness and safety and not worrying about what might happen next.

Later that day, Ari sat on the veranda and watched the evening cast its shadows across the farm. Swallows darted and swooped in the turquoise sky above the old milking shed, chasing the day's last insects. Orange-tinted clouds gathered above the darkening hills, and the sea spray swept swiftly inland, carried along by the onshore wind. A cobweb on the lantana bush was studded with dewdrops that caught the last rays of the sun. Everything about her home was as it should be: garden and farmyard, fields and scrub, all preparing to sleep as the day faded. Whatever darkness was threatening Stonehaven, it hadn't managed to touch Wyndham, not yet, and Ari was profoundly grateful.

That afternoon, Cass had made a cake and they'd sung "Happy Birthday" to her, Cass and Nick with their arms around each other and Alex holding Miranda as if she was used to cradling babies. Cass and Nick gave her a stack of new books and a voucher for the clothes shop she loved in Port August.

Everything about the birthday celebration was strange: having a birthday nearly four months late, having a new baby in the house, having Alex; but it was the most wonderful birthday Ari had ever had. She'd dressed up a little for the occasion and was gratified to feel Alex admiring her in her best jeans instead of her grubby underworld smock. Cass had insisted on washing the shroud-like garment, marveling at the hand-stitched seams and the embroidery across the bodice—details Ari hadn't noticed. She was glad to be out of it and didn't care what happened to it. Her medicine bottle and knife, however, were safely locked in her desk drawer. She had asked Alex if she thought the knife had any special powers, hoping, foolishly, that Mara had somehow given her the means to kill the lead dog, close the portal, save Stonehaven, and keep Alex alive.

But Alex shook her head. "It's just a knife," she said, turning it over in her hands. "Beautifully made, but not, you know, magical or anything."

Still, it was a knife, and Ari thought it wouldn't do any harm to carry it with her whenever she left Wyndham.

She still had on her thick woolen sweater and jeans, but the oncoming night was crisp, and she shivered and thought momentarily about going inside for a blanket to tuck over her lap. But there was a kind of magic in this fleeting late autumn twilight, and she wanted to stay in it, thinking of nothing, watching the horses pulling at their bale of hay, smelling the ocean on the wind.

Her time of peace and not thinking about things was almost over. Cass had called a family meeting for after dinner, and Ari had a feeling she'd be required to account for quite a lot of things, starting with where she had been for almost four months. Ari ran her fingers through her hair, which was still slightly damp from her shower. It had grown very long, and Cass had had to help her comb it. They had been forced to cut out several knots that refused to yield to Cass's patient fingers.

Cass was tight-lipped during this process, only once allowing her astonishment and her anxiety to break through: "Ari, have you been sleeping in a ditch or something? What on earth have you been doing to your hair? And how did it get so long so quickly? No. Don't tell me." Ari, trying to sit straight on the bathroom chair, sensed Cass grow very still; the comb shook slightly in her hand. "Not yet. We can talk about all of that later. Now stay still while I cut out this knot."

Ari sighed and went inside. Cass and Nick were sitting close together on the old green two-seater in the living room. Baby Miranda slept peacefully in her cradle, which Cass had pulled close. Alex had been given the best spot, in the recliner close to the enormous old stone fireplace, with her sore foot propped up on the ancient red satin footstool that had belonged to Cass's grandmother.

The fire flickered brightly, and Ari went to stand in front of it with her hands tucked behind her to warm them. Nobody spoke for a long time. Nick seemed very interested in a loose thread on his sleeve, and Cass looked at Ari, then at Alex, then at nothing in particular. Ari sat down on the warm hearth and wrapped her arms around her knees. She smiled at Alex and at her mother and Nick.

"Well, I'm going to start with an odd question, but it's been bugging me. Why is it so cold? I know it's the end of autumn now—I checked the calendar—but it feels like the middle of winter. And it can't be winter, because Alex and I found the most delicious apples on that old tree down by the beach track."

"You were lucky to find anything still growing," said Nick quietly. "Most of the trees in the area dropped their fruit while it was still green. But I'll believe anything these days. After the stuff that's been going on around here, ripe apples in winter are no big deal." He started to say something else, but Cass laid a warning hand on his arm.

Ari saw the glance they exchanged, and it chilled her. This was no family interrogation in which she would play the part of the teenage runaway and be grounded for the rest of her life. Ari knew her mother and Nick were frightened, and that was far worse, somehow, than her already fading memory of the underworld. If her mother was scared, that made it real. That meant there actually was something to be afraid of.

Ari bit her lip and watched Cass's face as she spoke, seeming to choose her words with caution. "It *is* still autumn by the calendar," Cass told her. "But strange things have been happening, especially with the weather. People are saying it's to do with the hole in the ozone layer and the world heating up, but that doesn't make any sense, because we're having our coldest autumn on record. There was actual *snow* on the hills last week and more yesterday. Not much, but still."

"Enough to cover tracks, but not enough to see any new ones." Nick gripped the arm of the couch, and his knuckles were white. He stood up, and Cass made a small sound of protest, but Nick was looking hard at Alex, then at Ari. "I know we're supposed to start with where you've been all this time, Ari, and how come you're here at all, Alex, and that we're to take it easy on the questions, but I'm afraid I'm not going to be able to stick around. I'm with the hunting party. We have hunters in Stonehaven now, and it's my rostered night to go out with the hunt. The guys are picking me up at seven-thirty. We only hunt till daybreak, so I'll be home for breakfast. I'll see you all then."

Cass gave him a pleading look, but Nick was already kissing her goodbye. He stroked Ari's hair and nodded at Alex.

"I'll see you in the morning. Make sure you lock the doors and the windows and check that the fireguard is secure. I don't think it was locked in properly last night."

"What fireguard?" asked Ari, turning to examine the fireplace. She saw that three heavy metal rings had been driven into the bluestone along each side.

"What are they for?"

"So we can attach the fire screen to the fireplace."

"But why?"

Cass and Nick exchanged another glance. "So that nothing can come down the chimney," Cass said finally.

Alex stood up. "May I come with you, Nick? I've tracked these dogs before. If I could borrow a jacket?"

"Forget it, Alex," Cass told her flatly.

"Not with a foot like that," added Nick. "Wait until it's completely healed, then we'll gladly take you out. We need all the hunters we can get." From outside, a car horn tooted twice. Nick gave Cass a final kiss, paused to gaze reverently at his baby daughter, and left. They heard him put on his boots in the kitchen and then the sound of a car pulling away down the drive.

Cass took a deep breath. "Right," she said. "I'm going to make us all a cup of tea, and then I want to know what's going on. I think you two might know something about the dogs already, so we could start with that."

"What makes you think we know anything about any of it?" Ari asked curiously.

Cass paused in the doorway. "Because, just now, young Alex over there was all ready to go hunt dogs with Nick and the others. But we hadn't told either of you what kind of animals the hunters are tracking."

Cass ran her finger along the edge of the doorframe. The wood was etched with years of children's height measurements. Ari knew, without having to look, that her name and Alex's were there together, about halfway up. They had argued for months when they were very little about who was taller. After a space of a couple of inches were her name, written in her childish ten-year-old hand, and Alex's, a good two inches above hers. Above that was nothing.

Cass touched the letters of Alex's name. She gave her a searching look. "I know you know something about the strange things that have been happening around here because, obviously, you being here is the strangest thing of all. So I'm going to make tea, and then you can tell me everything you know."

17. The Waning Moon

It took a lot of telling. Ari began with a brief and selective account of her first meeting with Alex. Cass was very quiet as Ari told her how they'd all agreed that the Ari's near death from snakebite should be kept from her until the baby was safely delivered. Alex tried, falteringly, to describe her years in the underworld and her role as a Summoner. Ari said very little about her own journey through the underworld. She tried, for Cass's sake, to play down her capture by Acheron, her dislocated shoulder, the desolate journey along the riverbank, and the horrors of the secret prison.

As she began to describe the trial and stopped, Ari tried anxiously to read her mother's expression. She saw disbelief in her eyes, followed by fear, and, above all, bewilderment. Alex took over, finishing with their impossible task and the cryptic advice that Atropos had given them at the trial. Little Miranda woke up twice for feeds while Ari and Alex were talking, and Cass took her off to the nursery the second time to put her in her crib. When she returned, Ari had her head on Alex's knee, and Alex was stroking her hair.

Cass stood near the fire, watching them. "So you have until the moon disappears, and if you can't close the portal and get rid of the dogs before then, Alex will die again and return to the underworld forever. Is that right?"

Ari and Alex both nodded.

Cass put her arms on the mantelpiece and rested her head on them. "You know," she said, her voice muffled, "I think I would have been happier if you really were some girl from school, Alex, and Ari had run away to be with you. I really think I'd prefer to go with that."

"No you wouldn't," said Ari. "You like to know the truth. And I know you believe us."

Cass lifted her head and nodded. Then she leaned over and tried to hug both of them at once. "I didn't mean what I just said. Of course I don't wish you were anybody else but you, Alex. It's just, I don't know. My brain somehow refuses to take it all in. You drowned. We mourned you. I thought, sometimes, that Ari wasn't ever going to be happy again. And now, after all this time, here you are, all grown up. And I can see that Ari loves you, and that you love her. Out of all of this madness, that's probably the best thing that could happen." She sat on the couch and looked at them. "There are two things we need to do right away. First, you both need to know what's been happening here since you left. And, Alex, you need to see Beth."

"I want to, more than anything," said Alex quietly, "but I'm afraid. What will it do to her, seeing me?"

Cass sighed. "I've been thinking about that. I don't know exactly how she'll react. But I do know, if it was me, that I'd want to see you no matter what. If I'd lost Ari, I would never, ever stop wishing that she could come back to me. Maybe Beth will surprise you by being able to believe the impossible. Look how well I'm doing!"

Alex smiled at her. "But you were always the strong one. And my mother is sick. Ari told me how long she's been in care." She stood up, took a log from the wood box, and began to fix the ailing fire. When she spoke again, there was steel-edged decision in her voice. She said with her back to them, still fiddling with the fire: "I can't see her yet. I have to wait until the moon wanes to dark, and we have fulfilled our part of the bargain. I have to be sure that I'm staying."

Ari was silent. She heard the brittle edge in Alex's voice and Ari's heart ached as she thought about what such a decision must have cost. She also knew that Alex was right. Why upset Beth and give her false hope when they might fail? When Alex might not be allowed to remain? Cass was quiet too, and Ari read by her expression that her mother was having similar thoughts.

"All right, then." Cass cleared her throat. "Let's talk about you seeing Beth when the time is right. I'm going to have to tell you some things now. Scary things. Are you ready?"

Ari and Alex looked at each other. "We do know about the dogs," Alex admitted. She told Cass about the day the dogs had threatened them in the pine forest and that the pack had played a major part in the disappearance of Tom Drysdale. Ari told her about Acheron and the way the dogs had chased her into the sinkhole.

Cass stared at both of them. "So this Acheron, he just appears when he feels like it, is that it?" Her voice was taut.

Ari told her mother and Alex about her dream. There wasn't enough time for concealment. She recalled the dream as best she could, adding: "It was a really vivid dream. The dogs were there, and Acheron was in charge of them, as he was in the forest. He, he said some cruel things, about how little time we have left."

Alex gave her a sharp look, and then took her hand and held it tightly. They sat holding hands on the hearthrug, looking up at Cass like two little children troubled by nightmares. But instead of soothing them, Cass just sighed and told them that the dog pack was huge now—estimated to be in the hundreds—and that no amount of baiting or trapping or hunting seemed able to control it. There were few families in the area who had not lost livestock or pets, and most animals were kept locked up at night now, except for the cows. The cows seemed to be too large to be easy prey, but some farmers were getting nervous about the size of the dog pack. It was generally considered only a matter of time before the dogs banded together to bring down a cow. Although few would admit it, the farmers who had to attend sick or injured animals in the fields now did so in pairs and carried rifles. Without their own dogs, they felt particularly vulnerable.

"Practically every dog around Stonehaven has run away and joined these monsters," said Cass sadly. "Only the sick ones and the very old ones seem to be immune. Maybe the pack doesn't want them." Cass glanced, as did Ari, at Sally's silvery-gray form stretched out across the doorway. "She never used to sleep in the doorways," said Cass. "It's like she thinks she can protect us from there. She's been so good. We only let her out to do her business, but she doesn't seem to mind. She always stays in the garden and comes straight back inside.

"Anyway, at first people just assumed their dogs, particularly the smaller ones, were being taken and killed by the pack, but then Owen Jones saw his kelpie, Jessie, with the pack. And she, she was changed. Owen had gone out with a hunting party, and they had tracked the dogs deep into the pine forest. Suddenly the pack appeared, just seemed to materialize out of nowhere, Owen said. The men started shooting, but they didn't hit even one dog. Nobody ever does. As the pack turned to flee, Owen saw Jessie, who paused as if to stare at him. He called her and whistled, but she snarled at him. Owen said..." Cass took a deep breath. "...Owen said her eyes were like black holes in her face. He raised his shotgun, he said, to put her down, but she disappeared into the pack. And most people with dogs have similar stories."

Ari's flesh crawled as she imagined their beloved family dog looking like that. For the first time, Sally's age was a blessing rather than something terrible that she tried not to think about.

Cass was talking, and Ari pulled her attention from Sally so that she could listen. "Apparently, the dog pack comes into town and starts howling. All the dogs who haven't been locked up, and even some who have, join them. And they kill everything. Chickens and other livestock, native animals, cats, anything unfortunate enough to be outside where they can find it. People are too scared to leave their houses except in groups. You see, the dogs have become so vicious, and the pack so big, that they've started to attack people too. Not often, and not fatally yet, but two people have ended up in hospital from dog bites.

"And little Emily Clarke, she's in grade six at your school, Ari, was knocked over and dragged. She was on her way to the post office with her mother, and they were passing that patch of scrub near the nature reserve. Two massive dogs just came out of nowhere, and the bigger one stood up on its hind legs and put its paws on her chest and knocked her over. When she fell down, both dogs grabbed her by the arms and started dragging her toward the bushes. She screamed, of course. Sara, Emily's mum, grabbed a stick and started hitting the dogs with it, and there were other people around, luckily, who heard the girl screaming. Between all of them, they threw enough rocks and pelted the dogs hard enough that they let go. But everybody thought the same thing afterwards: What if Emily had been on her own? Now nobody walks anywhere alone."

Ari picked at the short, knotted strands of the hearthrug. She didn't want to hear any more. She knew Emily Clarke by sight: a short, skinny little girl with thick glasses, an easy target. How many other people might also appear this way to the dogs, and how many animals had been lost? Ari tried to stop imagining what it might feel like to be dragged along the ground by those animals. She forced herself, again, to listen to what Cass was saying.

"Since what happened to Emily, they've had the parks and wildlife people baiting the entire forest and setting traps. The police sent in their dog squad, but of course the dogs turned on their handlers and ran away to join the pack. After that it was in the news, and the army even came, can you believe it? And when they went in with their automatic weapons and their helicopters and their jeeps, we all thought, 'Thank goodness. It's over. Now we can get on with our lives.'"

"And what happened?"

"Nothing. Nothing at all. The army troops came back, saying they hadn't even seen one dog. And what's worse, they found no traces of the pack, not one pawprint. They thought we were all mad, I'm sure. That was a few weeks ago. Now we're sending our own people into the plantation every night to try and shoot the dogs, and the government seems to be trying to decide whether to tackle the dogs again or try to subdue the lunatics who live in the town."

Ari and Alex looked at one another but said nothing. Cass cocked her head and seemed to be listening for something. "Was that little Andi? Where's the baby monitor? Oh, here it is." She shook the little walkie-talkie device and the row of lights around the speaker flickered on and off. Cass put her ear to it but seemed unsatisfied with the static and silence. "I'll be back in a minute. Just going to check on her."

When her mother left, Ari put her head on Alex's shoulder. "What are we going to do?"

"We'll find a way to stop them. After all, we've both faced them before."

"Yes, and both of us were driven or tricked into the sinkhole. And there were only a dozen or so dogs then. Now there are hundreds, apparently. And you don't have your superpowers anymore,

remember? You can't talk in a funny language and scare them off."
Alex said nothing. She put her arms around Ari, and they kissed, hurriedly, while glancing at the doorway. When Cass returned they were still sitting, a little self-consciously, on the rug in front of the fire.

"She's fast asleep," Cass reported. She looked closely at Ari. "Is there anything else you need to tell me? I want to know what both of you are planning to do next. And I don't want you to disappear again. This is serious. Nobody walks alone anymore. Do you understand that?"

Ari got up and went to sit next to her mother on the couch. She snuggled under Cass's arm and rested her head on her mother's chest. "I don't know what to do. Alex and I, we just don't know what to do next. All we know is that we don't have much time."

O

IT SEEMED TO ARI THAT the days were being nibbled away while she wasn't looking. The night after they talked to Cass, Alex went out with the hunters. Her foot was not completely healed, but it was useless to try and stop her. Ari was about to announce her own intention to go with them, but then she saw her mother's face and changed her mind. Nick just shrugged as Alex followed him to the door, wearing the new boots and jacket that Nick had bought for her in Stonehaven. Nick looked a lot older, Ari thought. The lines around his mouth were grim. Ari and Cass watched them through the kitchen window, which was now deadlocked every night. Sally growled softly in her throat as the first snowflakes of the night began their feathery attack on the windowpanes.

The same thing happened the next night and the next. Roster system or not, Nick seemed to be required at the hunt every night, and Alex always went with him. Ari was shocked at how quickly they all accepted the new routine. It was the same throughout Stonehaven. The hunters left at nightfall, well wrapped against the snow. Those left behind—the mothers with babies, the sick and the elderly, and the children—watched them leave and then they locked and bolted themselves in their houses until dawn. Everybody seemed to accept the snow in the same unquestioning fashion, but for Ari, the snow was like the dogs, something wholly unnatural. It certainly made hunting them difficult. Though there were many dog tracks, the constant snowfall covered them, confusing the pursuing townsfolk. Ari wondered if that was the intention.

Each night Ari asked to go with the hunt, and each night Cass begged her to stay. It was horrible to be left behind. Some of Ari's friends were out hunting every night, but Cass had pleaded with Ari not to go, and Ari still felt so guilty about causing her mother months of worry and about missing Miranda's birth that she promised she wouldn't join them.

Still, it was hard to watch Alex and Nick leave each night, and harder still to sleep not knowing whether they would return safely in the morning. It seemed to Ari they were all playing their parts in an old-fashioned fairy tale. The people of Stonehaven had become hunters. But they weren't hunting the big bad wolf or any familiar fairy-tale monster. Most of them were hunting their own dogs. The worst part was that, despite the nightly hunt, no dogs were ever caught, and the attacks and killings continued. Several kangaroos had been found near the edge of the forest with their throats ripped open. Any animals not locked away at night simply disappeared, leaving nothing but scarlet streaks of blood on the snow where they were dragged away.

Ari still couldn't quite believe that there was real, deep snow all around her. It had snowed once in Stonehaven when she was little. She remembered Cass, wrapped in a rainbow scarf, laughing as she scraped up the thin covering, more like ice than snow, and the tiny snowman they made on the frozen grass. That had been at the picnic area at Clearwater, the highest point in the hills. But snow down in the valley? Near the sea? Ari still found it hard to accept, even though some nights it fell in drifts so deep that Nick and Alex had to shovel their way to the front door in the morning. The horses and cows seemed warm enough in the shed, surrounded by hay, and most of the animals around Stonehaven were similarly protected. Ari tried not to think about the ones that didn't have a shed or barn to keep out the cold and the dogs.

The worst thing about the snowy nights was that there was no moon. Cass had borrowed one of Sam's nautical guides for Ari, and together they studied the phases of the moon. One night, after Alex and Nick had gone out with the hunt, Cass and Ari tried to figure out exactly how many days they had left. On the kitchen calendar they marked the day that Ari and Alex had returned, and Ari drew a full moon with a slightly flattened edge in that square. That was a week ago. According to the moon phase charts, this meant they were halfway to a dark moon. Ari thought it eerie rather than coincidental that the calendar's picture for June was a photograph of a snowy mountain landscape under a full, yellow moon. She found herself growing more depressed as she penciled in the few days that remained.

18.
Tracks in the Snow

The house was silent when Ari woke up. She pulled on her dressing gown and her Dorothy slippers and padded as quietly as she could down the hall to the guest room. They had swapped rooms, she and Alex, once she felt better. Cass had found them once sitting together in the guest room bed. They had only been kissing, but Ari couldn't bear the look on her mother's face as she shut the door without speaking.

"I don't think she really minds," Ari told Alex later. "But we'd better not get caught doing anything else. She's already got so much to deal with as it is. I don't think she expected me to grow up quite so fast."

After that they were much more careful, and the early mornings seemed to be the only time they could be alone. Alex and Nick would get back from hunting just before dawn, and, while Nick would collapse, exhausted, into bed, Alex didn't seem to be able to sleep straight away. She was worried, Ari could tell, although she tried to hide this from Ari. She had seen Alex in the kitchen looking at the calendar and her little moon drawings. Ari wanted to be with her all the time, and it hurt her to have to spend the nights alone. Ari thought perhaps this was what it was like to love somebody who had a terrible disease, one that came with a time frame: three weeks or six months and a death sentence at the end of all the waiting. Would people in that situation tick off the days as she was doing? As she lay snuggled close to Alex, Ari tried not to think about the passage of time and the disappearing moon.

We still have hope, she thought. That's what makes it bearable. We can still win. She made sure that she said this aloud to Alex every morning, and she made her repeat the words. But in her heart she was afraid, and she knew Alex was too.

Now, as Alex kissed her softly, longingly, and Ari kept one eye on the guest room door, she had to admit that she'd been trying to block it out, all of it. It was so wonderful to be home with her mother and Nick and baby Andi to cuddle and Alex always there that she hadn't done anything constructive about the situation. Watching Alex leave for the hunt each night and listening each morning as she described the useless trudging through acres of snow was not helping.

She pulled away and looked at her. Alex didn't seem affected by the hunting the way Nick was. She was smiling at her now, and her eyes, her face, everything about her was so familiar that it seemed as if she'd always been here, stroking her hair as they snuggled together on the guest room bed.

I never understood before now, Ari thought, what all the fuss was about when people talked about being in love. It wasn't that first flush of excitement that had made her lightheaded when Alex stood close to her in the beginning, although that was part of it. Nor was it that feeling of stepping into a new self, that momentous, life-changing night in the cave at Seal Cove, although that was part of it too. It was this, now, this closeness, this feeling of perfect indivisibility. But that was the feeling that lulled her into inaction. There *was* something that could come between them, and if they failed to close the portal and destroy the dogs, then Alex would die. And Ari knew, without any doubt, that she would not be allowed to follow her this time.

"Alex," she said, sitting up suddenly. "We have to try harder to figure this out. The moon is getting smaller. What did Atropos say right at the end? She said to watch out for Acheron and to pay attention to the old stories. Which ones?"

Alex thought. "She said to pay attention to the things that *recur* in all the old stories and that they could be like weapons."

"When other weapons fail us," added Ari excitedly. "Come on, think. What details can you remember from old stories? You read a lot of myths down there. They're the oldest stories, aren't they?"

"I guess so. Where's your book?"

Hours later, with half the family library spread out on her bedroom floor, Ari sighed in frustration and threw down her pen. "I love books, but a search engine would be helpful right now."

"A what engine?"

Ari just shook her head. "Never mind."

The sheets of notes had seemed so promising as she and Alex read furiously and found snippets of information that seemed significant. Now, though, as she watched the snow whirl past her window, Ari grew impatient. Was there was any point to all this research, while outside another precious day was quietly disappearing?

"It would help if we had some idea of what we were looking for." Alex picked up a richly illustrated copy of Grimm's fairy tales and began flipping through it again.

"Those aren't the oldest tales," Ari said, with some impatience. "I'm sure Atropos meant thousands of years old, not a couple of hundred years."

"They're still *old*," argued Alex. "And most of the Grimm Brothers stories were adapted from folk tales. Folk tales can be thousands of years old."

Ari found herself suddenly, irrationally, furious with her. "Well then, you just read your fairy tales and tell me when you find what we're looking for. I'm sure you have that figured out too."

"What's wrong? What's the matter with you?"

"What's the matter with *me*? You're the one who doesn't seem to care that we only have a few days left! All you do is go out with the hunt and spend the days sleeping." Ari struggled to stop the furious, futile tears from spilling down her cheeks.

She got up and went to the window. Outside, the garden had been transformed into a storybook tableau. Snowflakes settled on the windowsill, covering tiny stick-like prints where birds had tried to cling to the icy ledge. Beyond the fence line everything was white. Usually, Ari could see across the fields, hills and the forest all the way to the sea. It was difficult to believe that the world was still there under the snow.

Ari was beginning to feel hemmed in. She had visited Claire and Sam and been up to Stonehaven once or twice with Cass, but otherwise she hadn't left the house. It was hard to explain how helpless this made her feel. It was wonderful to be home and to be looked after by Cass, but Ari wasn't a child anymore. Her journey through the underworld had changed something fundamental inside her, and she thought perhaps this something might be making it hard for her to accept the old boundaries that used to make her feel safe.

Alex stood behind her. She put her arms around Ari's waist and rested her chin on her shoulder. "What are you thinking about?"

"Journeys," Ari told her absently. "How they change you. How, when you come back, everything looks different, smaller somehow. I wonder if knights used to feel like that when they came home from a quest. Not that my trip underground was like a quest or anything, but, well, you know what I mean." Alex lifted her chin from Ari's shoulder and clutched her excitedly. "That's it!"

"What do you mean? What on earth are you doing?" Ari watched, catching some of Alex's excitement as she began pulling jackets and boxes and bags from the top of the wardrobe.

"We've been looking in all the wrong places. We don't need to read every myth and fairy tale. We know this stuff, you and me. We knew it when we were kids. Look."

She dragged her old battered sketchbook down from the cupboard and opened it on the rug. Ari came to kneel beside her. There on the yellowed drawing paper was the title page of one of their epics. Ari's own writing filled the blank spaces, but Alex had done the title, in glorious, intricate detail, like the illustrated religious manuscripts she'd once seen in a museum.

"*The Quest for the Crystal Sword,*" Ari read, smiling. "We worked so hard on this one, didn't we?" She peered at Alex's drawing. "Look, there's the princess with her knights and servants riding away from the castle. I can't remember her name."

"It'll be there, if you read your story."

"I don't see how this helps," Ari said, turning the pages restlessly. "We're supposed to look for common details in the old tales that we can use as weapons. What's your sketchbook got to do with it?"

Alex placed her hand on a page just as Ari was about to turn it. "There." She pointed to a small drawing of the princess, now accompanied by another princess. They were standing in front of a dark cave, and the first princess held a flaming torch. In the next drawing, the heroes battled with terrible monsters in the depths of an underground cavern, and the final drawing showed them emerging triumphantly from the darkness. In the second princess's hand was a slender sword. Alex had colored it blue, and somebody, herself, Ari suspected, had added glitter to make it shimmer.

Alex turned to the next page and began to read the childish handwriting that accompanied the pictures: "*So Princess Star and Princess Moonlight went home to their kingdom with the crystal sword.*

When they got home they used the sword to kill the dragon, and so the kingdom was saved. The End."

Ari smiled, but she didn't understand what Alex was trying to tell her.

"It's the pattern. Don't you see? The basic quest pattern. We knew it, as children, because we had read so much of that kind of thing and seen so many fantasy movies, and those movies are all based on the same pattern. The heroes go on a dangerous journey to find something. They have to face danger and hardship but they're brave and they find what it is they're looking for. They return home and save the kingdom, just like Princess Moonlight and Princess Star."

Ari thought she caught a glimmer of something, a flash of understanding, but it slipped away just as she thought she had it. "I still don't get it," she admitted.

"*All the old stories*. Don't you see? It doesn't matter which stories because they all have something in common. Think about it: Orpheus and Odysseus and King Arthur and Ariadne, and even *Jack and the Beanstalk*. They all follow the same set of patterns."

"So," said Ari, as she began to follow this train of thought, "if it doesn't matter which stories, then all we have to do is figure out what the recurring elements are in all of them. And you think it's the quest pattern?"

"No, that's just an example. Besides, I don't see how we could use that as a weapon. I was thinking more along the lines of the crystal sword."

"An actual weapon?"

"Or something with special powers, like a goose that lays golden eggs, or a special thread that guides you through the labyrinth, or the Holy Grail."

"Recurring elements."

"Yes."

"Like a bottle of underworld medicine?"

Alex stared at her. Hope flared in her eyes. "Maybe." Then she shook her head. "But we both drank it and nothing special happened. It lessened the pain and kept us going when we had no food or water, but lots of herbal remedies can do that. It didn't magically heal my ankle or anything."

"And the knife? Mara's knife? You're sure that doesn't have any special powers?"

"I don't think so. It seems pretty ordinary to me. Enchanted weapons tend to have a strange vibration or a special glow or something."

"We'll keep looking," said Ari.

Cass opened the door. "Have either of you two seen Sally? Nick said he let her out to go to the toilet about half an hour ago, but he didn't let her back in. Did one of you let her in?"

Ari and Alex looked at one another. "We've been in here for hours," said Ari. "I didn't even know Sally was outside."

She was on her feet and running before Alex stood up. Wrenching open the kitchen door, Ari staggered under the force of the icy wind that blew great whirling gusts of snow across the threshold. As she stepped out onto the veranda the wind suddenly stopped altogether. It was bitterly cold, but still, and clear. A few snowflakes drifted down and melted on Ari's cheeks.

As Cass and Alex appeared behind her, Ari pointed silently at the smooth expanse of snow that used to be the scrubby grass of the garden. A deep set of pawprints ran in a straight line from the house to the white world beyond the garden gate.

○

CASS WATCHED IN SILENCE AS Ari pulled her gumboots on and zipped up her jacket. Ari could feel her mother's fear, but refused to meet her gaze. She concentrated on making sure that her gloves, which were a little too small, were pulled down each finger as far as possible. Alex and Nick put on their hunting gear, and Nick unlocked the new steel trunk that held the guns. He handed Alex a shotgun, and Alex took it without a word and without looking at Ari. Ari watched her mother out of the corner of her eye. Cass sat down on one of the heavy kitchen chairs and put her head in her hands.

"It's all right, honey," said Nick. "We'll bring old Sally-girl back. She can't have gone far."

Cass looked up. "I don't want Ari to go."

Ari stood still, her throat constricting. She drew a breath and croaked, rather than spoke: "But it's *Sally*. I have to go."

She had her hand on the doorframe, and her boots were on the threshold. Nick and Alex waited on the veranda. Guilt and remorse fought in Ari with fear for Sally and her frustration at being cooped up. Surely her mother could see that she had to go this time? Sally was old, and frail, and she would die of cold and exhaustion if they didn't hurry. And Sally might not come to Nick or Alex the way she was sure to come to Ari if Ari called her. But Cass just sat there, her bottom lip sticking out slightly in an expression Ari knew all too well. She fidgeted with her gloves, trying not to look at her mother.

But Cass got up and crossed the kitchen and put her arms around her, murmuring, "Please stay, Ari? Please? I couldn't bear it if something happened to you." Ari slumped against her mother. Cass was going to get her own way by crying, which wasn't fair. Ari gave her shoulders an angry little shake.

"Fine." She shrugged at Alex and Nick, and they turned immediately and set off through the snow. Cass tried to hug Ari again, but

Ari was furious with her mother and ignored her. She watched Alex and Nick until they were tiny black dots in the distance. Then she stomped off to her room, leaving Cass to shut the kitchen door.

Ari lay in bed; her sulk receding as she tried to follow Alex with her thoughts. Their invisible connection no longer worked, but Ari knew which way Alex and Nick would go. She had no doubt about where Sally's tracks were pointed. But how far would Sally get? She could barely walk around the garden, let alone as far as the pine plantation. Alex and Nick were sure to find her before nightfall. It was warm in her bed, and, although Ari told herself she should get up and apologize to her mother or offer to make dinner, sleep engulfed her.

She dreamed again that she was in the pine forest, deep inside, with the tang of pine resin in her nostrils and a crisp expanse of snow underfoot. The trees swayed and creaked above her, and, in the darkening sky, a sliver of moon hung above the black branches like the Cheshire cat's smile. Her dreaming self looked down at her feet, which were bare and yet not cold, making deep holes in the snow.

As she walked through the pines, Ari thought she could hear a voice, a man's voice, calling her. She spun around, but the forest was empty. There was nothing but trees and snow and the waning crescent moon in the evening sky. But the voice continued to call her by name. Ari followed it. She came at last to the sinkhole in the deep valley, and there was the Hunter, leaning casually against a tree as though he owned the whole forest.

"Hello, Ari," he said. "I knew you would come."

"But this is a dream," Ari replied. "Isn't it?"

The Hunter shook his shaggy head and gave her a sad smile. "Does it matter? I don't have very long, but I have to tell you something. It may help you when the time comes."

"When what time comes?"

"The end. Or the beginning."

"I don't have time for riddles." Ari's dream-self tried to look stern, crossed her arms and frowned. But the Hunter just gave her another of his enigmatic smiles. You know so much more than you are willing to tell me, thought Ari. Who are you?

And the Hunter answered, as though she had spoken aloud: "I can't tell you everything. But I do want to help you. Listen carefully." He looked around the clearing. "Acheron is close. He wants you, Ari, for the same reasons he wants Mara, but also for revenge. Be careful. Be wary if you have to speak to him."

Her blood froze as she imagined Acheron's light blue eyes staring into her own. And she wondered if it would be safe to confide in the Hunter something she could never admit to Alex, something she barely admitted to herself. The Acheron of the underworld was not the vile-smelling abomination who had laughed as she fell into the sinkhole. When he looked at her beside the river, Ari had been half-impressed by his power in spite of herself. She was afraid of him, revolted and terrified, but also acutely aware that he was a god, with all the power conferred by immortality. Those ugly pale eyes were just the outside, the grass and leaves that concealed the snare. He was the beast in the overgrown castle in the forest, the minotaur in the labyrinth, the wolf in grandmother's nightcap. And Ari worried that if Acheron caught her unawares she would be compelled to follow him, helplessly, into the dark.

The Hunter looked thoughtful, as if considering Ari's unspoken thoughts. Then he stretched out his hand and opened it. Ari looked. There, on the Hunter's weathered palm, was a single yellow leaf. It was strangely shaped, with tiny scalloped edges curving to a sharp point.

"It's a leaf from a special tree, Ari. The only tree that grows underground. Your medicine is distilled from it."

He reached into the pocket of his cloak and pulled out a tiny silver goblet. Ari watched as he placed the leaf ceremoniously inside and covered the mouth of the cup with his hand. When he took his hand away, Ari was astonished to see liquid, golden and fragrant, where the leaf had been.

"Drink," he said, passing it to her.

She took a cautious sip. "It tastes like my medicine."

She closed her eyes as the liquid sent familiar waves of warmth and strength through her body. When she opened her eyes, the Hunter was holding something else. She was shocked to see in his hand a long silver hunting knife, whose tip glinted wickedly sharp. He reached for the goblet with his other hand, and Ari passed it to him. The Hunter dipped the knife into the liquid. He stirred it and then he withdrew the blade and showed her the empty chalice.

"The knife absorbs the medicine, Ari. On its own, it is an ordinary knife. But it is a thirsty knife. It will drink this medicine. And then it is less . . . ordinary." The Hunter put the goblet in his pocket and passed her the knife. "Careful," he warned.

"But what's it for?"

"What do doctors and nurses do when somebody won't take their medicine?"

"But who? Everyone I know would drink this if I asked them to. Alex had heaps of it when we were in the underworld. It tastes good and it makes you feel good. Why would I need to force anybody to take it?" Ari blinked as the knife flickered like a candle flame and vanished from her hand.

The Hunter seemed to have stopped listening. He was fading. Ari could see the black trunks of trees through his body. "I don't have much time," he warned. "Listen carefully now. That liquid is a life-giving force. A little of it sustains and heals, as you know. But it only works on the living. It cannot bring a person back from death." He gave a short, bitter laugh. "Believe me, I have tried. Don't you see? It heals the living, but *only* the living. It has no effect on the dead. But life and death are not straightforward categories. They are not the only two modes of being. You know that by now, even if it's not clear at the moment."

Ari stared at him. There was something she should understand, but she couldn't quite grasp it. The Hunter was becoming more transparent, and his voice had shrunk to a whisper.

"What's happening? Please don't go. Hunter!" She reached out to touch him, but her hand passed through his chest. He was ghostlike against the snow, and when he spoke again his voice was ragged and faint.

"You're waking up, Ari. The dream is unraveling. The dark moon is coming. Listen to me. Keep the medicine close. Put Mara's blade in it. It may work as a weapon for you when other weapons fail."

"Those are the words Atropos used. What do they mean? Hunter?"

She blinked. The snow and the forest and the Hunter were gone. She was in bed, and the blanket had slipped down to her waist. She shivered and pulled the blanket back up around her head.

○

AT NIGHTFALL, ALEX AND NICK returned with loaded shotguns and no Sally. Nick looked so haggard and miserable that Ari hugged him before Alex, but he seemed not to notice her. He slumped at the kitchen table and stared at the window; his eyes were oddly flat and blank. Ari almost forgot the pain of losing Sally as she watched him. Cass put hot plates of food in front of Alex and Nick, and Alex ate hungrily, but Nick just moved his food around, saying nothing. At last he got up, scraping his chair across the floorboards, and left the room. Cass followed him, biting her lip.

"Poor Mum," said Ari. "She's got a new baby to look after and all of this as well. And Nick's not managing. Did you see his eyes?" She started to clear the table. Alex sighed.

"It's not just Nick."

"What do you mean?"

"It's all of them. All of the hunters." Alex took the plates and cutlery from Ari and filled the kitchen sink with water. "I figured it out a couple of nights ago. They seem fine when we gather at the edge of the pine plantation, but afterwards, at the end of the night, they change." She stopped washing the dishes and looked at her. "I don't like it, Ari. Something's not right. It's their eyes. Like Nick's eyes, but worse. A lot worse, some of them."

"We have to do something. Don't tell me you and Nick are still planning to go back out tonight?"

"I don't want to. It seems pointless. We never see any dogs. But I don't think Nick will stay home. I think…" She lowered her voice and glanced at the doorway. "I think they *have* to go, the hunters. I think something is compelling them to go and I don't like it."

"Let's test that theory. Stay home tonight. I bet Mum's begging Nick to do the same."

"All right. I'll tell Nick I'm staying, and we'll see what he does. But, Ari, time's running out. How are we supposed to stop the dogs if I can't even find them?"

Ari was just drying the last saucepan when Nick returned. He checked the clock, crossed to the stool near the front door, and began to lace up his hiking boots. He neither looked at them nor spoke, and Alex put a warning hand on her arm before Ari could say anything. They watched in silence as Nick fiddled with buttons and zips, and Ari was chilled by the mechanical familiarity with which Nick checked his shotgun. They all heard the crunch of gravel and the toot of a car horn from the white world outside. Nick left. He didn't even glance at Alex or ask why she wasn't coming.

Alex's fingers closed around Ari's hand and she held on tight. From behind her Ari heard her mother crying softly and she knew that there wasn't any more time. No matter what Cass said or how much she pleaded, Ari had to act. Tonight. Before it was too late: for Alex, for Nick, for Sally, for all of Stonehaven.

She sat Cass down gently and asked Alex to put the kettle on. Little Miranda was snuggled on Cass's chest, and Ari paused, struck anew by the wonder of this tiny person, all downy hair and rosebud lips and pink cheeks. Ari was not worried about Miranda's safety. Her mother's fierceness was the best shield any child could have. She kissed the baby softly on the top of her head and then she kissed her mother on the cheek. Alex put a cup of tea on the table for Cass. Ari dug her fingernails into the tops of her thumbs. There wasn't any more time for gentleness.

"Mum," she said, "whatever it is, we have to stop it. There are only two days left. Only two. I've stayed away from the hunt because you begged me. But now I have to go. And it's not just because of Sally. Alex says all the hunters are behaving like Nick. Something is terribly wrong, and I'm supposed to help fix it. I've been ignoring the instructions we were given in the underworld and I can't do that anymore. We may not be able to see it, but the moon is disappearing. Our time has just about run out."

Cass nodded slowly and rested her chin on the top of the baby's head. "I know you have to go, Ari." She reached out and stroked her cheek. "My beautiful, brave girl. I've been so afraid of losing you I've not let myself see how grown up you are. Of course you have to go."

She sipped her tea quietly, and Ari thought she could almost visualize it, that steel core that anchored her mother to the earth so that those around her could cling to her and not be swept away. Ari hoped she had inherited some of this strength and, if so, that it would help her in the forest tonight.

"Go," said Cass finally. "But you come back. Do you hear me? Both of you. Come back safely and bring Nick and Sally with you."

19. Dark Moon Rising

The lights from the house turned the snow golden, making it look almost homely. As they struggled past the orchard, past the deserted fields, Ari saw with a jolt of surprise that the sky was black and full of stars. The snow had stopped, and the lingering clouds had formed blue mounds of cumulus along the horizon. She looked for the moon but couldn't see it. We're out too early, Ari persuaded herself. Moonrise must be later on.

Ari checked on the cows and horses, envying them their sheltered, hay-filled barn and its heavy, padlocked door. Her heart ached as she thought, again, about Sally. Was she dead? Or worse? She undid the padlock, pushed open the heavy barn door and found the light-switch by running her fingers along the inside of the doorframe. The cows blinked their long-lashed eyes in the sudden brightness. Rusty and Bob looked over their stalls, whickering softly. Ari left Alex to stroke their shaggy winter coats while she opened the old filing cabinet that held all the animal remedies and first aid supplies. In her jacket she had stowed her underworld knife and the remains of the medicine, safely wrapped in one of Cass's woolen scarves. Ari had to search the drawer for a clean container but found one at last. Alex was watching her.

She unwrapped her bottle of medicine, removed the glass stopper, and tipped the golden liquid into the little plastic bowl.

"I didn't want Cass to see," Ari explained as she pulled out her knife. "The Hunter told me to do this. I had a dream this afternoon while you and Nick were gone. The Hunter said the knife and the medicine together might be a weapon for us when other weapons fail."

Alex gave Bob a final pat on the nose and came over to see. "Assuming we can find the dogs and assuming we could get close enough to stick a knife into the lead dog, what will the medicine do? Probably just heal all its scratches and make it stronger."

But she watched over her shoulder as Ari put the tip of the knife into the container. Ari heard her sharp intake of breath when the medicine disappeared. It did look as though the blade had drunk the medicine, sucked it all up so that the container was dry.

Ari sighed and wrapped the knife in the scarf. She handed it ceremoniously to Alex.

"Here, please take it. I couldn't, even if I had to. I'd freeze up or something. Besides, you don't have your shotgun."

"I hate those guns," said Alex vehemently. "I can't believe people in this town are carrying guns. We have to stop this, Ari. We have to stop it now. Let's hurry. I think the lead dog will come tonight, now that we're on our own." She unwrapped the scarf and held Mara's knife up to the light. No trace of the golden medicine showed anywhere along its silver blade. "Let's go."

They bolted the barn door, and Ari checked the padlock before hiding the key high on the doorframe. They crunched through the snow; the twin plumes of their breath clouded before them. The hillside had never looked so steep or the plantation so far away. Ari could just make out the dark shadow of the forest, as if somebody had drawn a thick black line to separate the land from the sky. She concentrated on telling Alex about her dream.

"The Hunter said the medicine only works on the living and that it has no effect on the dead. He was very clear about that. I think he was trying to tell me that the dog isn't alive or only alive in some supernatural way."

"I think most of the people in Stonehaven have figured that out by now. But I still don't understand why your medicine could do it any harm."

Ari told Alex as much of her dream as she could remember. The house lights faded to tiny points in the distance as they toiled up the snow-covered hill toward the forest. Ari tried to picture the expanse of the plantation and remember which roads bordered it.

"Where will the others go tonight? Where have you been getting in?"

"It changes night by night. Last night we drove along the highway toward Port August, then took a logging track, Gray's Track I think it was, and stopped a few miles in."

"There's not much chance we'll see anyone then. But I don't suppose it matters. Our part of the forest is still a part of it, of the plantation I mean. We might as well search there as anywhere else."

Alex was silent. Ari looked at her striding through the night and the snow. She didn't say anything, but Ari knew her so well that Alex didn't have to speak.

"No. Oh, no," she whispered.

Alex reached out and took her hand. "Be brave, Ari. You know where we have to go."

"But it's too far on foot! I had to take a bus and then I walked for ages. Besides, I was so hopelessly lost. I'd never find that valley again." With dreadful clarity, Ari saw in her mind the deep, wet valley where Acheron had first appeared. She saw the dark, gaping sinkhole and the ring of panting dogs. And Alex was right. That was where they had to go. She took a deep, painful breath of the icy air.

"How do we get there?"

"We walk. It's not as far as you think. I saw it, two nights ago. I saw the sinkhole. Everyone else just walked right past it without looking. But then, they do that anyway."

"How do you know it's the same one? There could be other portals."

"There could be," Alex agreed. "But I don't think so. I felt it, Ari. Like a shadow. Like a bruise that only hurts when you press on it. That's where the darkness is coming from. It's where Acheron is getting in and out."

They spoke very little after that. Ari struggled to walk through the deep drifts of snow. Her feet were frozen, and her jeans were wet up to the knees because snow kept slipping into the tops of her gumboots. She was warm from walking, but the cold pinched her nose, and her fingers were numb inside her gloves. The edge of the forest grew steadily closer, and Ari fought with the dread which sang in her nerves: Go back. Turn around and go home. You can't win this.

Alex squeezed her hand as they entered the first row of pines. Ari had never been in the forest at night. It had been dusk when she'd gone searching for Alex, and that was dark enough. But tonight the forest was even darker. Tonight the space between the trees was pitch black and full of unseen horrors.

Ari clutched her flashlight and hoped that the batteries would last. Alex had spares in her pocket, but Ari dreaded trying to change batteries in the dark. She shone her flashlight beam along the ground. The snow was less deep in here. It would be easier to walk, at least. Alex pointed the beam of her flashlight at the ground a yard or so from their feet.

"Here, Ari. You point yours where mine is and show us where to walk. I'll keep scanning from left to right."

"Which way?" Ari swallowed. Her voice had come out in a husky squeak.

"Straight in." Alex put her arm around her shoulders and kissed her forehead. "Come on, Ari. Think of how bad it was in that prison. You found me in there, remember? You saved me. You hold your head up and remember that. Remember how terrifying the underworld was and then look around. It's just our forest. Not nearly as frightening."

"It's not the forest that scares me," Ari began and then stopped. The back of her neck prickled. "What was that?"

There was a sudden crack and a rush and flurry among the treetops. Twigs and clumps of snow fell around them. Adrenaline charged through Ari's veins, and Alex pulled her close. They both swung their flashlight beams up into the trees. But it was only an owl, an enormous owl that swooped and dived into a clump of bracken right in front of them. In the forest's silence they heard the shrill, horrible squeal of a rabbit, and then the owl was rising with the rabbit twisted cruelly in its talons. Ari cried out and covered her eyes, but Alex just pointed her flashlight back at the ground and took her hand.

They walked on. It began to snow again, and the snowflakes looked like tiny stars whirling in the torch beams. Occasionally, Ari thought she heard voices carried on the night air, but they saw nobody. Alex kept scanning the forest floor for tracks, but the snow was crisp and clean and unmarked. Above them, the sky between the clouds was black and starry, but there was no moon. Still not up yet, Ari thought desperately. It can't have disappeared yet. It's not supposed to be dark until tomorrow night. We're okay. We still have time. Her legs ached with cold, but she ignored them. Time and distance dwindled to three things: the snow and the frosted black trunks of trees and the endless trudging.

Alex's hand was firm and reassuring around her own, but Ari wanted to feel her skin. She stopped, pulled off her glove and touched Alex's cheek. Her skin was icy, but her cheeks were flushed.

Alex kissed her, and Ari closed her eyes and tried to let herself forget the forest and the night. But although her eyes were closed, even while kissing Alex, Ari heard a branch crack somewhere behind her.

She spun around to point her flashlight in front of her, but the flashlight flickered and went out. She shook it, flicked the switch off and on, but it was dead. Alex banged her own flashlight against her hand, but it was no use. Her light had also gone out. They stood in darkness.

"Interesting devices, those lanterns of yours. But fallible. So very prone to expiring just at the wrong moment."

There was a hiss and a sudden flare of white light, and Acheron stepped out from behind a tree. He held a naked white flame in his hand. It quivered and flared as he strode toward them. He was dressed in his underworld garb: flowing dark cloak and heavy gold embroidery. A crown of some dull metal held down his hair, which looked white in the werelight.

Ari stood firm, her fingers interlaced with Alex's, but her knees were shaking. She couldn't meet Acheron's gaze. He lifted the hand that held the flame, and its ghostly light flickered across their faces.

"So," mocked Acheron. "I have both of you here where nobody else can find you. What happens next, do you think?" He cocked his head, and Ari dared a brief glance at his face. His predatory eyes and beak-like nose reminded her of the owl. He was sizing them up, she thought, trying to decide how best to torment them.

"Let us go, Acheron," said Alex. "My time is almost up anyway."

"Let you go? Let you go. Hmm. No, I really don't think so. In fact, I think I'll bring you both along with me. You seem to be in the wrong part of the forest. So tiresome."

Acheron raised his hand above his head, and the flame exploded in a shower of blinding sparks. There was a rushing noise and a confusion of swirling colors. Ari felt the ground move under her feet and then no ground at all. She closed her eyes. When the lurching stopped there was once again the cold crunch and slip of snow underfoot, and Alex was still there, beside her, gripping her hand. Ari opened her eyes.

Like a recurring nightmare, there was the sinkhole, like a gaping black mouth in the snow's white face. Its surface was covered in a thin film of ice, but there were holes and cracks all over it, and dark waters rippled under the starlit ice, just like in her dream. There were the steep, enclosing sides of the valley and the wet pines, now slick and gleaming with icicles. And there were the dogs: hundreds and hundreds of dogs, all lined up around the sinkhole, an expectant audience.

Ari looked for the lead dog but couldn't see it. She scanned the pack, hoping and fearing to see Sally among them, but though she saw several dogs she recognized, there was no Sally. And Ari was glad, for all the dogs were staring at them, and their eyes were black and hungry.

Acheron stood a little way off, caressing the dancing flame in his palm. Then he threw the flame carelessly into the air, where it burst and became a ball of flame, a searing globe of white fire that illuminated the little clearing. The dogs howled and cowered from the light, and Acheron laughed.

"My dogs are all here, as you see, but where are the hunters? They cannot find these tricky dogs, oh no, though they search and search. What a shame they became so preoccupied with tracking dogs. It made their minds so empty. Oh, look. Here they come now."

Acheron gestured at the top of the lowest ridge, and the werelight moved up the side of the valley until it shone on the figures scrambling and sliding down the hill. Ari saw all the men and many of the women of Stonehaven, some four or five hundred of them perhaps, come pouring into the clearing. They stood behind the dogs but seemed not to notice them. Their eyes were trained on Acheron. The last shreds of Ari's foolish hope shattered like cobwebs turned to ice. The hunters did not see her or Alex. They looked only at Acheron, and their eyes were as blank and as black as those of the dogs that crouched before them.

Acheron raised his hand, and the hunters put their shotguns to their shoulders, taking aim at Ari and Alex. Then he spoke a word of command, and they lowered their guns. At another gesture from Acheron, they planted the butts of their guns in the snow and put their mouths around the ends of the barrels. Ari was trying not to look for Nick in the crowd. She did not want to see his face, his eyes. But Nick was there, just a little way from the front of the crowd, and he raised and lowered his gun as Acheron commanded. He stood now like a zombie with his shotgun in his mouth. Ari felt sick.

"So what?" said Alex suddenly, loudly. Ari gave her a sharp glance as she pretended to yawn. "So you practiced mind control on a few hundred country people and their cattle dogs. Not such a great feat for a god. Really, I don't know why you bothered."

Acheron said nothing, though for a split-second Ari thought she saw his contemptuous expression slip, showing the barely controlled rage beneath. But he spoke calmly as he answered. "Stupid girl, this is only the beginning. These few are but a small part of what will become my army. Think of it: an army of the living, controlled by the lord of the dead. I will have both realms!" His voice rose, and the silent hunters fell on their knees in the snow.

"I will rule the realm of the living and all the earth shall bow down to me. And I will take my mortal army into the underworld and rule all of that also. I will decide who lives and who dies. The Fates will do my bidding. Atropos can wash my clothes. The other two will warm my bed. And all who hear my name will cower and lick the dust."

He turned to Ari and Alex. "Alex Cohen will die forever tonight. The moon is dark. You have run out of time. You know it. The old hag never changes the terms of any contract she makes. You have not closed the portal. See? It gapes, ready to swallow my army, one by one. You have not killed the dogs. They are ready to follow their leader, to herd more soldiers for my army. You, Arielle, will come with me, and I will do you the unimaginable honor of making you my mistress."

He laughed as Alex lunged at him. Ari could see Mara's knife concealed in her sleeve and she watched, holding her breath, as Acheron raised his arm and pointed at Alex.

"Kill her," he called.

A massive blur of hair and teeth flew past her toward Alex. She heard the splinter of a branch and a blood-chilling snarl as the black Alsatian leapt at Alex's throat. Then, like a flash of silver, a smaller dog rushed between them. The hellhound howled, and Ari saw Sally, her tiny teeth clamped on the monster's throat, swinging from its neck. Her muzzle was bright with the Alsatian's blood, but it swung its head and clawed at her, and she was flung wide, right over the top of Alex, who crouched motionless in the snow. Sally gave a small yelp, and then there was silence.

Ari screamed. "*Sally!* Nick! Nick, *do something*!"

Alex fell under the black dog and the beast howled with pain and rage. The bloodied knife skittered across the snow. Ari grabbed at it, and her fingertips just caught the handle. She couldn't see Alex, could only hear her muffled cries as the injured beast lowered its head for the kill.

Just as she turned the knife, ready to stab and slash the dog to pieces, there was a deafening crack and a sharp howl of pain, and the dog collapsed onto Alex's chest. Ari sensed somebody behind her. She turned, and Nick put his arm around her. In his free hand he held his gun, and the heat from its muzzle made the air smoke around them.

She bent over, loath to touch the dead beast but desperate to free Alex. Nick stood like a stone, his eyes blank and expressionless. Whatever sudden clarity had made him pull the trigger had vanished, wiped away by the force of Acheron's will.

Ari slipped out from under his arm and turned to face Acheron. Out of the corner of her eye, she could just see Alex, struggling to move the weight of the dog from her chest. The snow was splattered with the dog's blood.

Acheron's face was white, and his eyes burned like the flames that hung above his head. "Enough of this," he snarled. "Come here, girl. If you come willingly I might, perhaps, order the crone Atropos to change her sentence and let your precious Alex live. It would be interesting to have a mistress under such terms. Do you hear me? I will allow you to buy her life with your own. But you must come now."

Alex shouted in horror, "Ari, no!" and she thrashed around under the body of the monstrous dog, but Ari was already moving toward Acheron. She walked as slowly as she could, with her arms folded over her chest. The knife was concealed under her left arm, and its blade was slippery with blood. Acheron continued to jeer at her as she made her way around the sinkhole.

"So. In the end you will give yourself up for your friend, the girl whose death you caused all those years ago. Does it ease your guilt? Do you feel better now, Arielle? Does this final sacrifice make up for the lost years she spent in the underworld? Can you, even now, atone for what you did? How intriguing it will be to watch you struggle with these questions. And you will have eternity to do so. Come now..." He beckoned impatiently. "...I will send you down first, and the others can follow."

He held out his hand, ready to grab her, but Ari was quick. She pulled the knife from her armpit and slashed at the outstretched hand. The blade sliced through a finger, then another, and Ari quickly backed away as Acheron screamed.

He held up his hand and looked at her in disbelief. "How dare you? It is not possible! I cannot be harmed by a blade. I am Lord Acheron, god of the dead. You cannot harm me!" Blood, dark and thick, poured from the stumps of his missing fingers.

Ari stood up. She took a step toward him and held the knife up so that he could clearly see its point. A single drop of medicine, like a golden tear, clung to the tip of the bloodstained blade. She stared at it, struck dumb by the enormity of what she had done.

When she spoke again, she kept her voice low so that it wouldn't wobble. She couldn't look at the god she had wounded. "The knife drank my medicine, a medicine made from the leaves of the underworld tree. It healed me, that medicine, because I'm alive. I don't know what it will do to you, because you're not alive and you're not dead either. But I don't think it will do you any good."

Ari had a sudden vision of Atropos and she heard again the words she had given to help them. What had she said? That Ari had to confront her fears? What did she fear the most? She looked at Acheron, who was cradling his bleeding hand by the sinkhole. He seemed immobilized by what she had done. His glamour had vanished, and he seemed old, old beyond the count of years or even centuries—something ancient and diminished. She wasn't afraid of him, not anymore. What else did she fear? What was it that tortured her, more viciously than Acheron could ever torture her? Acheron's last taunts echoed in her mind.

The girl whose death you caused. All those years in the underworld. Your fault. Yours. He watched her as she approached. She knew what she had to say. It was so simple, but it took all her strength of will to say it aloud, and to believe it.

"It wasn't my fault," she whispered, and then she buried the knife up to the hilt in Acheron's heart.

20. SPINDLE

ACHERON FELL, CLUTCHING THE HANDLE of the knife, into the sinkhole. There was a tremendous cracking of ice. The werelight hissed and went out. Ari couldn't see the sinkhole in the sudden darkness, but she listened as the ice chunks resettled in the black waters.

As her eyes adjusted to the night, Ari stumbled around the sinkhole to help Alex. But she was already on her feet. The black dog's body had crumbled into thick dust that she was brushing from her clothes.

Looking around, Ari saw that it wasn't completely dark anymore. She found that she could see quite well by the starlight that filtered through the trees, and the snow itself seemed faintly lit from above.

Ari searched for Sally and found her, lying crumpled and still where the beast had flung her. Ari fell on her knees beside her dog. She stroked the short, silky hairs on her head and ran her fingers along her velvety ears. She kissed her while tears dripped off her face and wet the dog's fur.

"Poor Sally. Poor old girl. Good dog."

Alex put her hand on her shoulder. "Look," she said.

Alex had to help Ari to stand. Her feet and legs had joined in numbed protest against the cold, and she clung to Alex and stumbled as she led her gently a few steps away from Sally. They stood at the edge of the sinkhole and watched, silently, as the inky waters began to bubble and steam. The steep sides of the hole began to slip and collapse inward. Great chunks of mud and ice and clay tumbled into the water, and the earth shook. Then, as if somebody had pulled a gigantic plug, the sinkhole's waters swirled round and round, faster and faster, until the sinkhole dwindled and dissolved and shriveled away to nothing. Where the pool had been there was only a slight depression in the ground.

The people of Stonehaven blinked and stared at one another. The dogs shook the snow off their coats and began to whine and wag their tails. Ari looked away. She couldn't watch the many joyful reunions of the dogs with their owners. Nick called to her from across the clearing. He lifted Sally and held her body gently, carefully, against his chest.

Alex put her arm around her, and Ari suddenly remembered, with a terrible lurching fear, that it wasn't over. They were too late. Acheron had said so. Would Atropos appear out of the air and take Alex back to the underworld? Or would she just collapse on the way home? Why was Alex smiling at her?

"What is it?" she asked, confused. Alex pointed at the sky. And there, cradled in the curve of the Milky Way, was the faintest of crescent moons, a mere sliver of light etched onto the sky.

"You did it, Ari," she said. "The moon is still there. And you got rid of Acheron, closed the portal, and probably saved the world. Not bad for a night's work."

"Is he dead?"

"I don't know. But that knife and the medicine definitely killed the dog. Maybe it killed Acheron too. Who knows? Anyway, the portal is closed. The lead dog is gone. And I'm still here. It's done, Ari. It's over."

Ari couldn't speak. She closed her eyes and took a deep breath. Hope, tentative but steady, was beginning to unfold inside her.

Alex kissed her, quickly, fiercely, on the lips, and Ari saw all at once how a life together could be born from the briefest of kisses. They were only beginning, she and Alex, and a tightly wound spool of time uncurled itself at their feet. All they had to do now was to follow it and go home.

But something didn't feel quite finished. So Ari was not surprised to see the Hunter when he appeared from somewhere deep inside the crowd of people, and she smiled as he approached them.

He greeted Alex warmly and kissed Ari ceremoniously on both cheeks. "It was well done, Ari," he said, and Ari smiled. Her friend the Hunter was proud of her.

"I couldn't have done it without you," she told him. "But did it work? Is Acheron gone forever?"

The Hunter shook his head. "I'm sorry, Ari. You cannot kill a god of the dead with a knife and a few drops of healing elixir. But you have defeated him for the time being and for a long time to come. His portal is destroyed. It takes a long time and a lot of energy to maintain a doorway like that. He will limp back to his keep and lick his wounds. And I will watch him. Atropos is none too pleased with Acheron's arrogance, and she would prefer him watched while she considers how best to deal with him. That will be one of my tasks now."

The Hunter looked up at the sky, which was growing ever lighter. Somewhere, far off toward the sea, an early magpie was summoning the sun. The crowd began to thin out. People and their dogs were going home.

"I have something for you." He held out a small golden spindle, tightly wrapped with skeins upon skeins of olive-green thread. "Well, I suppose it really belongs to you, Alex, but since you'll be sharing it, here you are, Ari."

Ari held out her hand, and the Hunter placed the little golden cone on her outstretched palm. She held its weight for a moment, and then it disappeared.

"Don't worry," said the Hunter, smiling at Ari's stricken expression. "It was only a message, a token, sent by Clotho to let you know the Fates have honored their part of the bargain. The real spindle is underground, where the thread is spun and measured and cut by them, as all our lives must be." He smiled at her, but Ari thought his eyes looked sad.

"Where is Mara?" she asked. "Is she all right?"

"She is well. She sends her love. But Mara cannot enter the world of the living. She is a shade and not a Summoner and so she must remain in the underworld until she chooses to pass the last gate."

Ari looked at her friend, standing tall in the clearing, and she realized something she ought to have guessed sooner. "You're alive," she said, and the enormity of this struck her. "How long have you been living down there?"

"I suppose it has been a long time by the reckoning of years. But I had no choice. She was my daughter. My child. I would have followed her into the darkest circle of hell if such had been her fate. And when they offered me the chance to save her from Acheron, I agreed because I had no other choice. I had to save her, at any cost." He gave Alex a pleading look and hung his head. "I ascended the stair and came to say farewell to both of you, but also to apologize once more. I don't expect you to forgive me. But I am sorry, Alex. I stole your chance of a new life. You are not a parent yet, but one day you might be, and then you will understand why I had to agree to the terms."

Alex put her hand on the Hunter's shoulder. "I do understand," she said gently. "And if I hadn't become a Summoner, I wouldn't have been able to return to Ari. I wouldn't want to be living some other life without her."

The Hunter bowed his head and spread his hands wide, palms turned upward. Alex took his hands and placed them together, then put her own hands around them. They were silent. Watching them, Ari's eyes filled with tears. Alex was saying goodbye.

"Where did you come out from?" Alex asked the Hunter. "Where is the opening?"

"Nearby. But it will close when I have passed through it." He bowed to Ari. "Thanks to you, there is no more rift and the smaller doorways are guarded. I am a Summoner once more. Atropos came to me after your trial and told me that, as well as watching Acheron, I was to take up my old role, as penance perhaps. But it is also a reward beyond price. To breathe the fresh air and see the stars again! Next time I ascend, I may even feel the sunlight on my face. To one who has lived so long in the underworld, that is almost everything there is." He stopped and sighed. "But you know that, of course. Farewell, my young friends. I wonder if there was another purpose in Atropos' decision. Almost certainly we will not meet again. But I may be able to watch over you now and then."

Ari hugged him and let her head lie against his chest for a moment. She heard his heartbeat, muffled by leather and cloth and thought, a little wistfully, that it must be an extraordinary sort of love, this fatherly love that sustained the Hunter throughout countless years in the underworld. "I'll miss you," she said in a muffled voice.

He smiled and put his arm around Alex as well. "Take care of each other," he said, and then he walked away into the darkness between the trees.

Ari blinked. The sky was no longer black but deep blue, and the morning star glowed next to their tiny crescent moon. The forest was warmer, suddenly. Nick was still waiting for them with Sally in his arms, but otherwise the clearing was deserted.

"Let's go home," said Ari.

○

THE NEXT MORNING, THEY DROVE to Port August. The snow was swiftly disappearing, and everywhere she looked Ari saw bright, sunlit streams of meltwater. The cleared land began to show patches of muddy green between the mounds of melting snow, and great chunks of ice fell from the branches of trees as they drove up the winding road. They stopped in Stonehaven to pick up supplies, and Ari slumped low in her seat while Cass and Nick went into the general store. She didn't feel like talking to anybody or answering any questions. Alex didn't look out of the car window. She sat quietly stroking Ari's hand with her eyes closed.

Ari peeked out and saw that the temperature had risen so much overnight that people were walking around without jackets or scarves. There was a carnival atmosphere about the tiny row of shops. Ari watched the animated greetings and conversations with a growing sense of wonder. Had she and Alex really saved all these people? In the bright morning, in the ordinariness of her hometown, it was hard to believe in snowy forests and monstrous dogs and menacing gods. When she closed her eyes it was all there, of course, spread across her consciousness the way a horror film stains the mind. But Ari would not think about it, not this morning. This morning belonged to happiness and to Alex.

Cass and Nick chatted cheerfully from the front seat, but Alex was silent. Sitting in the middle of the back seat, squashed into Alex by the baby seat on her right, Ari was perfectly happy. But she knew that Alex was struggling with what was coming and didn't try to make her talk. She rested her head on her shoulder and held her hand as the Land Cruiser rattled over the hills and into the busy town center.

They pulled up outside the nursing home, and Nick reached over his seat to tuck the baby's blankets around her as Ari, Alex, and Cass climbed out. They stood, a tense little group, by the car.

Nick chuckled. "Look at you three. Don't worry so much. It will be all right."

He waved as he drove away, and Ari walked up the front steps with her mother and Alex. As they waited on the porch, Alex clutched Ari's hand so tightly her fingers hurt. A solemn looking nurse in a floral uniform led them through a maze of silent corridors to a tiny sitting room. The door was open.

Cass went in and sat close to her old friend. She spoke quietly to her, and Ari saw Beth look up, sharply, at the door. Ari watched from the doorway, and her eyes filled with tears as Alex crossed the room, knelt, and laid her head on her mother's lap.

Acknowledgments

My deepest thanks to the incredible team at Interlude Press: Annie, Candy and Choi. You each gave so generously of your time, talent and expertise, and guided me so well, that every step of the way was a revelation and a delight. Thank you all.

Thank you to Alex Brown and Tor.com for revealing the epic cover by C.B. Messer. This was the kind of book announcement that first-timers dream about. Special thanks to Alex for your kindness and generosity in supporting my debut. Your encouragement in the pre-publication phase was a much-needed gift of confidence. Thank you.

To Julia Ember and Mark Smith, thank you for reading *From Darkness* and for adorning it with such beautiful and encouraging words. It means a great deal to have the support of two authors whose books I admire so much.

To my parents, and to the family and friends who supported and encouraged me, thank you. Many of you knew about this book in its embryonic stages. I hope you like it now that its many transformations are complete.

Special thanks to:

Kirsty Buchanan, for sharing the most exciting parts of the journey, for naming Alex, and for teaching me about the importance of raking light. Thank you for the family holidays, the laughter and the tears, and for topping up my glass of wine all those times I was trapped under the cat.

Annie Hall and Simon Collings, for a lifetime of sharing your forest hidey-hole with me. I could not have imagined Stonehaven properly without all those research trips down south.

Maria Takolander, for your generosity and kindness and for telling me to keep going. This book would still be hidden away in a desk drawer if not for your encouragement. In my copy of *The Double* you wrote: "I can't wait for your book launch." That was a powerful invocation. Thank you.

Jo Langdon, for reading the manuscript in its earliest stages, for your patient and gentle guidance, and for believing in my writing. Thank you for giving me the gift of your sympathetic ear and keen insights. Heartfelt thanks for launching this book; it will go more bravely into the world because of your blessing.

Lyn Lea, for never asking me to translate or explain the most important things. Thank you for engaging with the various pieces of writing I've inflicted on you over the years, and for showing me how to transform the weak parts into words that ring true. Thank you for your uncompromising honesty and your honest praise, both of which I need in equal measure, and for the many sustaining joys of our friendship, on land and in the water.

Maya and Kendra, my amazing daughters. Thank you for believing in me, for answering millions of questions about what works and what doesn't in young adult novels, and for giving me sage advice. This book has so much of both of you in it. Thank you for reminding me every day that creativity is the connective tissue that binds the world, and for adding to it in your own unique and wonderful ways. Most of all, thank you both for being the strong, inspiring and delightful young women that you are. I am so proud to be your mother.

About the Author

Kate Hazel Hall has published short stories and creative non-fiction for adults, but YA fiction is where her heart is—especially fantasy, magical realism, and speculative YA with a healthy amount of Sapphic romance built in.

When she isn't writing, Kate often sneaks off to the forest or the beach with a sketchbook and a surfboard. Despite wearing out several wetsuits, Kate has yet to gain her advanced surfer qualifications, but she does have a PhD in Literary Studies from Deakin University, where she teaches graduate research skills, genre studies, and ecological fiction. Kate lives with her daughters and the world's naughtiest rescue cat in a small Australian coastal town, just across the Southern Ocean from Antarctica.

From Darkness is her first novel.

CONNECT WITH KATE ONLINE
katehazelhall.com
KateHH_writes
kate_hall75